I0543814

ABOUT THE AUTHOR

Maggie Anderson writes paranormal and contemporary romance, urban fantasy, supernatural crime thrillers and YA thrillers. She is currently working on the fourth book in her Dark Legacy series followed by the second book in the Moon Grove Paranormal Romance Thriller series. Maggie resides in Brisbane, Queensland. You can find out more about her books at: www.m-anderson.com.au

Romance titles
by Maggie Anderson
Driving Me Crazy
Love's Twist of Fate
A Night of Passion
A Night of Passion CR Edition
Christmas, Mistletoe and You
Christmas, Mistletoe and Me

Moon Grove
Paranormal Romance Series
Wolf Blood
Wolf Curse
Wolf Lover
Wolf Bonds

Dark Legacy
Urban Fantasy Series
(Writing as M. A. Anderson)
Reece: Prequel

Dark Legacy

Once Bitten

Soul Chaser

Evil Nature

Most Deadly

BOOK ONE

WOLF BLOOD

A MOON GROVE PARANORMAL ROMANCE THRILLER

MAGGIE ANDERSON

Bella Luna Books
Australia

This is a work of fiction. Names, characters, places and incidences are either the product of the author's imagination or, if real, are used fictitiously and with the utmost respect. Any resemblance to persons living or dead is entirely coincidental.

Revised Edition
Bella Luna Books, Australia

Copyright © 2022 Maggie Anderson
Brisbane, Queensland, Australia

All rights reserved. No part of this book may be reproduced, transmitted or stored in an information retrieval system in any form or by any means without prior written permission
from the author.

Front and back cover photos from
canstockphoto.com and pixabay.com
Cover design by
Maggie Anderson

ISBN-13:9780992513962

Published by Bella Luna Books
AUSTRALIA

PROLOGUE

The echoing, thunderous footsteps gained on her, the ground shaking beneath her feet. Paige pushed every ounce of strength she had left into her throbbing legs and propelled herself forward through the eerie trees, peering over her shoulder into the pursuing darkness, her blood pounding in her ears.

The creature was fast as lightning. It had matched her speed in micro seconds. She had hoped she'd have enough time to get some distance between them but it had remained at her heels with every terrifying step.

Her heaving chest constricted and she forced dry mouthfuls of air into her lungs to keep the oxygen flowing through her body so she could continue to run. To save herself. To flee for her life from – she wasn't sure what. All she knew was the creature was big. Massive.

It's gaining on me. I can't go any faster! Tears stung the backs of Paige's eyes and her throat burned as she rocketed through the gloom. She pushed her body to its limit, every tortured fiber screaming in agony. She tripped and stumbled forward, arms thrust out, fumbling to retain her balance. Her breath caught in her throat, her knees buckled, and she crashed to the forest floor, skinning her hands and knees on jagged tree roots and rotting fallen branches.

She tried to scramble to her feet, the soles of her running shoes slipping on the soggy leaves beneath them, and landed flat in the mud. A huge clawed hand reached out of the dark, shredding her blouse and the skin beneath it. She opened her mouth to scream but the monstrous palm slid across her face, smothering the sound before she could make it.

Paige sucked in a strangled breath, her heart thumping against her ribs, her sweat-soaked nightdress clinging to her trembling body. She sprang up in bed, nervous eyes flitting around the dark bedroom. Gulping in another mouthful of air, Paige attempted to calm her ragged breathing and racing heartbeat. "It – it was just another nightmare," she assured herself with a shaky breath.

In the peculiar half-light, Paige studied the familiar shapes and shadows around her room and gave a relieved sigh. *Nothing out of place.* She'd been having these nightmares since she was a child and had no idea what they were supposed to mean. Even her psychiatrist couldn't interpret them. He'd told her it had to be related to some kind of childhood trauma locked inside her subconscious. But what? As far as she was concerned, she was a happy, well-adjusted young woman who had lived a normal childhood.

Paige threw back the covers, climbed out of bed and padded bare foot across the room to the window. She gazed up at the beautiful, iridescent full moon hovering above the soft, gray clouds and sighed. Maybe a change of scene would help. She'd been considering it for a while now.

ONE

Paige O'Connell sat opposite her fidgeting patient scribbling notes and intermittently doodling swirls around the edge of the page. Mrs. Franklin believed her husband was trying to kill her, that her son moved to a different state to college because he hated her, and her daughter never visited because she blamed her for God knows what. Paige did her best to be supportive and empathetic but sometimes she felt like killing the woman herself. There were people out there with far more serious conditions who needed legitimate help. Mrs. Franklin wasn't one of them. Paige had referred her to a psychiatrist but Judy preferred to remain her client and without the assistance of medication.

A knock echoed into the room and her receptionist stuck her head around the door. "Dr. O'Connell there's an important call for you on line one."

Paige breathed a relieved sigh. "Thank you, Steph." She glanced at her patient. "Time's up for this week, Judy. Make an appointment for the same time next Thursday." She stood up, walked over to the door and opened it.

"But I didn't finish telling you about…"

"You can tell me next week."

"Very well." The woman gave her a disgruntled scowl and marched out of the office.

Paige closed the door, walked over and dropped the notebook and pen on the desk blotter, then sat down in her high-backed, leather executive office chair, kicked off her heels and gave another sigh. Perhaps she really should consider a change of location. Some of her patients were driving her crazy.

The door opened and Stephanie stuck her head in. "Are you going to answer the call on line one?"

"Oh?" Paige straightened. "I thought you were rescuing me from Mrs. Franklin again." Her eyes moved to the telephone on her right. "Thanks. Yes, I'll take it." She picked up the digital handset. "Hello, Dr. O'Connell speaking."

"Miss O'Connell, my name is Myles Chesterfield. I was your uncle's lawyer. Can we meet?"

Was her uncle's lawyer? What did that mean?

"Can you tell me what this is about?" Paige leaned back in the chair and rubbed her aching left temple. The beginnings of a headache were forming there.

"I'd prefer to discuss it with you in person, if you don't mind."

She sighed. "Ok. When and where?"

"I'm across the street at the café so whenever you have some free time. I don't mind waiting."

Paige jumped out of her seat, rushed to the window and peered through the blinds. "I'll be there in five minutes." She stepped into her heels, hurried across her office, opened the door and rushed out into reception. "Steph, can you reschedule this morning's appointments and hold my calls. Something's come up and I have to leave for a while."

Her receptionist, who was also her best friend, frowned up at her from her desk. "Everything ok?"

"I'm not sure yet. I'll let you know when I get back." She headed for the stairs.

Standing on the sidewalk, Paige's stomach did anxious flip flops. The man on the telephone had said he *was* her uncle's lawyer. Was? Had something happened to Jake? She inhaled in a calming breath, put on her professional face and crossed the street.

When she entered the café a man in his mid-forties, wearing a dark blue suit stood up at one of the booths. "Hello, Paige, thank you for meeting me on such short notice." He extended his hand. He was mildly attractive with pleasant gray eyes, bushy eyebrows, and his dark hair graying at the temples.

Paige shook it and sidled into the bench opposite him.

"Can I get you something?" Myles offered. "Coffee?"

She shook her head. "No thanks. I'd just like to know what this is about."

He reached into the top pocket of his suit jacket, retrieved a pair of metal-framed spectacles and placed them on the bridge of his nose. "I'm sorry to have to tell you this, but I'm here because your uncle has passed away and you are his sole beneficiary."

Tears stung the backs of her eyes. She hadn't spoken to her uncle in a while and now she'd never have the chance to. She swallowed the painful lump in her throat and asked in a quiet voice, "What happened?"

"The investigation is ongoing so I'm afraid I can't discuss it."

Paige's eyes widened. "Investigation? I don't understand. What investigation? What happened to him?"

He cleared his throat. "I wish I could tell you more, but I'm sorry I can't."

"You said I'm his sole beneficiary?"

"Oh, yes." Myles reached into the black leather briefcase sitting beside him on the padded, green vinyl seat, pulled out a folder, sat it on the table and opened it. "As he wasn't married and had no children that we're aware of, you are his sole heir… or heiress as is the case."

Paige eased her body back against the seat. "Oh."

"He left you his house and land and a hundred thousand dollars in cash."

"What?!"

"Yes, it's all yours."

Her tearful gaze moved to him. "Has there been a funeral? Why didn't someone let me know before now?"

Myles shook his head. "Not yet. As I said the investigation is ongoing. They won't release the body until the case has been solved. And I'm informing you now."

"But you can't tell me anything?"

"I'm afraid my hands are tied. I'd be breaking the law."

Paige attempted to take it all in. Her uncle Jake was dead by suspicious circumstances and she now owned his house in Moon Grove, Illinois. From what she could remember from visiting her uncle a few times over the years, it was a small town of no more than twelve hundred people, give or take, but the scenery was beautiful and, as she recalled, the townsfolk friendly. Maybe this was the change of scene she'd been looking for. Could she set up her practice there? Would it be worth the move? Something she'd have to consider. Washington was far removed from a backwater town in the middle of nowhere. And she had a thriving practice and close circle of good friends. Would she leave it all behind and move back to a place she didn't know?

"It was obviously a crime, right?"

He nodded.

"Was he... was he murdered?"

He nodded again. "I've said too much already."

Paige gasped and her eyes moved to the file sitting on the table then back to him. "Why? He was a good man. I doubt he had any enemies. He'd give people the shirt off his back if they needed it."

Myles gave her a pained look. "I'm sorry. Truly I am. I wish I could answer all of your questions. I understand how overwhelming this must be for you, Paige." He reached across the table and rested his hand on hers.

Paige eased her hands out from under his and placed them in her lap. "So what happens now? With the will, I mean."

"I have a couple of things for you to peruse and sign and then I can hand you the keys to the house and the banking information, which has already been transferred into your name."

She blew out a noisy breath. How could this have happened? She loved her uncle Jake. He was a kind, gentle man who had always been there when she needed him. His death would leave a huge hole in her heart.

The lawyer slid the paperwork across the table. "It's pretty standard stuff. What I do need you to read is here," he said, pointing to several clauses marked with a sticky, red 'SIGN HERE' arrow, "and here. If you have any questions don't hesitate to ask."

"I think I'll have that coffee now," she said, gazing up from the papers.

"Of course." Myles waved the waitress over and ordered their drinks.

After reading the important clauses and signing the documents, Myles handed her the keys and other information. "It's been good meeting you, Paige. I'm sure I'll see you again when you visit Moon Grove." He stood up and extended his hand.

She shook it. "Thank you."

Once the lawyer was gone, Paige sat in silence feeling numb. Her uncle was the last family member she had. Aunt Ruth, her mother's sister, had passed away in a car accident five years before, leaving Paige on her own, and now this. She'd never considered marriage and kids because of her career so she was the last of their bloodline, as far as she knew.

TWO

Six weeks later

Eli Blackwood sat behind his desk going over the report on Jake O'Connell. They'd been friends for years and he couldn't get his head around why someone would want him dead. Moon Grove had its fair share of secrets and its crazies too, but Jake wasn't one of them. There had been a similar death over the past two months and Eli wondered if they were related. Both victims were male and each one had had their heads taken off. Well, ripped off.

He'd heard Paige O'Connell was moving into her uncle's place and remembered her fondly from kindergarten: red, wavy hair and rosy cheeks. She had always been a happy little girl as far as he could remember. She'd been taken away to live with her aunt after her parents disappeared. The case was never solved, and Eli had recently pulled the files to see if there was anything the investigating officers had reported that had been missed by their sheriff. He knew there were certain aspects that had to remain undocumented but, nonetheless, the whole scenario was suspicious because there had been blood in the house. A lot of blood – and no bodies. And now that her uncle was dead in similar, suspicious circumstances, he deemed it necessary to dig deeper.

Eli wondered what Paige was like now. She'd be close to thirty, if his calculations were correct. He was thirty two. Not the little girl tucked away in his memory. He heaved his six foot four inch, solid frame out of his office chair and gathered up the folders on his desk to take home. He figured he'd find out what Paige was like soon enough as she'd be arriving in town the day after tomorrow. Would she remember him? They were just kids when they'd known each other, she around five years old and he around seven or eight. Did she remember what had taken her from the town? She had lived a very different life all of these years, why had she decided to come back now?

It was late, and as Eli switched off the light in his office the station fell into deep shadow. It didn't bother him; he was comfortable in the dark.

When Eli arrived home he found one of his deputies sitting on the steps of his front porch. He pulled his four wheel drive up to the garage, turned off the engine and gave a heavy sigh. All he wanted to do right now was have a bite to eat and fall into bed before another day began with its own set of problems. *What could Craig possibly want at this time of night?* Eli glanced at his watch. 11:26. He pulled the keys from the ignition, stepped out of the vehicle, and walked up the path to the porch. "Craig." He could hear the tightness in his voice. There was a certain, unspoken animosity between them and no matter how hard he tried to alleviate the tension Craig wouldn't yield.

"Eli." He fingered the neck of the empty beer bottle in his hand before sitting it on the step with the other three and standing up.

"What brings you here so late?"

"Jake's murder."

"What about it?" Eli dug his hands into the pockets of his dark blue, police issue anorak and sighed.

"I've been thinking about who would do that to him. Maybe he had a secret just like the rest of the town."

Eli frowned. "You don't know what you're talking about. Jake was a good guy. He didn't have secrets. Like the rest of us."

"Come on, Chief, this town is full of secrets. Everyone here has skeletons in their closets."

"You need to go home and sleep it off, Craig."

"I'm not drunk!" He stumbled on the step and Eli gripped his arms to prevent his fall.

"Let me take you home," Eli offered, wrapping an arm around his deputy and leading him toward his car.

Craig pulled out of his grasp. "I don't wanna go home. You have to listen to me. I think someone thought Jake was…"

"Stop!" Eli grabbed him by his jacket front and pulled him close. "You don't want to go around saying the things you're thinking. You need to keep your mouth shut. It's dangerous."

"See." The deputy swayed, stumbled backwards and landed on his butt on the front lawn.

Eli grabbed his coat front and hauled him to his feet. "I'm taking you home or I'm putting you in a cell. Up to you."

Craig's harsh gaze met his. "Put me in a cell. I'd be

better off there. At least I'd be safe from whoever's killing everyone. You know there'll be more, right?"

Eli frowned. "What are you talking about?"

"Someone's picking us off, Chief. And I don't wanna be the next in line."

"You don't know what you're saying. Let's get you home." He wrapped a supporting arm around his deputy once again and led him to his four wheel drive. "Get in."

Craig gave him a dark glare and climbed into the passenger seat.

The ten minute drive to his deputy's house was in silence. Craig was brooding. Eli didn't want to play into the politics of the town. He knew the darkness that lay beneath it. Yes, Jake had been butchered, but it wasn't because he was anything other than in the wrong place at the wrong time. They'd found his blood behind Pete's Tavern and his body in the woods. Later on, his head was discovered in the dumpster out the back of the bar by the proprietor throwing out food scraps.

Eli pulled up outside the timber clad, two story house and kept the engine running. "Well, here you are, safe and sound. Get some sleep. I'll see you in the morning."

Craig gave his boss a sour sideward glance, unclipped his seatbelt, flung the door open and slammed it after he got out.

Eli sighed. Once the alcohol wore off Craig would feel pretty stupid. He always did.

The little girl couldn't have been any more than five years old. Why was she out in the woods alone? As she ran through the trees, her long, wavy red hair flowed behind her like a cape and she giggled. Were they playing hide and seek or a game of chase? He continued to follow her through the legion of tall trees which grew darker the further they ran. Cold fingers of apprehension crawled up his spine and he shivered. "Wait for me," he called after her.

She didn't stop.

Her giggle echoed around him.

"Wait!"

She glanced over her shoulder. "Come on," she said and disappeared into the gloom.

"No. Wait. Come back." His eyes studied the eerie haze around him. He could hear her giggling in the distance. He followed the sound. "Where are you?" The road map of nerves winding through his body tingled with fear and his anxious gaze roamed the shadowy woods. "Please answer me!" he shouted, a nervous quiver in his high pitched voice.

The giggling grew distant.

He broke into a run, pushing through the tangle of low-lying branches. The woods grew even darker. His stomach shrank, his heart raced and tears stung the backs of his eyes. *Where is she?*

A shrill scream shattered the dense silence and he raced through the trees, clambering over twisted, rotting roots and underbrush.

Then he saw it.

A jagged trail of blood.

Splashes of red leading deeper into the woods.

He called her name frantically, over and over and over…

Eli launched himself out of bed, his breathing ragged, his heart pounding so fast he thought it would claw its way out of his throat.

He sucked in a strangled mouthful of air and ran his hand through his tousled, wavy, dark brown hair. It had been a long time since he'd had that dream. Why now?

THREE

Paige waited on the porch for the moving van to back up the driveway. The rhythmic beeping of the reversing alarm would surely stir prying eyes to their windows or the street, but there was nothing she could do about that. She glanced at the keys in her hand, opened the glass paned, white washed door and swung it back. It was strange being here without her uncle. It felt like a violation of his privacy.

The removalists had all of her belongings inside the two story white and gray house in no time, and after they were gone Paige stood in the kitchen with her hands on her hips wondering where to begin.

It had been a big decision returning to this small town after being away for so long, but she wanted to get back to her roots. Would she be welcomed or would she be a stark reminder of tragic circumstances people would prefer to forget? A knock on the door pulled her from her thoughts and Paige wandered through the spacious home to the front of the house. She moved the curtain aside to see who it was, not that she would remember anyone because she had been too young, and frowned when she saw a tall, ruggedly handsome man standing on her front porch.

Paige turned the lock and pulled the door back. "Can I help you?"

"Hi, I'm Eli Blackwood, sheriff of Moon Grove. I wanted to personally welcome you back and ask if you needed anything while you're settling in." He turned the fawn colored, police issue Stetson around in his hands. He'd removed his hat to speak to her. A nice gesture.

Her eyebrows rose. "Well that's very kind of you..."

"Eli," he reminded her.

"Yes, Eli, but I think I have everything covered. Thanks for stopping by though. Have a good day." She eased the door forward. He blocked it with his hand.

"You don't remember me, do you?"

"No, I'm sorry, I don't." She gave him a curious frown.

"We went to the same kindergarten. We used to play together along with Becky and Bobby."

Paige's forehead wrinkled even more and she tried to recall the friends she'd had all those years ago. The names didn't ring any bells. "It's been a long time."

"Yeah, you're right. I remember you though... I just thought, maybe, you'd remember me." Even though her long, wavy red hair was straightened into a practical, shoulder-length bob, Eli couldn't help but notice that she had grown into a beautiful woman.

"I wish I did remember you." Glancing over her shoulder to the boxes still needing to be unpacked. "I really have to get back to it."

"Oh. Yeah. Sure."

"Once again, thanks for coming by. I guess I'll see you around town." She smiled.

He nodded and eased his wide-brimmed hat back onto his head. "Guess so."

Paige didn't want to be rude and close the door in his face now that she'd spoken to him. She stood waiting for him to turn around and leave. He didn't.

"Thanks again," she said, hoping he would take the hint.

Eli peered over his shoulder at his vehicle. "Yeah. Right. See you round." He turned on his heel and headed down the front path to the street.

Paige sighed and closed the door. There was work to be done.

It was just on sunset when Paige put the last book on the bookshelf and collapsed the box they'd been packed in. She carried it and the other few empty, flat boxes down to the cellar and stacked them against the wall under the staircase. A sudden chill wrapped itself around her as she stood beside the stairs with only the lightbulb shining a dull yellow glow in the center of the underground room. Her eyes ran around the stacked boxes and other covered items. Most of her uncle's furniture had been sold off, but there were still some odd pieces that she needed to look at before getting rid of them. The dream she had rushed vividly to mind and she raced up the stairs, slammed and locked the door. Goosebumps travelled up her arms and she shivered. What was her subconscious so afraid of?

Paige popped the kettle onto the stove and wandered into the living room to turn on the small, electric space heater she'd brought with her from her apartment. The nights here would be so much colder than Washington and once winter truly set in there would be regular heavy snowfalls. She loved the snow but dreaded the cold.

After making a cup of hot chocolate, she headed upstairs to the room she had chosen, set the mug down on the bedside table and unpacked the suitcase with her pajamas and underwear in it, placing them in the top bureau drawer.

She climbed into bed around ten thirty and hoped tonight she would have a peaceful sleep.

Eli lay on his back with his hands behind his head staring up at the ceiling. Paige O'Connell didn't remember him. How could he change that? He hoped to get to know her all over again. Maybe he should ask her to dinner to break the ice. And while he was at it, see if she remembered anything about her parents' disappearance. Perhaps that would be pushing his luck on a first... it wouldn't be a date, though, would it?

Moon Grove had its fair share of secrets, ones many in the town wanted to remain buried. It was a close-knit community and most would consider Paige an outsider, after twenty three years of living elsewhere. Eli didn't expect that they'd be welcoming. He flicked on the lamp and pulled her parents' file out of the stack. What information did the investigating officers alter to include in their reports?

He ran his eyes over the pages but nothing unusual jumped out at him. It seemed the police back then had followed the correct protocols. Still, something didn't sit right with him. It was all too perfect. So what was he missing? Forensics had matched the blood to Paige's mother and father from their medical records at Doc Hoskins' office. And the amount of blood found at the scene confirmed that they would have died there. So where were the bodies?

One of the investigating officers still lived in town. Wil Wallace was in his seventies now. Eli made a mental note to go find out what he remembered and if he'd be willing to talk. He had every reason not to.

FOUR

Paige jolted awake and sat bolt upright, her ragged breathing and heartbeat causing her head to spin. She closed her eyes and inhaled a deep breath, filling her lungs, then blew it out in a slow whoosh. Her trembling body was covered in goosebumps. The dream had been different this time. She threw back the covers, swung her legs over the side of the bed and sat on the edge of the mattress. What had changed in her dream? She remembered seeing her uncle's face. She closed her eyes and tried to recall what she'd seen. Jake had been warning her about something. What was it? He'd said something about her being in danger. But how would that be possible?

She stood up and walked over to the window. The night was dark and the quarter moon gave off very little light. It was quiet outside. Too quiet. Something Paige hoped she'd get used to.

Maybe she should take up the sheriff's offer to help and see what she could find out about her uncle's death.

Eli Blackwood: Tall, dark, and way too handsome to be sheriff of a small town. She wished she could remember him and the other friends he'd spoken of. Were they still living in Moon Grove? She would have to make a point of asking him.

Paige gave a heavy sigh and wandered across the room. It was already after 4 AM, would she be able to go back to sleep for a couple more hours? She climbed into bed and pulled the snug covers up over her head the way she used to when she was a child. She felt safe cocooned inside their warmth. The drowsy warmth of sleep finally wrapped itself around her and she drifted into the same dream.

Later that morning, Paige was up at 6 AM with all thoughts of the dream far from her mind. She threw herself into settling in as she still had quite a bit to do to get her new home in order. Once finished, she head into town to check out the local realtors and find some office space. She'd decided to set up a small practice. Even though she could wait a while, because she had her own savings and the money her uncle had left her, she felt as though she needed to be doing something productive. After finding the perfect space, she'd place an advertisement in the Moon Grove Tribune for a receptionist and hoped the process would be painless.

By two o'clock things were looking much more comfortable and Paige figured the rest could wait. She took a quick shower, put on a warm, cream colored sweater and a pair of black pants and boots and applied a light coat of makeup. Despite the town being small, she felt she should look her best when conducting business. She grabbed her gray wool jacket from off the coat rack by the front door and headed to her car.

As she cruised along the main street, Ashton Real Estate came into view on her right. Paige pulled into the curb in front of the medical center beside their office and stepped out. She gazed along the street, taking in the various shops, cafés and other stores and also noticed an old fashioned movie house. *That could be fun.* Something else stood out to her, a huge spire over the tops of the buildings. Was it some kind of church or did the town have a city hall? Something she'd have to investigate when she had the time. She pushed the button on the remote to lock her car then realized in a town this small no one would bother stealing it.

Stepping into the realtor's office, the warmth of the air conditioning wrapped itself around her and she gave an appreciative sigh. It was chilly outside and the dark gray clouds threatened rain… or snow.

"Good afternoon, can I help you?" the woman behind the reception desk offered brusquely. She was in her early to mid-fifties, plump, with short curly brown hair and rosy cheeks. She had on a pink floral, long sleeved, button through dress and yellow cardigan and seemed disgruntled about something. Perhaps her day wasn't going as expected.

Paige's eyes moved to her. "I hope so." She smiled and stepped up to the counter. "I've just moved into town and I'm…"

"Yes, I know who you are. You're Jake's niece from Washington." The woman gave her a knowing look and the left corner of her mouth quirked up into a smirk. She didn't bother to introduce herself.

Paige gave her a thin smile, her stomach doing nervous flip flops. She was the new attraction in Moon Grove, it seemed. "I guess I should have realized. It's a small town after all."

"And there's nothing wrong with that." The woman's forehead wrinkled and she gave Paige a curious stare. "You were saying?"

"I didn't mean... I'm looking for office space..."

"Oh?" The woman's green eyes bore into her. "And why would you want to do that?"

"I'm thinking about opening my practice here. I'm a psychologist." She had trained in the area of forensic psychology but decided to pursue a role in helping others rather than work for the justice system. She felt it would be far more rewarding.

"You don't say?" The woman's eyes remained on Paige. "We already have a psychologist here, so probably not worth your while."

Paige considered turning around and trying another realtor. But she wasn't about to allow this woman to intimidate her. She mustered her professional visage and spoke. "Yes, I do say. Now, do you have any properties I can inspect or do I need to go elsewhere?"

The woman's eyes widened and she folded her arms. "No need to take that tone with me, Paige O'Connell." She stood up. "Let me speak to the property manager." She walked down the narrow hall and disappeared into a back room.

Paige felt a burst of pride for standing up for herself. Why should she be treated like an outcast? This town was once her home, although she didn't remember it, and she wasn't about to let people treat her like she didn't belong.

FIVE

Eli spotted Paige's car parked near the realtor and wondered why she would be doing business there. Was she planning on leaving so soon? He crossed the street and stood outside Dot's Diner, waiting for Paige to come out of Ashton's. He hoped she wasn't looking into selling her uncle's place and heading back to Washington just yet. He wanted a chance to get to know her again and had planned to ask her out to dinner as a welcome home. Eli also hoped to subtly quiz her about the night her parents disappeared. She'd been in the house, after all.

Ten minutes later, Paige came out of the office.

Eli walked up to her. "Hello. Good to see you again."

"Oh!" Paige spun around. "H – Hello. How are you?" she said, flustered by his sudden approach.

"Good. You?"

"Great, actually. I've just about settled in and it feels good."

He glanced through the realtor's window and spotted Beryl watching them. "That's great. Moving is always the hardest. Can I offer you a coffee?" He motioned toward the diner.

"Sorry, I can't." She held up a set of keys, giving them a jingle. "I'm on my way to look at a property."

He frowned. "Oh? Are you thinking about moving already?"

"No, no, nothing like that. I'm looking for office space. I want to set up my practice."

Eli's frown deepened. "Your practice?"

She noticed he had pale, light brown eyes, almost honey colored. Very attractive. She had never seen irises that color before. They drew her in like quicksand and for a moment she forgot what she was saying. Regaining her composure, she said, "Uh, yes, I'm a psychologist. I had my own practice back in Washington and I thought I might set one up here."

"We already have a shrink in town." He folded his arms and glanced down the road.

"Yes, so I've been told. But it can't hurt to have options, can it?" Paige pushed the keys into the right hand pocket of her jacket. "Maybe we can have that coffee another time." She glanced along the sidewalk at her car. "I really have to go. They want the keys back in half an hour."

Eli didn't want her to leave just yet. "Can I drive you?"

She smiled. "I need to do this on my own. But thanks for the offer."

"Ok, if you're sure?"

Paige nodded.

"Well I'd better let you get on with it then. I'll keep you to your word about having that coffee some time."

"Ok. That would be nice."

He watched Paige walk to her car, get in and drive away before heading into Ashton Real Estate.

Ten minutes later, Eli walked back to his four wheel drive and climbed in. As he wasn't having coffee with Paige he thought he'd utilize the time by going to see Wil to find out what he could remember about the night Paige's parents disappeared. The reports were cut and dried but there was something about them that bothered him. He hoped the ex-cop could shed some light on what the house had looked like and what he suspected had actually happened to the O'Connells.

Wil Wallace lived on a property twenty minutes out of town. These days, he chose to steer clear of the folks in Moon Grove. Eli wondered what his reasons were for staying away. Was he afraid of something? Or someone?

Eli listened to his police radio as he drove along the country road. He hoped everything remained quiet while he was gone. He wasn't concerned because he knew his deputies could handle whatever came up. He was on a mission and needed answers. Not a lot went on in the town, but on occasion things could get a little out of hand when the mood took certain members of the community, especially around the time of the full moon. The word lunatic came to mind and he gave a humorless chuckle. It was a well-known fact that the moon could influence certain types of people, causing them to do things they wouldn't normally do. He'd witnessed it with his own eyes. There was also an undercurrent in the town, one that no one talked about but most of everyone knew.

He pulled the wagon up in front of the run down, weathered, timber clad house and turned off the engine. Would the old man be willing to tell him what he remembered?

As he climbed out of his four wheel drive, Wil appeared on the porch. "Eli."

The sheriff tipped his Stetson. "Wil."

"What brings you all the way out here uninvited?" It wasn't a friendly greeting.

"I need to talk to you." He closed the car door and rounded the hood of the vehicle.

The older man's brow wrinkled. "What about?"

Eli pointed to the front screen door. "Can we go inside?"

Wil sighed. "Yeah, s'pose so." He opened the door and motioned for Eli to go in ahead of him. Once inside, he closed the wood paneled door and turned around. "I hear Jake's niece is back in town."

"Yeah, she moved into the house a few days ago." Eli waited to be offered a seat.

"Are you gonna sit or remain in the middle of the floor?" Wil asked, giving the sheriff a severe stare.

Eli sat down on a threadbare armchair and cleared his throat. "Now that Paige is back, I've been going through the archived reports on her parents' disappearance."

Wil's weathered face wrinkled even more. "Why do you want to dig up the past? There are people in the town who'd prefer things stayed buried. Let it alone, Eli, nothing good can come of it."

Eli thought he'd appeal to the man's loyalty to his job. He'd been an honest law enforcer for over forty years. "You were a good cop, Wil. There had to be things you saw that didn't sit right with you. Things you couldn't do anything about because your hands were tied."

The older man's eyes rested heavily on Eli. "What's your point?"

"I've gone over the files and all I can see is that the I's have been dotted and the T's have been crossed, but I don't think that's all there was. We both know the secret to this town. Do you think it could've had something to do with why the O'Connells were killed?"

Wil gave him an astute stare. "Assuming that's what happened."

Eli's right eyebrow arched. "You think with the amount of blood found at the scene they got up and walked away? Why wouldn't they take their daughter with them?"

"I'm not saying they walked away. You and I both know what her father was. Maybe they were taken for a reason. Maybe someone helped them get outta town." The old man frowned at him. "Does the O'Connell girl know any of this?"

"Not to my knowledge. I don't think her aunt was aware either."

Wil's discerning gaze met Eli's. "But you're not sure?"

"She didn't remember me and she doesn't remember much about the town, as far as I can tell. I wanted to query her about what she remembered but I haven't had a chance to ask her yet."

"Don't. If she doesn't remember what happened leave it that way."

Eli stood up, towering over the old man. "Why?"

"Because she's gonna find out soon enough, especially now she's back in Moon Grove."

SIX

The office space was perfect. Paige wandered around the interior imagining where everything would go. The reception desk here by the left wall, the patient chairs there on the right, the coffee machine over there in the center of the opposite wall. She smiled and gave a happy sigh. As she continued through the door and along the short hallway toward the private offices, kitchen and bathroom, someone entered the building through the front door. The hair rose on the back of Paige's neck and her stomach flipped over. She was sure she'd locked it when she came in. "Hello? Who's there?" she called, turning and walking back to the doorway.

A young woman of similar age stood smiling at her. "I couldn't believe it when they said you were coming back here. How are you? It's been such a long time."

"I'm sorry, but I don't know you."

She waved the comment off. "Oh, of course you don't. How silly of me." She extended her hand. "I'm Rebecca. Becky to my friends."

Paige shook the woman's hand. So this was the Becky Eli had mentioned. "We used to be friends, didn't we?"

Rebecca's eyes sparkled and her smile widened. "Yes, we were. In kindergarten."

"I wish I could remember the people I knew back then. I feel really bad that…"

"Don't worry about that. We can start fresh." She gazed around the room. "So are you planning on opening a store?"

"I'm going to open my psychology practice."

"Oh? You're a doctor."

"Yes, of sorts." Paige smiled. "I think this place is perfect.

"We already have a psychologist here in town."

"So everyone keeps telling me. But, like I say, it can't hurt to have options."

"Doc Taylor's been looking after the minds of Moon Grove for a long time now. I don't know if he'd appreciate the competition."

Paige gave her a curious frown. "There may be some women in this town who'd prefer to talk to another woman, don't you think?"

"Maybe, I couldn't really say." Rebecca gave her a thin smile. "I guess you've got to do what you must."

"I don't want to appear rude, but I've got to get the keys back to the realtor. Maybe we can catch up for lunch some time?"

"I'd like that." Rebecca leaned in and gave her a brief hug.

Paige felt her body go rigid and tried to relax. The woman was just being nice. She eased herself out of

Rebecca's embrace, took her cell phone from the pocket of her jacket and swiped the face. "Why don't you give me your number and I'll call you."

"No need. I work at the inn. We can have lunch there anytime. Just come by."

"Which inn?"

Rebecca chuckled. "The only one in town. You can't miss it."

"Oh, ok. Sure." Paige's eyebrows went up. "Maybe in a day or two?"

"Whenever. Lunch is between 12 and 2. And I can take a break any time during those hours."

"Great. Then I'll see you soon."

Both women walked out the front door and Paige locked it. When she turned around to say it was lovely meeting Rebecca the woman was gone. Paige glanced along the street in both directions but there was no sign of her. She shook her head and crossed the sidewalk to her car. The town and the people in it seemed – odd. Maybe it was her. Moving from the hustle and bustle of a big city to a quiet little town could have been the reason. She'd reserve judgement for a while longer, but there was definitely something about Moon Grove that unsettled her.

Back at the realtor, Paige entered the office with a smile on her face. She wasn't going to allow the receptionist's sour disposition to influence her. The woman glanced up at her and raised her index finger then lowered her head again. Paige frowned at her hand and spoke anyway. "I'd like to lease the property."

Beryl's head shot up and she gave her a severe stare. "Do you not understand when I raise my finger I'm asking you to wait a bit?"

"Have you forgotten I'm a client and that you should have a more amicable approach when interacting with people?"

The plump woman popped up out of her chair, her mouth open, her cheeks flushed. "Well, I never," she huffed in a disbelieving breath.

"No, I imagine you haven't. Look, I don't know what you've heard about me or what you think you know but I'm here and I'm staying so get used to it." Paige felt exhilarated giving the belligerent woman a piece of her mind. "Now, are we going to do business or am I going to look elsewhere? I really don't care which."

The older woman sized Paige up with a dark stare and a pout to match. "The property's been leased already. I wasn't aware. Sorry." She held out her hand for the keys.

Paige inhaled a deep breath through her nostrils and let it out slowly, counting to ten in the back of her mind and not allowing frustration to get the better of her. "Fine." She pulled the keys from her coat pocket and dropped them on the counter. "I'm sure one of the other realtors will have what I'm looking for." She turned on her heel and marched out of the office.

"Don't count on it, honey," Beryl said, as the door closed.

After visiting the only other realtor in town, and they also having no properties she could inspect, Paige climbed into her car and smacked the steering wheel. There were empty shops and buildings sitting intermittently along the main road so why couldn't she lease one? She started the engine, gave a heavy sigh and headed for home. After first deciding to give the town the benefit of the doubt, now she was certain there was definitely something wrong with it.

As Paige cruised along the street toward her house she noticed Eli's car parked outside. *Damn! What does he want now?* She pulled into her driveway, turned off the engine and blew out a noisy breath. After the day she'd had she just wanted to go inside, close the door and sulk for a while. Even psychologists had the right to do that on occasion. Pulling the keys from the ignition, she was about to open the door when it swung out of her grasp.

"How'd the property hunt go? Find something you like?" Eli smiled at her.

Paige got out of the car, pulled the door from his hand and slammed it. "Don't you know? I'm sure the grapevine would've spread the word by now." She sounded angry and she knew it. She inhaled another long breath and let it out. It wasn't his fault the people of Moon Grove were unkind. Not at all as she remembered them when she'd visited her uncle from time to time.

Eli frowned at her. "No, I haven't heard. I've been on the road. What happened?"

Paige looked up into his honey colored eyes and her stomach flipped over. She ignored the feeling. "With all the empty properties on the main street of town why doesn't anyone want to lease me one?" She folded her arms and gave him a disgruntled stare.

"I have no idea. I assume they're not all leased."

"You know you should never assume anything." She headed for the front porch.

Eli followed. "Wait a minute." He reached out and grabbed her arm.

She pulled free and swung around. "You have no right to touch me."

"I – I'm sorry. I just wanted to stop you so we could finish our conversation. I didn't mean anything by it." She rubbed her arm. "I didn't hurt you, did I?"

Paige gave him a thin smile. "You have a firm grip. But, no, you didn't hurt me. I'm made of tougher stuff than that."

"Good to know," he said, giving Paige a broad grin. "Do you want me to check with Beryl and find out if there are other offices available?"

Paige's right eyebrow arched. "I don't think that's a good idea. The woman hates me. She was so rude to me today."

"She can be like that sometimes. Not that I'm excusing her behavior."

"Glad to hear it. Thanks for the offer, but I'm a big girl, I can take care of myself."

"I don't doubt it. I was just trying to be neighborly."

Paige climbed the front steps and unlocked the door. "Well, I'd better let you go. You must have a million things to do, being the town cop."

"I have some free time up my sleeve." His gorgeous grin widened even more. "Why don't I show you around?"

"Thanks, I appreciate it but I'm not in the mood for a Moon Grove tour right now. Perhaps another time?"

"Like the coffee, you mean?" Eli folded his arms. "If you don't want to have coffee with me or…"

"It's not that. I still have a bit to do before I'm properly settled in and I want to get it done so it's not hanging over my head for the next few weeks."

Eli frowned into her eyes. "Ok, fair enough." He knew

she was trying to avoid them sitting down together to talk. "When do you think you'll be free? Maybe we could have dinner some time as a welcome."

Dinner? That would mean spending a couple of hours with him.

"Can I call you?"

Eli gave her a skeptical frown. "That usually means never, doesn't it?"

"No, not at all. I just need some time to get myself sorted and find a place to work and then we can have that coffee."

"So you don't want to have dinner with me?"

Paige let out a soft sigh. He wasn't going to let it go, was he?

SEVEN

The next evening, Paige was getting ready to go out with Eli. She'd felt bad about continually putting him off and decided to go with the dinner plan, at least it would stop him from asking. He'd be coming by to pick her up within the next half hour. She glanced in the mirror and freshened up her lipstick then sprayed the pulse points on her throat, between her breasts and at her wrists with Calvin Klein's Secret Obsession.

Because of the freezing weather conditions, she had chosen to wear a mid-length, black wool skirt, crimson sweater and knee high black boots. She also didn't want to give Eli the impression that she was interested in him in any way other than friendship. He seemed nice enough, but she wasn't looking for a relationship right now.

The brass ship's bell beside the front door clanged and she rushed downstairs to answer it. When she opened the door she couldn't believe the same man was standing in front of her. Eli Blackwood cleaned up nicely. He was dressed in washed denim jeans, a white button through shirt and a casual black jacket. *Very nice.* And he smelled good too. The cologne he'd chosen to wear drifted into

Paige's nostrils sending a tingle through her body. Why did he have to be so attractive?

"Hey, sorry I'm early. I guess I'm excited about our dinner date." He realized what he'd said and attempted to rephrase it. "I didn't mean an actual date…"

"I know what you mean," Paige assured him with a chuckle, grabbing her jacket from the coat rack and pulling it on as she closed the front door.

Neither knew what to say on the drive into town. It really did feel like an awkward first date. Paige hoped Eli wouldn't see it that way, but figured he probably did. Considering what he'd said when he arrived.

Eli pulled his four wheel drive into the curb outside The Jade Dragon Chinese Restaurant, took the keys from the ignition, climbed out and walked around the vehicle to open the door for Paige. A nice gesture. "I hope you like Chinese," he said, extending his hand to help her out of the car.

She smiled. "I love Chinese."

"Good. I wasn't sure so I had a plan B." He gave her a wide grin. His smile was gorgeous and her heart gave a little shudder.

"Really? What was the plan?" She took his hand and stepped onto the sidewalk.

"The Moon Grove Inn."

"I thought they only served lunch."

"To the public, yes. But I'm a resident of the town and the owners have known me since I was a kid. They serve dinner to guests in the evenings so I thought if you didn't like Chinese we could go over there. Home cooking always hits the spot." He patted his abdomen. He had attractive hands too. Long fingers… and clean nails.

"Yes it does. Maybe I can drop your name when I have lunch there with Rebecca." She watched him close the door and set the alarm before he took her by the arm and escorted her into the restaurant.

The Jade Dragon blew her mind. She never considered a restaurant of its caliber would be in such a small town like Moon Grove. The subdued lighting, well dressed tables and oriental music playing softly in the background reminded her of Chalin's Restaurant on Connecticut Avenue. The place had only one other couple seated at a table and Paige wondered if they did a good trade.

The proprietor walked up to them. "Good evening, Eli, your table's ready."

Good evening, Liu. Thanks."

Liu led them to the back of the restaurant to a corner table. Once they were seated he offered them menus and said he'd return to take their order.

Paige gazed around the elegant, Asian décor impressed with the wonderful ambiance of the place.

"You like?" Eli asked, his eyes taking in everything about her.

"Yes, it's lovely. I never expected a restaurant like this in such a small town."

"We do get the odd tourist or two." His tone had been tighter than intended.

"I'm sorry. I didn't me to belittle Moon Grove. It's a lovely little town. It's just… well I guess I expected it to be more… countrified."

"Most people do. But we can hold our own."

Paige felt as though he had taken what she'd said as an insult, but she hadn't meant it in that way. "I am sorry, Eli."

"It's ok. You've come here from the big city so what could I expect."

She gave him a disgruntled frown. "What's that supposed to mean?"

"I guess you're used to high class venues, living in Washington. Maybe you think our *countrified* town isn't up to your standard."

"That's not fair. I really wasn't trying to belittle Moon Grove, it's very quaint…"

"Quaint?" Eli's eyebrows shot up.

"Well, yes, it has an old world kind of charm to it. It's sweet." She realized she was making things worse. "Will you please accept my apology and move on?"

Eli sat back and folded his arms. He studied the woman opposite him before speaking again. He wanted to get to know her but he wasn't sure he could accept her superior attitude, whether she knew she had one or not. "Maybe us having dinner wasn't a good idea after all."

Paige's mouth gaped. "What?!"

"You've been here all of five minutes and seem to have formed an opinion of what this town is like before giving it a chance."

"Wait a minute." She dropped the menu onto the table. "I wasn't being horrible. I think the town is…"

He frowned. "Sweet. Yes, I heard what you said."

"Well it is. I don't think I said anything wrong so why the sudden hostility?"

"Moon Grove has as much to offer as anywhere else. Maybe you should get to know the town before passing judgment."

"I think you're making too much out of what I said. I just meant…"

"I can see this wasn't a good idea. Perhaps I should take you home."

She scowled at him. "Are you serious? You offer to take me to dinner, I get dressed up and come here with you and now you want to take me home."

"You may have moved away and created a different life for yourself, but I've lived and worked in this town my whole life and it's a great place to be." Why was he defending Moon Grove when he knew what lay beneath it? Because of Paige's attitude, that's why. He hated it when people from outside came in and tried to tell them what was wrong with the place. If it wasn't good enough for her then maybe she should consider going back to Washington. "If you're not happy here then perhaps you should go back to where you came from."

Paige's eyes widened, along with her mouth. "How incredibly rude!" She popped up off her seat. "Don't bother taking me home. I know the way, I can walk." She threw the white napkin she'd placed on her lap onto the table and marched to the door, tears stinging the backs of her eyes. She wouldn't allow herself to cry and give Eli Blackwood the satisfaction of knowing he'd upset her.

Eli inhaled a deep breath, his muscular chest expanding so wide that he almost popped the buttons on his shirt. The woman was frustratingly annoying and beautiful at the same time. "Wait." He pushed back his chair and strutted toward her. "I'll drive you. It's not safe out there after dark. The wildlife often wanders into town and I wouldn't want you being attacked by something on my account."

She turned and glowered up at him. "As I've already said, I'm a big girl and can take care of myself. Don't do me any favors." She opened the door and a blast of freezing night air hit her in the face. She stepped onto the sidewalk.

Eli followed her. "Fine. If you're sure that's how you feel." He climbed into his four wheel drive and drove away.

Paige stood on the sidewalk watching the red taillights disappear into the distance. She gave a huff. "Well, of all the nerve." She knew she shouldn't have accepted his offer of dinner. She shook her head, pulled her coat around her and began the mile or so walk back to her uncle's house. It was difficult calling it her home, but she guessed she'd get used to it in time. Lucky for her she'd chosen to wear flat-heeled boots otherwise she'd have blisters to go along with her rising blood pressure. Eli Blackwood was a rude, incredibly handsome jerk.

As she continued further along the main street, Paige remembered the woman at the grocery store telling her there was a short cut through the woods. The trail was well marked and it would cut about ten minutes off the walk. When she reached the beginning of the path, she pulled her cell phone from the pocket of her jacket and pressed the flashlight. *Am I really going to do this?* She swallowed the nervous lump in her throat as a shiver ran through her and stepped between the trees onto the well-trodden, dark dirt path.

EIGHT

Night sounds around her caused Paige's stomach to squeeze into a tight ball of fear and creeping apprehensive fingers trailed an icy path up her spine to the nape of her neck. Had she made a mistake taking this short cut? She picked up her pace. An owl hooted somewhere nearby and Paige spun on her heel, her eyes darting around the overhanging tree branches as she shone her flashlight into them. Glowing beady eyes stared back at her from all angles: the birdlife of the woods. She breathed a relieved sigh, turned and continued moving.

The chill wind whipped around her and she shivered, pulling her collar up around her jawline. She'd be relieved when she reached the front porch of the house. A twig snapped and something brushed past the low-lying shrubbery. Paige's belly squirmed, the rolling sensation rising in her throat. She stopped in her tracks and fanned the flashlight across the scrub. Nothing. She sucked in a shaky breath and blew it out. *It's a small town. Nothing ever happens in small towns,* she told herself and pushed onward with caution, her eyes and phone light darting around the legion of trees.

About five minutes from the exit she broke into a jog. That would get her out onto the street faster. The woods were ominous at the best of times, but more so at night, and her stomach continued to squirm. She held her flashlight out in front of her so she could see the path and caught sight of a pair of animal eyes glowing in the dark not far ahead. She came to an abrupt stop, her nerves buzzing through every fiber of her body. Was it a dog? Or could it be something more dangerous?

Taking a step backwards, Paige contemplated turning around and running. Could she? Should she? What if it was a coyote or a wolf? Their speed would outmatch hers. Her lungs tightened causing her breaths to come in short bursts, pluming white in front of her face. *What should I do?* She took another step backwards. The eyes moved forward. Paige's heartbeat knocked against her ribs. She stepped back again. The glowing eyes came toward her through the gloom.

Fight or flight?

Paige chose flight.

She took off running as fast as she could in the direction she had come from. The dream she'd been having for years popped into her head and her stomach rolled in a wave of nausea. *This can't be happening.* She flew through the trees, the gleaming eyes in hot pursuit. "Help!" she screamed. Would anyone hear her in here? She picked up her pace and rocketed through the dense woods toward the main street, the animal behind her gaining ground. She peered over her shoulder, her heart in her throat. The eyes were now glowing red. "Somebody help me!" She raced through the scrub and low-lying branches.

Paige tripped on a jagged tree root and threw her hands forward, fumbling to stay on her feet. Visions from her dream rushed through her mind and she let out a shrill scream as she streaked through the trees, the low branches and leaves connecting with her face, scratching her skin.

The large dark creature kept coming. Was it a wolf?

All of a sudden the thing leapt into the air over the top of Paige and landed in front of her.

She skidded to a stop, shining the light into the huge wolf's snarling face. It didn't turn away. Instead, it gave a throaty growl, bared its canines, and crept toward her.

Paige stumbled backwards, her eyes never leaving the creature for a second, her pulse pumping in her throat. She was about to be torn to shreds by the monstrous beast. She had nowhere to run.

A shot rang out shattering the eerie silence and the wolf's huge form dissolved into the dark trees.

Paige let out the breath she'd been holding and lowered her head to her knees, the blood whooshing in her ears.

Eli and one of his deputies stalked toward her. "Are you all right?" Eli helped her straighten up.

"How did you know where to find me?" she asked between shaky breaths.

"Joe at the gas station heard you scream while he was out checking the pumps and called it in."

The deputy stood with a hand on his hip and shone his flashlight into the surrounding, shadowed woods. "Looks like whatever it was is long gone."

"It was a huge black wolf." Paige's face was a pale shade of white.

"There aren't any wolves around here. Maybe it was a coyote or a bobcat," Craig told her.

Paige frowned at him. "I know what I saw."

"Are you sure 'bout that? Being from the city and all." Craig lowered his flashlight and gave her a condescending stare.

Eli stepped in. "Let's get you home." He wrapped an arm around Paige's shoulders and helped her through the woods to the main street. "What possessed you to go through there at night? Didn't I say it wasn't safe out here after dark?"

Paige stepped out of his supportive embrace. "I wouldn't have had to if you hadn't left me standing on the street."

Craig's left eyebrow arched and he smirked at Eli.

"Can we discuss this later? Let's just get you back to your place and make sure you're not hurt."

"Ok. Fine."

Eli opened the car door and gave her a hand up. After closing it he turned to Craig, his index finger raised, and said, "Not one word. You got that?"

"Whatever you say, boss." He gave Eli another deliberate smirk.

"I want you to round up the others and have them do a thorough sweep of the woods. See if they can pick up the scent. We need to locate the lone wolf and find out what it wants... or eliminate it if it doesn't want to cooperate."

Craig glanced over his shoulder into the woods and nodded then stalked back to his vehicle, got in and drove away.

Eli walked around his four wheel drive and climbed in. He looked at Paige and noticed the scratches on her face and hands. "We'll need to clean those up." He pointed to the injuries.

Paige gave a heavy sigh. "Can you please just take me home now? I've had quite enough of tonight."

"You'll have to come into the station tomorrow and file a report." Eli started the engine. "We need to keep track of animal attacks." *For more reasons than one.* He knew the wolf tonight wasn't just any wolf, although he didn't know who it was. Why had it gone after Paige?

When Eli pulled into Paige's driveway, she opened the door and stepped down out of the car. "Don't bother coming in with me, I can take care of the scratches myself. Thanks for dropping me home." She closed the door and headed for the porch.

Eli sat and watched her through the windshield as she walked away. What was he going to do about her? If she wasn't careful she'd get herself killed. Or worse.

NINE

When Paige opened the door, stepped inside and turned on the light she couldn't believe what confronted her. Furnishings and belongings were strewn everywhere. Her home had been ransacked. She heard Eli start his car and back down the drive so she turned on her heel and rushed outside. "Eli, wait! Wait!" she called, waving her arms in the air to attract his attention.

Eli pulled on the parking brake, turned off the engine, and flew out of the car. Racing across the lawn he said, "What's wrong?"

Paige motioned to the doorway.

Eli scowled as his eyes met the chaos inside. "What the...?" He climbed the steps and entered the house. Paige right behind him. "What were they looking for?"

She frowned at him. "How would I know?"

"Man, they sure did a number on your place." He stood with hands on hips gazing into the living room then the dining room from the entry hall. "I'll call it in and get our forensic guy out here to fingerprint. We need to go through everything to see what's missing. But that'll have to wait until after the crime scene's been investigated. You'll need to be fingerprinted too."

"Ok." Paige sighed. Could the night get any worse? "I can't believe this. Who would do such a thing? And why me?"

Eli gave a heavy sigh. "I hate to say this but it could be someone who thinks you're an outsider."

Paige folded her arms. "Well that's just peachy, isn't it?"

"I didn't say it was right, I just said it could be the case."

"Nice welcome." She trudged up the stairs to grab the first aid kit.

"You shouldn't go up there," Eli said, climbing the staircase behind her.

She glanced over her shoulder. "Then why are you following me?"

"Did you consider that whoever did this could still be in the house?"

Paige stopped short on the landing and spun around, her eyes wide. "Well, no."

"Let me go ahead of you." He stepped around her and continued to the second floor. After a few minutes he called, "You can come up now."

Paige continued up the stairs and wandered along the hallway to the bathroom. She retrieved the first aid kit and followed Eli back downstairs.

Just as they reached the entry hall his phone went off. "Blackwood. Craig. Can you contact Paul and have him come over to Paige's place and come over yourself? We've got a break and enter."

After he finished with the call, Eli walked Paige out to

the front porch and sat her on the swing seat. He took the first aid kit from her hand, opened it and picked up the small bottle of antiseptic and some cotton wool balls. "Let me clean those scratches on your face while we wait." He squatted down in front of her and poured some of the liquid onto the cotton.

Paige's eyes met his and she folded her arms. "The attack wouldn't have happened if you'd been a gentleman and drove me home."

Eli sighed and dabbed the moistened cotton swab onto one of the cuts on Paige's face.

She jerked away. "Ouch!"

His serious gaze met hers. "Sorry, I should've warned you it would sting. But you stung first."

"Well it's true." She straightened and allowed him to continue tending her wounds. Even though she didn't want to admit it she liked him touching her.

"I came back for you but you'd left. I even took a drive along the main road to see if I could find you."

"You did?"

"Yeah. I never intended for you to walk home alone. I took offense to something so trivial and it shouldn't have happened. I'm sorry." He continued cleaning her cuts. "You know, we could start over."

Paige gave him a thin smile. "I'm sorry, too, but maybe that's not a good idea."

"If you're concerned I'll leave you to walk home again you could meet me there." He finished cleaning up the scratches and closed the first aid kit. "But I assure you it won't happen again."

"I appreciate that, but I think we'd better leave things the way they are. I'm not looking for…"

At that moment, two police units pulled into the curb outside Paige's house.

"Finally," Eli said, climbing to his feet and walking down the path to the street.

After several minutes, the trio stepped onto the front porch and Eli introduced his colleagues. "This scruffy looking character is Craig Campbell, one of my deputies. You met him earlier in the woods."

Paige eyed him darkly. "I remember." *I remember his condescending manner when I said I'd seen a wolf. Which I had.*

"And this is Paul Burke. He'll be fingerprinting you and the rest of the house."

Paul extended his blue latex-gloved hand and smiled. "Good to meet you, Paige."

She shook it. "Thanks. Nice to meet you, too." Were all the men in this town built like Eli? All tall, muscular and good-looking?

Craig and Paul entered the house.

Eli's gaze returned to her. "Why don't you sit here while we do the preliminaries? Then you can go through everything and tell me if anything's missing. Ok?"

Paige nodded and sighed. "Sure."

Eli headed to the open front door.

"What about my fingerprints?"

"Paul will take them after he's fingerprinted the house, that way he can eliminate yours first."

"Oh, ok." Paige shivered as she sat outside in the crisp, cold night air. She'd almost finished settling in and now she had to start all over again. And she was sore and injured from her incident with the wolf. It *was* a wolf! She was sure it was.

Forty five minutes later, Eli came out onto the porch. "Want to come in now?"

Paige eased herself out of the swing seat and followed him inside. He led her into the kitchen where Paul was waiting to take her fingerprints.

"Where's the ink pad?" Paige asked, staring at the small black and gray box sitting on the table beside a laptop.

"We don't use them anymore. We do electronic fingerprinting these days," Paul offered.

"Wow. I didn't know that. Saves the mess, I guess." She gave him a smile.

"Yeah, it does. May I?" He pointed to her hands.

Paige nodded. "Sure."

Paul took her right hand and pressed her thumb onto the panel on the device then followed with each finger of both hands. "There, all done."

"Thanks." Paige turned to Eli. "You'll let me know if you find out who did this, won't you?"

He nodded. "Yes, of course."

Once the forensic and basic report was done Craig and Paul left.

Eli assisted Paige with the clean up and going through the things strewn throughout the house. He felt bad that someone in his town would do something like this to her and wondered what the motive was as nothing appeared to be missing.

A loud crash echoed up from the cellar. Eli pulled his weapon and headed to the closed door in the entry hall beside the staircase. "Wait here," he told Paige, throwing the door open, switching on the dull yellow light and flying down the stairs. The cellar had been turned over too.

Boxes were open, their contents spilled all over the floor. Old chairs had been flipped and cut open, the white stuffing lying on the concrete like a layer of snow. "What the hell?" They'd smashed the ground level window to get out. Shards of broken glass lay on the ledge and the floor below. That was the noise they'd heard. What were they searching for? And how did they get in?

"Everything all right down there?" Paige's voice echoed into the cellar from the top of the wooden stairs.

"Uh, yeah, but they've been down here as well."

Paige groaned. "Of course they have."

Eli made his way back upstairs. "I'll need to secure the window in the cellar. That was the noise we heard."

She gasped. "Oh, no!"

"I'll head out to the garage. Jake would have some timber and tools out there. Won't be too long. Close the door after me and lock it." Eli stepped outside and headed down the front steps.

Paige closed and locked the door behind him. She shivered as she turned around and studied the open cellar door. Eli had been right about someone still being in the house. What were they looking for?

TEN

It was almost two in the morning by the time they finished securing the cellar window and cleaning up the house. It had taken hours to get everything in some kind of order again and Paige was exhausted. She told Eli how grateful she was for his help and walked him to the door. She needed to try and get some sleep before the sun came up.

"Are you sure you'll feel safe being here by yourself?" Eli gave her a concerned frown.

"I'll be fine." She opened the front door and sighed. "What I need right now is some rest."

"I could camp out on the sofa if it would make you feel better." His eyes moved to the slate colored three seater under the window in the living room then back to Paige.

"Thanks, but I'm sure whoever broke in is long gone by now. I doubt they'd come back twice in one night." At least she hoped they wouldn't.

"Ok, if you're sure?" His gaze met hers and lingered longer than it should have. She had beautiful, pale blue eyes and a splash of light colored freckles across the bridge of her nose and the tops of her cheeks. She was a redhead after all. He cleared his throat, "Well, goodnight then." He stepped out onto the porch.

Paige eased the door forward. "I really appreciate you staying to help me. You didn't have to."

"No problem at all."

"Goodnight."

Eli gave her a brief smile and headed across the lawn to his car. He wasn't about to leave her unprotected.

Paige closed the door and leaned against the curtained glass. Romance was the last thing she needed right now, but she couldn't help being aware of the intense attraction between them.

Eli backed out of Paige's driveway without turning on the headlights, pulled up under the tree outside her house and released the backrest to recline his seat. If he couldn't camp out inside then he'd keep watch outside. Despite Paige's assumption that whoever had ransacked her home wouldn't come back, he wanted to make absolutely sure she was safe. You can never be too careful, especially in Moon Grove.

He reached between the seats, pulled his jacket through the gap and tucked it around himself. Even though he didn't feel the cold, because Lycan blood ran hot, he had to make it appear as though he did in case Paige found him outside in the morning before he woke up.

Was she putting on a brave face? He was sure of it. Would she get any sleep tonight? If he were in her shoes he wouldn't, being a woman alone in a two story house. Eli spotted the subdued yellow glow of a lamp flash on in the living room and got his answer. She was spooked and wasn't planning to sleep tonight.

Why was the little girl out in the woods alone? Were they playing hide and seek? He continued to follow her through the legion of towering trees. It grew darker the further they ran. Cold fingers of apprehension crawled up his spine and he shivered. "Wait for me," he called after her.

She didn't stop.

As she ran through the trees, her long, wavy red hair flowed behind her like a cape and she giggled even more.

The sound echoed around him and he couldn't understand why she was giggling. The woods were frightening.

"Wait!" he called again.

She glanced over her shoulder. "Come on, silly, keep running. You haven't caught me yet," she sang as she disappeared into the gloom.

"No. Wait. Come back." His eyes surveyed the spooky darkness surrounding him. He could hear her giggling in the distance. He followed the sound. "Where are you?" The road map of nerves winding through his body prickled with fear and his anxious gaze flitted around the shadowy trees. "Answer me!" he shouted, a nervous quiver in his voice.

The giggling grew distant. She was too far ahead of him now.

He broke into a run, pushing through the tangle of low-lying branches. The woods grew even darker. His stomach shrank, his heart raced, and tears stung the backs of his eyes. *Where is she?*

A shrill scream shattered the dense silence and he raced through the trees, clambering over twisted, rotting roots and underbrush.

Then he saw it.

A jagged trail of blood.

Splashes of red leading into the legion of tall trees.

He called her name over and over but she didn't answer.

He followed the trail deeper and deeper into the woods. The further he got the more blood appeared on the path.

Another ear piercing scream shattered the silence and he stopped short, sucking in a sharp nervous breath.

"Paige?" His high-pitched frantic voice resonated around him. "Where are you?"

Eli sprang forward cracking his forehead against the windshield, his heart racing, beads of sweat dotting his brow. He raised his hand to his head. No blood. It was still dark outside. What time was it? He turned the key in the ignition and the dashboard digital clock lit up. 4.05 AM. Visions of the dream circled his brain. He'd called Paige's name, hadn't he? That was new. What did it mean? And where was the place in his dream?

His eyes roamed the street and the front of Paige's house. The light was off. Maybe she had finally gone to sleep. Eli eased his six foot four inch frame back against the seat and closed his eyes. Somehow he needed to find out what the dream meant.

Around sun up, Eli was awakened by tapping on the driver's window. He peeled back his left eyelid, sat bolt upright and pressed the button on the armrest to roll the window down. Paige was on the sidewalk in her pink robe with a steaming mug of coffee in her hand. "Did you sleep out here all night?"

"Uh, yeah, I did." Eli gave her a sheepish glance, straightened in his seat and eased the cup out of her hand.

"Thanks." He took a cautious sip. "I wanted to make sure you were ok. Get any sleep?"

"Not much. I kept turning it over in my mind who would do such a thing and what they could possibly be looking for. I don't keep drugs at my house. As a psychologist I can't even write a prescription for them." Paige thought it endearing that he'd slept outside her house in the freezing conditions. If she'd had any idea he was going to do it she would have agreed to him sleeping on her sofa.

"I don't think they were looking for drugs."

She shrugged. "What then?"

Eli shook his head and sighed. "I don't know but I will find out. That's a promise."

"I appreciate it." She gave him a thin smile. "Want to come inside? I made waffles."

"Thanks, but I'd better go home, take a quick shower and change my clothes before heading to the station. Wouldn't want the grapevine to get the wrong idea and sully your reputation." He gave her an amused grin and handed her the half empty mug. "I'll talk to you later when you come in to file that report."

"Ok." Paige couldn't hide her disappointment. She'd hoped to spend some time getting to know him better. Even though she'd promised herself she wouldn't get involved in a romantic relationship, she was finding it more and more difficult to find reasons not to now that Eli had entered her life.

Eli clipped in his seatbelt. "Oh, before I forget, I had a chat to Ted Ashton the owner of Ashton Realty. He said the application for the office you were looking at fell through and if you're still interested to come by and see him personally and he'll organize the paperwork."

Paige's eyebrows rose. "Really? I am definitely still interested. It's perfect." She knew Eli had something to do with the realtor's change of heart. "How did you manage it?"

He leaned out of the window and gave her a heart-melting smile. "I just used my small town charm."

Her pulse quickened. He was so attractive. And those eyes. She pulled her thoughts back to the conversation. "Thank you so much!"

"I'm glad you're happy about it. Maybe you'll reconsider a second attempt at dinner. I'll see you later." He started the engine and drove away.

ELEVEN

At ten o'clock that morning, Paige drove to the police station and pulled into the small gravel parking lot on the left hand side of the single story building. The red and white timber clad house with gray front porch and white railing sat amidst a cluster of tall Ash trees, and if it wasn't for the police department emblem on the white wood and glass paneled door no one would recognize it as a place of law enforcement, because it looked like every other house in the neighboring streets.

She pushed open the door and stepped into the heated office out of the freezing cold. The warmth of the room caressed her chilled face and she gave a contented sigh.

A woman in her forties sat behind a dark wood desk talking on the phone. When she noticed Paige she quickly ended her conversation. "I'll have to call you back, Charmaine. I got a customer... uh client." She plonked the receiver down, clasped her hands in front of her and pasted a pleasant professional smile on her face. "Well, good morning. I'm Rosemarie. How may I help you?"

"Eli... um, Sheriff Blackwood asked me to come in to file a report about an animal attack." Paige's eyes roamed the small office looking for him before returning her gaze to the woman in front of her.

"Oh? That's right. You were attacked on the trail last night by a…?"

"Wild animal, yes," Paige finished the woman's sentence. She didn't want to be ridiculed again for saying it was a huge black wolf. Which it was.

Rosemarie pointed over her shoulder. "Sheriff's out back in the… I'll just go get him for you. Won't be a tick." She got up, walked across to a closed brown wood door, pushed it open and stepped through, closing it behind her.

Paige glanced around the office once more and sighed. She thought Eli would be here to greet her because she'd called ahead to let him know she was on her way.

A blast of cold air met the backs of her legs as the front door opened and a cop trudged inside out of the chilly wind. When he spotted Paige he smiled. "Pretty cold out there, huh?"

"Yes, it is."

He walked up to her, hand extended. "I'm Bobby McBride. But I'm pretty sure you don't remember me either." He smiled. Also as tall as Eli and with similar colored eyes, Bobby was ruggedly handsome with sandy colored hair and a stubbled chin.

Paige shook his hand. "I'm sorry. I really wish I did remember everyone I knew back then."

"Pay it no mind. You'll get to know us again. And then you'll really be sorry." He chuckled as he walked over, shrugged out of his police issue, dark blue jacket and hung it on the coat rail in the right hand corner of the office, then removed his hat, scarf and gloves and walked over to a desk on the opposite wall and sat down behind it.

Eli came through the door, followed by the receptionist. "Hello Miss O'Connell. Would you please come this way?"

Paige smiled at Bobby before turning and following Eli into a glass office behind the desk Rosemarie occupied.

Eli gestured at the chair in front of his desk, closed the door and took his seat. "Have you been to see Ted yet?" He opened the second drawer and rummaged through the paperwork.

"Yes. All signed and sealed."

"That's great. I'm glad you got the place you wanted."

"Thanks. Now all I have to do is get the office set up and advertise for a receptionist."

"You'll want to head over to the Moon Grove Tribune after you finish here. Wendy Ellis can help you place the ad."

"Thank you. Is it far from here?"

"It's on the opposite corner to the bank. You can't miss it."

"Great. I'll do that."

Eli found the form he'd been looking for and slid it and a ballpoint pen across the desk. "If you'd like to write down your version of last night's events we can make an official report."

"Ok. Sure." She picked up the pen and paper and began filling out the basic information on the form first: Name, address, phone number.

"Can I get you some coffee?" He stood up. "We have donuts too if you're hungry."

"Thanks, coffee's fine." Paige smiled up at him.

"Coming right up." Eli rounded his desk, stepped out of the room and closed the door.

Paige stopped writing and studied the office. Typical male décor. And slightly untidy. Well, perhaps not untidy but he had a fair amount of paperwork strewn across his desk. Her eyes returned to the form in front of her. What was she supposed to write down?

The door opened and Eli came in carrying two mugs. He walked over and set one down in front of Paige then returned to his seat. "Doing ok?"

"I'm wondering what I should actually say. I know what I saw but..."

"Perhaps just state that you were attacked by a large, wild animal. That leaves it open to anything from a coyote, to bob cat, wolf, or bear."

"But I saw a huge black wolf. Shouldn't I say that? It is a legal document after all. And what if it attacks someone else?"

"It won't."

Paige's eyebrows rose. "How can you be so sure?"

"Gut instinct." He sipped his coffee. "Animals don't stay in one place too long. It's probably already moved on."

Paige's inquisitive stare lingered on him. "What do you know that you're not telling me?"

There was a long silence as Eli's serious gaze remained on Paige. Should he tell her? "What could I possibly know that I'm not sharing with you?" He leaned back in his chair and folded his arms. "There are no wolves around here that we know of. If there was one then it's a long way from home."

"So it's not impossible that there's one in Moon Grove right now?"

"It *may* be possible, but highly unlikely."

"I know what I saw. I didn't imagine it."

"Look, we haven't had this kind of attack in town before, so it's new territory. I don't doubt you saw something, but…" His gaze moved to the window then back to her. At least not in a while, but he wasn't about to tell her that.

"Then I'm going to say I was attacked by a large black wolf." She continued writing. "It's the truth."
Eli sighed and didn't argue. He figured nothing he could say would change her mind.

When Paige stepped into the office of the Moon Grove Tribune she was once again pleasantly surprised by the elegance of her surroundings. The well-appointed office was warm, welcoming, and painted in a low sheen Full Moon shade. Paige recognized the color by a sample she'd picked up when she repainted her apartment in Washington before selling it. A coffee colored sofa with a magazine table sat to Paige's left. There were three oak desks lining the right wall by the side window and white-framed pictures of water colored roses along the left. Very chic.

The only person in the office was a blonde woman in her thirties, around Paige's age. So she could only assume it was Wendy Ellis. The woman walked over to her, hand extended, and gave a welcoming smile. "Hi, Paige, it's great to finally meet you."

"Nice to meet you too. Eli suggested that I come and see you. I want to place an ad in your paper."

Wendy's left eyebrow arched. "For what?"

"I'm opening my practice in town and I'll need a front desk receptionist."

The journalist frowned. "What kind of practice?

"I'm a psychologist."

"Oh? You know there's already a shrink in town, Doctor John Taylor, right?"

"Yes, a few people have mentioned it."

"Ok. Well, I can certainly help you with the want ad." She motioned for Paige to follow her over to the back desk. "Please, have a seat."

"Thank you." Paige sat down opposite Wendy. She had the feeling there was something else on the woman's mind but would wait to see if the topic came up.

"What would you like the ad to say?" Wendy's fingers hovered over the keyboard of her computer.

"I suppose it should say front desk receptionist needed. Good interpersonal skills. High level of confidentiality. Able to work odd hours due to appointment schedule. Resume and references required. Please contact Paige O'Connell. Here's the number." She slid a business card across the desk and frowned at Wendy. "Does that sound ok?"

"Yes, should be fine for the people in Moon Grove."

Paige's frown deepened. "What do you mean?"

Wendy shook her head. "Nothing." She finished typing in the phone number. "There, it's set for the next edition, which comes out Friday."

"Great. How much do I owe you?"

The woman gave her an odd grin. "What I'd really like to do is interview you."

Paige's eyebrows rose. "Why?"

"Because your story is interesting and worth telling."

"I don't understand. What story?"

"Your past and what happened to your parents. It would make a great front page feature article."

Paige stood up and reached into her purse for her wallet. "No, thanks. How much for the ad?"

Wendy sighed. "Twenty five dollars." She picked up a business card and offered it to Paige. "If you change your mind give me a call."

Paige dropped the twenty five dollars on the desk and didn't take the card. "I won't. Thanks for your time." She turned on her heel and marched out of the Moon Grove Tribune. When she reached her car, she heard someone call her name. She glanced along the street to her left then turned her head to the right.

Rebecca came up to her. "Hi, what brings you into town?"

"Hi, Rebecca…"

"Please, call me Beck or Becky. We're old friends."

"Ok, thanks." Paige felt odd calling her Beck or Becky. They hadn't been friends for many years, but she'd keep things friendly. It seemed that everyone in town knew what she was doing before she did. "I just placed a want ad."

"Oh? What are you looking for?" Rebecca's eyes moved to the Tribune window.

"I need a receptionist for my office. You wouldn't happen to know anyone who's looking for a front desk receptionist job, would you?"

The young woman's gaze moved back to Paige. "Sorry, no." She pasted a sweet smile on her face. "But if I hear of anyone I'll be sure to steer them in your direction."

"Thank you, I'd appreciate that."

"Did you figure out when we could catch up for lunch?"

Paige glanced at her watch. 12.18 PM. "I'm free now." She had a feeling Rebecca had come along the street to her for that very reason.

"Great. Follow me." She waved Paige on and both women walked back to the Moon Grove Inn.

TWELVE

Eli called Craig into his office and asked him to close the door. The young man gave the sheriff a serious glare then scraped back the chair in front of the desk and dropped into it. They had never gotten along. Not from day one. And even though Eli was his superior, Craig felt compelled to make his life difficult. It felt good. He figured the situation would come to a head at some point and he couldn't wait. He'd love to get into a physical altercation with his boss. Winner take all.

Eli folded his arms and leaned back in his chair. "What did the others find out last night? And why didn't you get back to me?" He could sense the animosity oozing from Craig. He hated being an underdog and Eli knew the challenge for leadership would rear its ugly head one day. But until that day, he would remain the Alpha until someone stronger and faster could defeat him in a fair fight.

"Are you even sure there is a lone wolf out there? Wouldn't it be part of another pack?" Craig challenged. "The woman could've seen a big dog and thought it was a wolf. She was pretty shaken up."

"I believe her. She knows what she saw and we have to find it and contain it until we can figure out what it's doing here." Eli leaned forward resting his elbows on the desk. "It might be scouting."

"You believe her because you've got the hots for her, that's all."

"You don't know what you're talking about, as usual. If Paige said she saw a wolf, she saw a wolf."

"The guys didn't pick up any scent or tracks." Craig folded his arms and crossed one leg over the other. "What if she got spooked in the dark and thought she saw something?"

"There has to be some kind of evidence out there. The fact that Paige's house was broken into on the same night isn't just a coincidence." Eli's gaze remained on his deputy. "You could be right about the wolf belonging to another pack though." His frown deepened.

A self-satisfied smirk crossed Craig's face. It elated him to hear his boss acknowledge that he'd said something right for once.

"Let everyone know there's a meeting tonight. We need to get a handle on the situation before Paige or someone else is attacked again."

His deputy pulled himself out of the colonial-style, wooden chair and stood up. "I'll get right on that, boss." The sarcasm in his tone wasn't lost on Eli. His deputy strutted to the door.

"Craig."

"What?" He opened the door and glanced over his shoulder.

"Stop being a smartass and take your job seriously. Both jobs. You're not second in command for nothing.

Why can't you get it through that thick head of yours?"

If looks could kill Eli would be six feet under. Craig stalked out of the office slamming the door behind him, the thin pane of glass shuddering in the wood.

A couple of seconds later Rosemarie popped her head in. "What was that all about?"

Eli looked at her. "Just a battle of wills, Rosy. That's all."

She entered the office. "Can I get you anything? Coffee, a donut... maybe some lunch?"

"Thanks, but I'm fine."

"I don't know what's wrong with that boy. Doesn't he realize you're an amazing leader? He'd be hard pressed to find someone better."

"I appreciate that." Eli eased himself onto his feet and came around the desk. "I think he's tired of being told what to do."

A look of alarm crossed Rosemarie's face. "That could mean trouble, Eli."

The sheriff's gaze moved through the window of his office to his disgruntled deputy sitting at his desk. "Yeah, I know."

Around two o'clock, Eli stopped by Paige's house. He wanted to make sure she was all right after the previous night's scare and also wanted to take a look around the property in daylight hours to see if he could find the entry point. When he pulled into the curb he noticed the empty driveway. Paige was still out.

He pulled the keys from the ignition, climbed out of his

wagon and wandered up the path to the front door. He scrutinized the lock and the frame. *They didn't get in here.* He headed for the sideway, opened the gate and continued down the path, checking the windows. *No sign of forced entry here either. How did they get in?*

Eli headed around the back.

The chill wind caused the screen door on the small enclosed porch to swing back and forth, bumping against the frame.

Climbing the four wooden steps, he checked the lock. The latch bolt didn't connect with the strike plate and looked as though it had been forced. He could see new metal gleaming through the scratches. He sniffed the air. Nothing. The forensic report had said no finger prints other than Paige's and her uncle's were found on the premises. Whoever broke in knew what they were doing, leaving no trace evidence anywhere in the house.

Eli moved to the glass paneled back door and studied the lock.

There it is!

The keyway had been tampered with. Maybe by a small, flat blade screwdriver.

Just as he leaned in to take a closer look the door swung open.

Paige squealed and jumped backwards. "Oh, my God, I thought…"

Eli straightened. "Sorry. I was just doing some investigating of my own."

She breathed a relieved sigh. "Thank goodness it was you and not the ones who broke in."

"Amen to that." He gave her an awkward smile. He hadn't meant to spook her even more than she was already.

"Want to come in for some coffee? It won't take a minute to prepare."

"Sure, that'd be great." It was the least he could do after frightening her half to death. He followed her into the kitchen.

"How do you take it?" Paige glanced at Eli over her shoulder as she took two mugs from an overhead cupboard and sat them on the counter. She had set the coffee maker before she went out and it was hot and ready to drink.

"Cream, two sugars." Eli wandered over to the small table pressed against the wall, slid back a chair and sat down.

"Not sweet enough, huh?" Paige quipped.

"What was that?"

"Nothing." Paige brought the mugs over to the table and sat down opposite him. "Do you think it'll snow?"

"Yeah. There's a cold front coming across so we should get some in the next few days." He sipped his coffee.

"Moon Grove will look pretty in a layer of white." She eased her spine against the backrest and took a cautious sip of her black brew. She didn't like cream in her coffee.

"Yeah, it usually does. And seeing as it's getting close to Christmas it'll make it all that much more..." He winked at her. "Magical."

Paige chuckled. "Did you just say that?"

"Why, yes I did." Eli chuckled too. "My mom used to tell me that when I was a kid. I always remember it around the holidays."

Paige didn't know if she should ask about his parents.

"You want to know about my parents." He gave her a knowing look.

"How did you…?"

"You picked up on the 'used to' part of what I said. I noticed your eyebrows go up."

"Really? I'm sorry."

"Don't be. There's nothing to be sorry for. You want to know?"

"Only if you're comfortable with telling me."

"I don't mind. Truth is I didn't know my father. He was out of the picture before I could even walk and talk. My mom raised me on her own. She worked two jobs to give me a normal, comfortable life. And I knew I was loved. She was the best. When I was fifteen she got sick and within two years she was gone."

Without realizing it, Paige reached across the table and rested her hand on his. "I'm so sorry."

Eli's gaze moved to their hands then back to Paige's face.

She blushed, easing her hand away from his and picking up her mug of coffee. Touching him made her feelings all too real and she didn't want to entertain that kind of scenario right now. She couldn't.

Eli felt the electricity between them. It was difficult not to notice it. But he had demons of his own to deal with and wouldn't inflict those demons onto anyone else. Especially someone he was growing too fond of.

He attempted to query her about her childhood. "What do you remember about your parents?"

Paige set her mug down, sighed and said, "Not much. Just glimpses really. I have photos that my aunt left me but the people in them don't seem real to me because I don't remember being with them."

"Do you remember your house?"

She shook her head.

Eli gave her an empathetic frown. "It's abandoned. Been that way since…" He stopped himself. He didn't want to upset her.

"Since they disappeared?"

He nodded. "Yeah."

Paige moved her mug aside and rested her elbows on the tabletop. "Do you have any idea what happened to them?"

"No." Eli gave a heavy sigh. "When I heard you were coming back to Moon Grove I pulled the case files so I could go over them. I'd like to be able to give you some answers and close the case, if possible. It's been a cold case for far too long."

"I appreciate that. Yes, it would be good to solve the mystery." She waited a beat then said, "Do you believe they're dead?"

Eli didn't want to get into the logistics of the case and the amount of blood found at the scene but there was no way around the question. "Yeah, I do. The crime scene points to that scenario."

Paige frowned. "What do you mean?"

"I don't want to upset you."

Her cheeks flushed. "Let me worry about that."

"Ok." Eli folded his arms and watched her for a moment before continuing. "There was enough blood on the premises to indicate that your parents were killed before their bodies were removed from the house."

Paige's frown deepened and she moved uncomfortably on her seat.

Now it was his turn to reach across and rest his hand on hers. "I'm sorry. I did say I didn't want to upset you."

Paige's gaze moved to their hands and remained there. "I was there that night, right? I mean, I was only five where else could I have been?"

Eli gave another heavy sigh. "Yes, you were there."

"Then why don't I remember it?" Paige pulled her hand free and popped up off her chair. "Surely seeing something like that would stay in my memory."

Eli stood up. "You're a psychologist. You know it doesn't work that way. Your mind suppressed what you saw. If it hadn't you'd probably be a basket case by now." He grimaced. "Sorry, but it's true."

"You're right." Her eyes moved to the floor in front of her as her mind searched for a solution. After a few seconds, her gaze shot up to meet Eli's concerned stare. "I need you to take me to the house."

"Do you think that's wise?"

"How else can we find out the truth?"

"What if it doesn't work?"

"Then I'll call Doctor Taylor and make an appointment to go under hypnosis."

Eli's left eyebrow arched. "You'd do that?"

Paige nodded. "Yes." Her eyes glazed over as she recalled the dream. "I should've done it a long time ago."

"What is it, Paige?" Eli reached out and rested his hands on both her arms.

She looked up into his honey colored eyes. "I've been having nightmares for as long as I can remember." She trembled. "Similar to what happened in the woods last night."

Eli frowned into her eyes. "Me too. Only they'd stopped, until recently."

Paige's eyebrows rose. "Since I came back, you mean?"

He thought about her question for a moment then said, "Yeah."

She reached out and gripped his arm. "Take me to the house."

THIRTEEN

The gray remains of the once whitewashed, two story timber clad house stood amidst a cluster of tall, wiry leafless trees. The cracked concrete path still carved a straight line through the overgrowth up to the weathered front porch, and as Eli and Paige trudged along it through the waist high weeds and grass covering the front yard a shiver ran through her. Was she doing the right thing? Should she be here? Could it cause more harm than good? As a psychologist, she knew the dangers of opening up the mind too quickly to long hidden secrets that had lain dormant in the shadowed recesses of the brain for too long. What would she remember? And could she handle what she discovered? Her stomach flipped over sending a nervous quiver through her belly.

When they reached the steps, Eli held out his hand to help her up the crooked, rotting wooden treads. The place had stood unoccupied for over twenty three years and had succumbed to the elements. No one wanted to buy it after what had happened here. The rusted metal sheets that once covered the veranda were lying on the ground or swinging precariously in the chill breeze from the porch rafters.

Eli shoved one aside as he led Paige up the steps and onto the decaying porch. The weather beaten front door lay wide open, welcoming them into the disintegrating home. Inside, the water stained, peeling floral wallpaper clung in ripped curls to the damp plaster walls, the cream, burgundy and green pattern in the threadbare carpet unrecognizable, and creeping ivy vines coiled their way up the staircase banister to the second floor. The earthy smell of sodden soil and decay wafted into their nostrils and the pair reluctantly stepped across the scuffed, gray wood threshold into the crumbling entry hall.

Paige pressed herself against Eli's back, the blood pulsing rapidly through her veins. Something about the place gave her the creeps. Every nerve ending in her body prickled with apprehension and her breath caught in her throat. Eli glanced over his shoulder, eyeing her with concern. "Maybe this wasn't a good idea."

"I – I'm fine." Her eyes moved around the gloom. Skeletal fingers of a lone tree branch stretched into the living room through the decimated ceiling like a giant child's hand reaching into a doll house to play with the toy furnishings. It gave the house an eerie, inhabited feel. Mother Nature was reclaiming what belonged to her. The icy wind picked up, whooshing past the pair along the hallway and the back door slammed shut with a loud, wall shuddering bang. Paige jumped forward and Eli wrapped his arms around her.

Perhaps he was right. Perhaps she shouldn't have come.

"You don't seem fine," he said, his caring eyes resting on her beautiful face. As Eli held her in his arms, their bodies close, he knew he wanted to kiss her more than ever.

Paige averted her eyes to the stairs and she stepped out of his embrace. "I guess we'd better go up. The blood was found in their room, wasn't it?"

"Yes." Eli sighed. "Paige, you don't have to do this. We can find another way."

"What other way? The case files have sat untouched in police archives for years. Someone has to find out the truth." She stood with her hands on her hips. "No one else but me and whoever murdered my parents were here that night. I *need* to remember what happened."

"You might not have seen anything. You may have been asleep."

"Well, then, there's only one way to find out." She started up the overgrown staircase, tearing at the vines to make a path as she climbed the rickety stairs.

Eli followed her.

Paige stopped on the top landing and exhaled the deep breath she hadn't realized she'd been holding. "I really don't remember this place at all." She turned and frowned at Eli. "It's as though I never lived here."

"It has been over twenty years and you were only five at the time." Eli stepped up beside her. "We need to be careful up here. Some of the floor boards might not hold our weight."

Paige's eyebrows rose in alarm. "Oh? Do you want me to go first? I'm lighter."

"We'll go together. Keep close to the walls."

"All right." The pair moved cautiously down the hallway toward Paige's parents' bedroom.

A loud crack echoed around them and a section of the floor in front of them crumbled, raining powdery plaster down into the living room below.

"Oh!" Paige jumped backwards.

"Just stay close to the walls." Eli moved around her and took the lead. "Give me your hand."

Paige grasped his hand and shuffled along behind him.

When they reached the bedroom, Eli turned the handle and pushed the door open. It squealed on the rusted hinges and stopped half way. Shoving it all the way back, he stepped into the bedroom pulling Paige alongside him. The blood stained double bed stood in the center of the floor and when she saw it she gasped.

"I didn't expect it to still be here," Eli told her. "I'm sorry you had to see that."

Paige's face turned a gray shade of white. "There's so much blood!"

Although the faded, dark stain was watery now there was no mistaking what it was.

"Let's go. It was a bad idea coming here to begin with."

"No!" Paige yanked her hand free. "I need to stay and see if I can remember anything." She found it difficult to tear her eyes away from the blood-soaked mattress but forced her gaze to the hallway. "Which… room's mine?"

Eli's eyes moved to the hall and he motioned with his head. "The door on the right."

Paige gave a heavy sigh and stepped out of the room, Eli right behind her. She reached out with a shaking hand and when her fingers connected with the cold metal door knob she froze. An image flashed across her brain and she jerked her hand away.

Eli spun her around and gripped her shoulders with both hands, frowning into her eyes. "What is it? What just happened?"

"I – I don't know. I thought I saw… something."

"What did you see?" His frown deepened.

"I think it was me as a child."

FOURTEEN

When Rosemarie came back from lunch, she caught Craig in Eli's office going through his desk drawers. He seemed to be looking for something specific and each time he didn't find it he cursed. Rosemarie dropped her purse onto her desk and walked silently over to the open doorway. "What are you doing in Eli's office, Craig? And why are you going through his desk?"

"That's none of your business." Craig slammed the bottom drawer shut, came around the desk and stalked up to her. Raising his index finger in front of her face he said, "You'd do well not to say anything."

Rosemarie's right eyebrow arched and she folded her arms. "Don't give me attitude, Craig Campbell. I don't answer to you." She frowned into his menacing gaze. Even though he scared her she wasn't about to let him see it. He had a dark soul.

"Just remember what I said." He pushed past her, slamming into her right shoulder, and strutted out of the police station.

The door opened a couple of minutes later and Bobby

entered the warm office accompanied by a chill blast of winter air and a few stray brown leaves. "What's with Craig? He drove outta the parking lot like a man possessed."

Rosemarie shrugged and came around her desk. "I found him in Eli's office when I got back from lunch. I don't know what he was looking for or how long he'd been in there but he was doing an awful lot of cussing while he was at it."

Bobby's eyebrows shot up. "Are you going to tell Eli?"

"Don't you think I should?"

"There's enough tension between them. It's getting harder and harder to be around those two." His eyes moved to Eli's office. "I wonder what he was after."

"I don't know, probably a way to get at Eli. Some kind of evidence he could hold against him."

"He'd have a hard time finding something like that on Eli, why the man doesn't even date." Bobby shrugged out of his jacket, hung it and his hat on the coat rail, walked over to his desk and sat down. "Craig's becoming a big problem."

Rosemarie returned to her desk and took her seat. "Yes, he is."

"I wonder if Eli'll do something about it. He's put up with Craig for a long time now."

"Eli has the patience of a saint. I think he'll just let it run its course. Something is bound to happen eventually. Craig won't want to stay the underling for long. You can see he hates Eli telling him what to do, here and within the pack. Look at what happened at the meeting the other night. If you hadn't stepped in there would've been an all-out brawl in the church."

"Yeah, I know. Despite what we are we still have to respect the laws. And, to answer what you said, Craig doesn't have much of a choice. Eli's our Alpha... unless he plans to challenge him."

Rosemarie gave Bobby a serious stare. "I think that's exactly what he's planning to do."

As Eli pushed the door open to Paige's childhood room the corroded hinges gave way and the splintered, white paneled door crashed to the floor of rotting leaves and debris. The window had been shattered by a falling tree branch, allowing the wind to carry the surrounding vegetation into the house. Paige jumped backwards and as she did they both heard the floor crack beneath her feet.

Eli grabbed her around the waist just as the section of floor under her disintegrated and fell in chalky clumps onto the weathered kitchen counter below. "Ok?" he asked, pulling her into his arms.

"It's dangerous here, maybe we should go." She frowned up into his attractive, caring eyes.

"Are you sure? Don't you want to find out if you remember anything?" He needed the information as much as she did. It would be good to finally have the answers he was looking for to close the case.

Paige sighed. "You're right. Might as well get it over with."

"Only if that's what you want. We can leave anytime you like."

She shook her head. "No, I need to stay and see if something comes back to me."

They stepped into the room and Paige's gaze roamed

the empty space. Something flashed before her eyes. "Oh!" She jerked backwards.

"Did you see something?"

Paige's breaths were short, nervous bursts of white fog. "Me."

"Anything else?"

She shook her head.

Eli led her into the center of the room. "Close your eyes."

Paige's wary gaze narrowed.

"Trust me."

"All right." She gave a heavy sigh and did what he asked.

"Ok, now focus on how your room looked when you lived here."

Her eyes snapped open. "But I don't remember being here."

"Humor me. Just open your mind. Give it a try." He squeezed her hand.

"Ok." Paige wriggled her shoulders, inhaled a calming breath, and closed her eyes.

Eli continued to hold her hand. "Focus on your breathing: breathe in, breathe out... and again. Good."

Paige listened to the rhythm of her breath, the tension ebbing away. She was already familiar with this technique. Eli was good at getting her to relax.

"All right, now I want you to let your mind wander. Just continue listening to your breathing." He gave her a minute then asked, "Do you see anything?"

She shook her head. "No."

"Ok. Just keep listening to your breathing and relax. You still feel tense to me."

"I'll try." She wriggled her shoulders again and inhaled a deep breath.

"Now, what do you see?"

Although her eyes were closed they were moving under her lids as though she were gazing around the space in front of her. "I see this room." She raised her arm. "My bed used to be there. It was white with a pink curtained canopy overhead." Paige pointed to the center of the back wall next to the broken window. "And my dresser stood over there." She motioned to the left wall. "Wait. I hear something." Her face wrinkled into a frown. "I hear people arguing."

"Who's arguing?" Eli took her hand in both of his. It was Ice cold.

"I – I don't know."

"Concentrate, Paige. Are the voices male or female?"

"Both, I think. No." She cocked her head to the side. "Male. No, wait. I hear a woman's voice too."

"Can you make out what they're saying?"

Paige's frown deepened and she shook her head.

"Concentrate. What are they arguing about?"

Her breathing grew short and sharp. "One man is saying the other man was in a lot of trouble. That he hadn't delivered what his boss asked for."

"His boss? Do you recognize any of the voices?" He knew it was a long shot but he had to try.

She stood still, her chin tilted upward as though she were listening to them right now. "Yes. I think the second man is my dad." Her eyelids flickered.

"Keep your eyes closed, Paige. Is your mom talking?"

She shook her head. "No." Her body jerked backwards and she gasped, "Oh, my God!"

"What happened?"

"I heard a gun go off."

"Are you sure?"

She nodded frantically. "Yes."

"How many shots?" Eli pulled her to him.

"Several."

"Is anyone speaking now?"

"No." She pressed herself against Eli's chest, her body trembling. "Why were they in my parents' room?"

"I don't know." He wrapped his arms around her. "Where are you?"

"Behind my bedroom door. I'm holding a Snakes and Ladders game to my chest. I'm terrified that someone will come in and shoot me too."

"What's happening now?"

"Nothing. No one's talking." Paige's eyes snapped open. "They killed my parents and I was in the next room."

FIFTEEN

Wendy Ellis stepped out of the Moon Grove Tribune and locked the door. It was the end of the working day and she was on her way home when she decided to take a drive over to Paige O'Connell's. The young woman's story was too good to pass up, and if she could talk her into an in-depth interview it would put the newspaper on the map. The disappearance of her parents had been nationwide news back then. A mystery everyone in the United States wanted answers to.

As she turned the corner to make her way to the parking lot behind the office building, Wendy felt that disconcerting tingle between her shoulder blades as though she were being watched. She stopped and gazed along the street in both directions. No one. She inhaled a deep breath, shrugged off the feeling and continued to her car.

Wendy was aware of the dark undercurrent of the unassuming little town. As a journalist, it was her job to delve deep into the quagmire of lies and unspoken secrets that kept Moon Grove thriving, even though she couldn't make what she'd discovered public knowledge. She knew about the wolves and she also knew about the hierarchy keeping the people of the town segregated from the rest of the country. The tourist trade had all but dried up and new residents were never welcomed. She knew first hand because she had been a new arrival to the town five years before. Most of the townsfolk were still wary of her today, which she suspected had something to do with her occupation. No one wanted to talk.

Wendy already had her car keys in her hand, force of habit from once living in a big city, and when she reached her hatchback she pressed the remote, scurried into the vehicle, slammed the door shut and locked it, then shoved the key into the ignition. The feeling of someone's eyes on her grew more intense and a shiver ran through her. Wendy's anxious gaze circled the empty, four car parking lot and the street. Still nothing. She started the engine, backed out of her spot, turned the car around and drove out onto the side street. She'd leave visiting Paige for another day. Maybe it wasn't a good idea, after all.

The fine hairs on the back of her neck stood static and her pulse quickened as she drove along the main street and connected to the urban highway heading out of town. She lived in a country cabin thirty minutes away and couldn't wait to get there and lock herself inside. The anxious feeling lingered as she drove and her eyes flicked to the rearview mirror every few seconds to make sure she wasn't being followed. One car and a dark blue pickup that she didn't recognize were behind her, but that didn't mean it wasn't someone that knew who she was or where she lived. Wendy pressed her foot down on the accelerator and watched the speedometer needle move up to sixty five miles an hour. She just wanted to get home.

Eli and Paige stepped out the front door of her childhood home and descended the steps, him offering her his hand as she clambered over a large hole on the second stair tread. She stumbled and fell into his arms, her coy gaze moving to his. He smiled and helped her straighten before letting her go. He didn't want to, he liked having her in his arms.

As they were about to head back to his four wheel drive, a gunshot blast echoed around them and a bullet zipped past Eli's left ear. The pair dived into the tall grass and stayed low.

"Who's shooting at us?" Paige's voice was high-pitched and anxious, her breath choppy.

"Good question." Eli dragged his hat off his head and threw it into the grass then craned his neck just enough to try and see where the shooter was.

"Do you think they're gone?" Paige swallowed the lump of nerves lodged in her throat threatening to choke her and sucked in a deep breath, trying to calm her erratic breathing.

"I don't know." Eli continued to peer over the top of the four foot high grass to see if there was any movement amongst the trees. Whoever had taken a pot shot at them was laying low. "Stay here, I'm going to make my way over and see if they're still there."

Paige's eyebrows rose. "What?! Are you crazy? You could get yourself killed and then what happens to me?"

"I won't get myself killed. Just stay here till I get back." Without waiting for a response, Eli spread the grass carefully and kept low, making his way over to the trees.

Paige bit the corner of her bottom lip and tried to peek over the swaying overgrowth. She couldn't see Eli or anyone else. Maybe whoever it was did it to scare them. But why? Thunder rumbled in the distance sending a shiver up her spine. Paige hated thunderstorms and hoped she'd be back home before the lightning and rain hit.

A hand pressed across her mouth stifling the frightened scream she would have let out if she'd had the chance and her heart sank.

Eli came around her with his finger to his lips and Paige nodded. He picked up his hat but didn't put it on. "There are two men standing in the trees straight ahead. I can't get a good look at them because they're keeping to the shadows. We need to get moving before they come looking for us." He gripped Paige's hand. "Let's just stay low and leave as quietly as we can. They'll hear the car but I'm hoping we'll have a good head start before they come after us. Assuming they would.

"Are they trying to kill us?" The word *kill* hiccupped out of her mouth. Paige couldn't believe this was happening to her.

"Yeah, that would be my guess."

Paige gave him an anxious grimace. "But why? Neither of us knows anything."

"Maybe we've opened an old wound that someone would prefer to stay healed." He led her through the overgrowth, keeping low so as not to disturb the grass and let their attackers know where they were.

"I don't understand. They couldn't possibly know that I remembered something. Anyhow, it didn't get us any further than we already are... did it?"

"It might have. I need to go over the files again."

"Eli?"

"Yes?" He glanced over his shoulder.

"We're going to make it out of here, aren't we?"

The gaunt look of terror on Paige's face caused Eli's heart to stutter. "Yes, we're going to get out of here. But I'm staying at your house tonight and I'm putting a car out front."

Paige squeezed his hand. "No argument from me on that."

SIXTEEN

Nothing unusual or dangerous occurred for the next week and Paige hoped that it had been a couple of hunters out in the woods the day she and Eli were at her parents' house, not someone actually trying to kill them, although she knew it was wishful thinking. She eased herself onto the kitchen chair with her mug of coffee and nibbled at a piece of cold toast. Who was she trying to kid. Whoever was out at her parents' property weren't there for sport, at least not the animal kind. Someone had tried to kill them. Why?

The bell outside clanged and Paige's eyes moved to the hallway. *Who could that be on a gray, rainy Saturday morning?* She was still in her pajamas and robe even though it was after ten o'clock. She set her mug of coffee down on the table, pushed back her chair and wandered out to the entry hall. Before opening the door, she peered through the curtain.

Wendy Ellis.

Why is she here? Paige had a sneaking suspicion she knew the answer. She opened the door. "Hello, Wendy. What brings you here on such a cold, gray day?"

The woman's eyes ran over Paige's attire before answering. "I'm here to tell you something important."

"Like what?"

Wendy gestured to the open doorway. "May I come in? I won't take up much of your time."

Paige contemplated letting the woman into her home. Why should she? And what could she possibly have to tell her? "I'm not dressed and…"

"That's perfectly fine. As I said I won't stay long."

Paige stepped aside. "All right. You've got ten minutes."

Wendy eyed her sideways as she stepped across the threshold.

Paige closed the door and ushered her uninvited guest into the living room. "Have a seat." She motioned to the sofa before sitting in an armchair opposite.

"Thank you." Wendy sat down on the left side of the three seater couch and dropped her purse on the floor by her feet. "I wanted to tell you about a strange thing that happened to me a few nights ago."

Paige leaned forward, rested her elbows on her knees and clasped her hands. "What do you mean?"

"When I left the office I had the distinct feeling someone was watching me. I couldn't see anyone, but I know they were there."

"How do you know?" Paige's frown deepened and her stomach squirmed.

"You know that tingle you get between your shoulder blades? I had that feeling all the way home."

"So you think you were being followed?"

Wendy nodded. "Yes, I do."

"What does you being followed have to do with me?"

Paige didn't like where the conversation was heading.

"It was the same day you came into the office to place your ad."

The heavy feeling sitting in Paige's chest sank into her stomach.

"I heard about what happened out at your parents' place and I had to come and warn you."

Paige's brow wrinkled even more. "About what?"

"It's not safe for you here. The people of this town are…" A loud thud echoed into the room from outside and both women jumped to their feet.

"I'm calling Eli," Paige said, snatching her phone from off the bookshelf nearby and pressing speed dial. Eli had set his cell phone number to one in case of emergencies. "Someone's outside the house. Ok. See you soon." She pressed end and pushed her phone into the pocket of her robe. "He's on his way."

They heard the sound of breaking glass coming from the kitchen and dashed out the front door into the street. "Jump in my car. We have to get out of here." Wendy raced around to the driver's side and climbed in, Paige clambering into the passenger seat beside her.

Wendy shoved the key into the ignition and turned it. The engine coughed, made a feeble whirr, but didn't kick over. She tried again and again. Nothing. "What are we going to do?"

Both women's nervous gaze moved to the open front door. A man dressed in a black hoodie stormed toward them, his face hidden beneath the deep hood. The pair squealed, flung open the doors and flew out of the car into the pouring rain. Just as they took off running, Eli's police wagon screeched into the driveway.

Paige and Wendy raced back along the sidewalk and across the lawn to his car, but Eli was out of the vehicle and in hot pursuit of the intruder who had disappeared down Paige's sideway. After a couple of minutes, he returned to the women. "He's long gone. I wish I'd gotten hold of him but he was too fast." He stared at the dripping pair. "Let's go inside."

Once in the entry hall, Paige went to the linen cupboard along the hallway and pulled out some towels, wrapping one around her wet hair and another around her shoulders before taking the others back to Eli and Wendy. She passed a towel to each of them. "Why is someone trying to scare me? What do they want?"

Eli took one of the towels. "I wish I had an answer for you, Paige, but I don't. This is such a strange situation. You haven't been here long enough to make enemies so I don't understand what's going on."

"Well that makes two of us. There's nothing here anyone could possibly want." She shivered and it wasn't because of her rain-soaked clothing. The thought of being shot at out at her old family home, the break in, and now this really frightened her.

Wendy glanced outside and noticed that her car doors were wide open. She passed the damp towel back to Paige. "Thanks for towel. I'd better get going."

"But your car won't start."

"Oh darn, that's right."

"I can take a look at it for you. I do all my own repairs," Eli offered.

Wendy gave Eli a flattering smile. "Really? So you're a man of many talents." She handed him the keys.

After ten minutes or so, Eli came back into the house

and passed the keys back to the journalist. "All fixed."

"What was wrong with it?"

"Loose sparkplug cap."

"Well thank you for finding it." Wendy glanced at Paige. "I hope we can have that chat some time."

Paige was concerned for the woman after what had happened and what she'd told her. "Are you going to be all right?"

"I'm driving straight home and I'm not stopping until I get there, so I should be fine." She gave Paige a thin smile.

"Will you give me a call when you get there, so I know you're ok?"

Eli frowned at them. "What's going on?"

Paige's eyes moved from him to Wendy. She wasn't sure if the journalist wanted her to say anything.

"It's nothing, Sheriff Blackwood. I'm fine." Wendy stepped out onto the front porch. "I'll call you once I'm in the house."

"Thank you. Be…" Paige thought twice about saying be careful in front of Eli, especially when she realized Wendy didn't want to say anything about what she'd experienced. Was she wary of him? If so, why?

Paige stood at the front door and watched the other woman drive away before turning to Eli. "I don't think she wants me to tell you this but I think I have to."

Eli reached out, gripped both her arms and frowned into her eyes. "Tell me what?"

"Wendy thought she was being followed a few days ago. That's why she was here."

Eli walked Paige into the living room and sat her down on the sofa then sat beside her. "What does that have to do with you?"

"She thinks her being followed and us being shot at are related somehow."

The sheriff let the idea roam his brain for a moment. "How did she know about that?"

"I didn't think to ask her." Paige shrugged. "Small town, I guess."

"What makes Wendy Ellis think the two incidents are related?" He stretched his arm along the back of the sofa behind Paige.

"She wanted to interview me about my parents' disappearance and what I could remember about that night. Maybe someone doesn't want her to find out, and maybe someone doesn't want me to remember what happened."

"I'd like to know why someone keeps trying to break in here." His eyes roamed the room. "Your uncle wasn't..." He stopped himself before he said something he couldn't take back. Her uncle hadn't been part of his pack. He wasn't a werewolf.

Paige prompted, "My uncle wasn't what?"

"Nothing. I was just thinking out loud." Eli gave her a smile and huffed out a humorless laugh. "Goes with the territory."

She straightened. "What were you going to say about Jake?" She folded her arms and gave him a severe stare. What was he hiding? "Tell me."

"I wasn't going to say anything about Jake. He was a decent man and a good friend."

"I don't believe you. You know something. What is it?"

"Until we find out what's going on here it's better for you not to know any more than you need to."

Paige leaned away from him and frowned. "What does that mean?"

"Will you please trust me? That's all I'm asking right now." He reached out and drew her to him, resting his chiseled jaw on top of her head. "We're going to get to the bottom of this. I promise." He was starting to doubt Paige's safety in Moon Grove.

SEVENTEEN

When Wendy didn't call Paige became worried. It wouldn't have taken any more than half an hour for the journalist to get home, and it was now late afternoon, so why hadn't she been in touch? She pulled her cell phone from her pocket and keyed in Wendy's number. It went straight to voicemail. A sickening wave swelled in Paige's stomach. She knew something was wrong.

Eli came into the living room with two mugs of coffee and set them down on the table. He could see the look of concern on Paige's face. "Still no answer?"

She shook her head. "I'm starting to get really worried." She frowned into Eli's eyes. "Maybe we should go out there and make sure everything's ok."

"If it'll make you feel any better we can."

Paige nodded. "It would. I'll just go change and grab my purse."

"Ok." Eli picked up his mug of coffee and took a generous sip. While Paige was upstairs, he tried Wendy's number. Voicemail. He didn't know a lot about the journalist except that she'd moved to their town about five years before and took over the operation of the Moon Grove Tribune after Joshua Kendal passed away unexpectedly from a heart attack. She had been in a few scrapes over the years, sticking her nose into things that were none of her concern, and Eli wondered if that's what had happened this time. Had she stepped across someone's line? Nevertheless, he hoped she was all right.

Paige came downstairs dressed in skinny blue jeans, a pale blue cable knit sweater and brown knee high boots. Eli thought she looked amazing.

He helped her into her black wool jacket and she plucked her burgundy knit cap from the coat rack as they walked out the door.

When they reached his four wheel drive, Eli opened the passenger door for Paige and helped her in. She liked that about him.

He rounded the front of the car and climbed in beside her. "All set?"

She nodded. "The sooner we get out there and check on her the better I'll feel."

By the time they turned off the road and drove down the drive they could see Wendy's house was in complete darkness. Her car was out front, so she had to be inside. Maybe she was too scared to turn on the lights in case someone was lurking nearby. Her house backed up against an expansive cluster of tall trees which made it easy for someone to sneak up on her without being seen.

Paige was the first one out of the car. She flung open the passenger door jumped out and headed for the front porch.

Eli fingered his pistol under his regulation police jacket. Would he need to use it? Ever since Paige had moved into town a lot of crazy things had happened and the sheriff was ready for anything.

"Don't go up there yet. I want to take a quick look around first." He pulled a small black flashlight from a pocket in his jacket and flicked it on. The charade was for Paige's benefit. Even though he didn't need the light to see he had to appear normal to her. "Wait here. I'll be right back."

Paige stood at the bottom of the steps with her hands pushed deep into the pockets of her coat, her stomach doing nervous flip flops under her sweater. Her eyes roamed the surrounding fence line and trees. It was almost dark now and the shadows played tricks with her vision. Birdwings fluttered somewhere overhead and Paige spun on her heel in the direction of the sound. What was taking Eli so long? Wendy's cabin wasn't that big.

The porch light flashed on and he came out through the front door. "I've called my team."

The color drained from Paige's face and she asked in a trembling voice, "Why?"

Eli pulled her to him. "It's not good."

Tears stung the backs of her eyes. "Where's Wendy?" A thick, painful lump formed in her throat and she tried to struggle free but he held her to the spot.

"She..." he gave a heavy sigh, "she's dead, Paige."

The tears she'd tried to hold back tumbled down her face. "How? What happened to her?"

"It's better that you don't know." He frowned into her tear filled eyes. "I think it would be a good idea if I stayed at your place for a while."

She pressed her trembling body against his firm muscular frame and slid her arms around his waist. The action was intimate but Paige didn't care. She didn't want to be alone tonight. "You'll get no argument from me."

Eli wrapped his arms around her. He liked holding her. He wondered if there could be anything more between them some time in the future when all this craziness settled down, but then he remembered why he kept women at arm's length. He couldn't risk their lives.

Paige sat in the four wheel drive, her sad eyes focused on the small wooden cottage, while Eli and his team conducted a thorough search in and around the house. An ambulance coasted past the wagon, its red and blue lights strobing into the darkness, and pulled up at the front steps. Paige felt a tear slide down her cheek. Poor Wendy. Why her? She now wished she'd given the woman a chance to tell her what she had come to say. Is that the reason she was killed?

Eli attempted to remain poker faced as he approached the passenger window but what he'd seen in the house made him sick to his stomach.

Paige pressed the button on the armrest and window glided into the door. "Did you find anything?"

"Nothing useful."

"Eli?"

Knowing what she was about to ask his eyes locked onto hers. "Yes?"

"What happened to Wendy?"

"You don't need to know." He rested a hand on her arm.

"But I do." Her voice was strained, thin. "This all

started just after I arrived here so it must have something to do with the break in, the wolf almost attacking me, us being shot at and now this."

"Look, let me get finished up here and we'll talk about it back at your place. Ok?"

Paige's gaze remained on his eyes. They were mesmerizing. She could drown in those gorgeous honey colored pools. "Ok."

Eli kept side-glancing Paige on the drive back to her house. She seemed deep in thought and had been quiet for the whole trip. He pulled his car into her driveway, turned off the engine and faced her. "Want to tell me what's going through your mind?"

Paige eyed him sideways. "What if what happened to Wendy happens to me? What do they want?" Her voice was tight.

"Nothing is going to happen to you, Paige. I won't let it." Eli meant every word.

"How can you promise something like that?" She folded her arms. "You can't be with me 24/7. Whoever broke in is bound to try again if they're so adamant about finding whatever it is they're looking for. I wish I knew what they were after. I'd give it to them so they'd leave me alone."

"As I said before, if you don't mind a house guest for a while I'm happy to stay here at night. At least until we can work out what's going on or find whoever's doing this."

She'd had time to consider that option. As much as she would love having Eli around it would be a distraction and she needed to keep a clear head. "I know and I appreciate the offer but…"

"Don't tell me you're worried about your virtue." He gave the kind of smile that made her stomach turn to water and her heartbeat kick up a notch.

"I think people are talking about me already, so no, not at all. But aren't you worried about the backlash you'll get from your superiors?"

His dark eyebrows came together and he stared into Paige's eyes for some time before answering. "I couldn't care less about that. You're safety is my main priority right now."

Her eyes teared up and she turned toward the window so that Eli wouldn't notice. He did.

"Paige." He reached across and turned her face to meet his sincere gaze. "I won't let anything happen to you." He found it difficult not to lean in and kiss her but knew now wasn't the time. A tear slipped down her face and he brushed it away with his thumb. God, she was beautiful. "We're going to figure this out. Together."

EIGHTEEN

The next morning, Paige walked into the living room with two mugs of coffee and found Eli still sleeping; his six foot four inch frame looking awfully cramped on her five foot, three seater sofa. She sipped her drink as she moved across the room to the coffee table between the settee and armchairs and was about to set a mug down for Eli when he turned over and gazed at her with beautiful, sleepy eyes. When he threw off the blanket and stood up, wearing only a pair of figure hugging, black boxer shorts she almost choked on her mouthful of coffee. It slid down her throat on a bubble of air and she couldn't catch her breath. His lean body was sculpted in all the right places and she couldn't help home in on his six pack abs. He was in great physical shape.

"Good morning," he said, pulling on his jeans then easing the mug out of Paige's hand and taking a sip. "Thanks."

She could finally breathe again. "Y – ou're welcome." She averted her roaming eyes to the mug in her hand. "Want some breakfast? I have bacon and eggs in the refrigerator."

Eli sat his mug on the coffee table and shrugged into his blue denim shirt. "Sounds good. Need any help? I'm pretty handy in the kitchen."

Paige's eyes met his and he gave her a broad, handsome grin. "If you want to make some toast to go with the bacon and eggs that'd be great."

"Done." Eli picked up his mug of coffee and headed to the kitchen.

Paige turned around and followed him, noticing how cute his butt was on the way.

Eli was good in the kitchen. He went to work grabbing the food from the fridge and popping the toast into the toaster. "I make mean scrambled eggs," he said, giving Paige a dazzling smile she couldn't ignore. Her heart thumped against her ribs and she hoped he couldn't hear it.

"Great. Why don't you do that while I fry the bacon. Crispy, right?"

He shrugged. "Does anyone have it any other way?"

They sat across from each other enjoying their breakfast and conversation, and Paige realized it was nice to have a man around the house. Well, maybe not just any man.

"Oh, by the way, the Christmas carnival will be under way in a couple of weeks. Will you be going?" Eli asked.

"Christmas carnival? I wasn't aware Moon Grove had one." She tore a strip of bacon in half and popped a piece in her mouth.

"We sure do. This year it's the Winter Wonderland Christmas Carnival."

Paige gave him a dubious frown.

"I know it sounds cliché but what can you do?" He gave another shrug.

"I guess that's true. And Moon Grove will be a winter wonderland by then. The snow is already dusting the town. Sure, why not." She scooped scrambled egg onto her fork and took a bite. "Mm, these are amazing. What did you do to them?"

"Secret recipe. If I told you…"

She smiled. "Ok, I get it."

"A man's gotta have some culinary secrets."

"It's nice to see a man cook." She set her knife and fork down, wiped her mouth on her napkin looked into Eli's eyes, the conversation taking on a more somber tone. "There's something I've wanted to ask you about Jake."

Eli set his cutlery down and gave her a serious frown. "Like what?"

"I was wondering if I could see him. To say goodbye." Tears glistened in her eyes.

"I don't think that's such a good idea, Paige."

"Why not?" She dabbed the corner of her right eye to prevent a stray tear from sliding down her cheek.

"Because he sustained some very serious injuries. He doesn't look the way you remember him."

"How much longer do you need to keep his body? I would really like to organize a funeral."

"Unfortunately, he has to remain in the coroner's office in the next town until we apprehend his… the person or persons who took his life." He tried to be tactful.

"What did they do to him?"

"You don't want to know. Trust me on that."

"But…"

"Please, Paige, promise me you won't go over there. As next of kin you have the right to view his body but I'd appreciate it if you didn't. For your sake."

Paige could hear the genuine concern in Eli's voice. Her frown deepened. "Ok. I won't go."

"Thank you. I'd like you to come into the station today. I don't want you being here alone."

"I won't be here. I'm going into town to start putting my office together. The furniture I purchased will be arriving later this morning and I thought it would do me good to keep busy and be in a place where there are people around outside."

"Good thinking. I'll stop by during my lunch break and see how you're doing. If you need anything heavy lifted or moved I can do it then."

Paige smiled. "Thanks, I appreciate that."

"Gives me an excuse to keep an eye on you. But now that I know, I'll have Bobby do a cruise by every once in a while just to be safe." He grinned. "And I'll bring lunch."

"That makes me feel much safer. Thank you."

"No problem."

While Paige was hanging some prints on the wall in the outer office she realized that no one had replied to her want ad. *Doesn't anyone need a job in this town?* She couldn't open her practice without a receptionist. Well, she could but it would make things a lot more difficult for her. She stepped back to take a look at her handy work. The two frames lined up perfectly and looked great above the smoky gray sofa. She wanted her office to be warm and welcoming, not clinical.

She wandered over to the reception desk and picked up her cell phone. *I wonder if Steph will want to come here for a while and help me out until I can find a replacement.* She sent her friend a text saying she would call her at seven o'clock Washington time which would be nine o'clock Illinois time. Stephanie text her back: Everything ok?

Paige replied: Need your help.

Her cell phone chimed and she pressed the button. "I didn't expect you to call me right away. It can wait until later."

"What's up? I know you wouldn't have messaged me if it wasn't important."

"I placed a want ad a couple of weeks ago and haven't had a single application. I'm setting up the office as we speak but I won't be able to open until I have someone at the front desk."

"Are you asking me to come to Illinois?"

Paige could hear the apathy in her friend's voice. "It wouldn't be for long. I know I can trust you…"

Stephanie's tone changed to concern. "What do you mean? Is everything going ok there?"

"Not exactly. There have been a couple of incidents that have been off-putting, to say the least."

"What kind of incidents?"

Paige brightened up. "Look, I didn't get in touch to worry you. Everything's ok for the moment. Eli is looking out for me."

"Who's Eli?"

"The town sheriff."

"I bet he's cute, right?" Stephanie knew without a doubt because all the good looking guys always chased after Paige.

"What does that have to do with anything?"

Stephanie knew she shouldn't have said anything. "Nothing."

"We were childhood friends."

"Really? So you've rekindled your friendship?"

"Not exactly. He's doing his job, that's all. Will you come?"

"Yeah, of course I'll come. I'm in between jobs so I can give you a hand for as long as you need. I know it's only been a few weeks since you left but it'll be good to see you. I miss you."

"I miss you too. Thanks, Steph. You don't know how great it'll be to have you here." She realized she could use a friend right now.

Later in the morning, as Paige sat at the front reception desk setting up the computer, she noticed Bobby drive by in a patrol car. It was comforting to know someone was watching out for her. After what had happened to Wendy Ellis, Paige was afraid whoever killed the journalist would come after her next. But why? And why had someone broken into her house twice? She wished she had some idea of what they were looking for. Was it something of value or something that could incriminate them? And, if so, why would her uncle be in possession of such a thing? Had she known Jake as well as she thought she did?

Her thoughts were pulled back into the present when she heard a knock on the glass door and looked up to see Eli standing there. Her heart skipped a beat. He was so attractive and his smile caused her stomach to go hollow. In a good way. She found it difficult to keep her heart in check where he was concerned. She knew she liked him but now wasn't the time to contemplate starting any kind of relationship. Things were too crazy.

She popped up off the office chair, crossed the room

and unlocked the door. Eli stepped inside carrying a bag of Chinese takeout. "As we didn't get that dinner I promised at The Jade Dragon I thought I'd bring some here for you."

"Thank you, I'm starved." She checked her watch. 1.07 PM.

"Great. Where do you want to eat?" He glanced around the office. "Wow. You've done a lot in a short time. It looks fantastic."

Paige gave a satisfied smile. She had worked hard and appreciated that Eli noticed. "Thanks. It's a labor of love. I want clients to feel comfortable coming here. I don't want it to be clinical." She relocked the door and directed him to the compact kitchen at the back of the building. She'd set up a small table and two chairs out there.

"How'd you go with the want ad? Anyone apply?" Eli motioned for her to go ahead of him. Always the gentleman.

"No, not a single one. I called my friend Stephanie in Washington to see if she could come out and give me a hand for a while and she said yes, so she should be here in the next couple of days."

Eli wasn't pleased about that. Having another outsider in Moon Grove only meant more problems for him and his deputies. "Oh. She is?"

"Yeah. And it'll be great to see her. She's my best friend as well as my receptionist." Paige eased a chair out from under the table and sat down.

Eli placed the bag on the tabletop, unpacked it then sat down opposite her. "Do you think it's wise after everything that's happened?"

Paige frowned. "What do you mean?"

"Well, we know someone is either trying to frighten

you or…" he didn't want to say the words out loud. "What if something happens to your friend as a result?"

She hadn't given that any consideration. "Do you think it's possible?"

"They took pot shots at me as well out at your parents' place, what's to say they wouldn't do the same thing to…"

"Stephanie."

"Yeah." He opened the white containers with a green dragon motif and passed a pair of plain wood chopsticks to Paige.

"Thanks." She gave a heavy sigh. "I need someone on the front desk otherwise I can't open for business. Steph's excellent at her job and it would take a load off my mind having her here. But you're right. I certainly wouldn't want to put her life in danger. If anything happened to her I wouldn't be able to forgive myself."

"Let me ask round and see if I can rustle up someone for you."

"If no one answered the ad I can't see how anyone would want to help me now. I have the distinct feeling I'm off limits somehow." She wondered if opening her office was going to be worthwhile. Would anyone actually use her services?

Eli's dark eyebrows came together. He knew she was correct in her assumption.

NINETEEN

Stephanie insisted she wanted to come despite what Paige had told her about the incidents so far. It had made her friend more determined to be there with her. Safety in numbers, she'd said. Paige was worried. What happened to Wendy had frightened her and she wasn't even sure she wanted to remain in Moon Grove anymore despite her growing feelings for Eli. *Perhaps that's what whoever's doing this wants – me to leave.*

It was after nine o'clock and Eli was still at the station. He'd called to make sure everything was ok and told Paige to check every window and door and that he'd be there as soon as he could get away. He'd kept her on the phone while she'd gone through the whole house before hanging up. She appreciated that he was concerned for her well-being. She liked having that comfort.

When it got to ten o'clock Paige couldn't keep her eyes open any longer. After a day of shifting and lifting furniture and other items around the office she was exhausted. Bone weary, she climbed the stairs and wandered along the hallway to her room. After taking a quick shower to loosen up her muscles, and putting on a fresh pair of pajamas, she climbed into bed and pulled the warm covers right up to her chin. Giving a relieved sigh, she drifted into a dream...

Her uncle Jake was on the porch in the swing seat drinking a beer. It was summer. The sun was shining, the breeze was warm but appealing, and everything looked lush and green. Paige came out of the house and sat next to him, sipping an iced tea. The day was gorgeous and she hadn't felt this relaxed in a long time.

They were talking and laughing together when all of a sudden the sun disappeared and heavy, dark clouds rolled in leaving them sitting in the gloom.

Jake turned to her and said, "Wake up, Paige."

She gave him a peculiar frown and said, "I am awake."

"No you're not. Wake up. Wake up now! Someone's in the house."

Paige frowned over her shoulder, her gaze meeting the open front door. No one was in the house. When she turned back her uncle was gone. Her nervous eyes roamed the porch and the dark street. Where was he?

A wave of nausea turned Paige's stomach over as she jumped to her feet and ran for the door.

"No, Paige, get out of the house!"

...Paige sucked in a strangled breath, threw off the covers and leaped out of bed. She stood breathless trying to gain her bearings. A loud bang echoed up the stairs and along the hallway. Paige's heart jumped into her throat and she snatched her cell phone from off the bedside table and pressed speed dial for Eli.

The phone rang for a long time. "Come on, come on, please pick up." Her heart shuddered at the thought of not being able to reach him. Not knowing what else to do she was about to ring off when she heard his voice. "Thank God! Eli, someone's in the house."

"Open the bedroom window and hide in the closet. I'm on my way."

Paige raced over and threw the window up. A sharp blast of chill breeze hit her in the chest and she closed her mouth to stop herself from coughing. As she rushed over to the closet she noticed the time. 12.07 AM. Another loud bang. Paige whipped one door open, dashed into the closet and pulled the white louvers closed as quietly as she could. She squeezed herself into the tight corner behind the hanging clothes, held her breath and hoped she wouldn't be seen if whoever was out there opened the doors.

Footsteps.

Coming up the stairs.

Heavy footfalls along the hallway.

Outside her room.

The door swung open.

Someone stepped into her bedroom.

Paige pressed her hand to her mouth.

"She's gone out the window," a male voice said.

"Take a look and see if she's on the veranda roof," another male voice told him.

Paige's ears pricked up. Was that Craig's voice? She felt her heart rate quicken even more, the thudding, anxious beat pulsing in her throat depriving her of oxygen. *What if they find me?*

A siren screamed in the distance, the sound moving closer with every second.

"Let's get out of here," the second male voice said.

The pair scrambled down the stairs and through the house.

The seconds seemed to stop. Paige strained her ears to listen. Were they gone?

"Paige? Paige where are you?" Eli's voice was a welcome comfort.

Paige let out the breath she'd been holding, shoved the closet door open, climbed to her feet and raced out of the bedroom. "I'm up here."

Eli bolted up the stairs two at a time and met her on the landing. "Are you ok?" He reached for her and his eyes roamed her body from head to foot.

She nodded. "Yes, thanks to you."

"Which way did they go?"

"Out the kitchen door, I think."

Eli took off down the stairs and through the house. The back door was wide open, the lock hanging from the wood. He closed the door and wedged a kitchen chair under the handle then went back to Paige who was now at the bottom of the stairs.

"How did you know they were in the house?" he asked.

They entered the living room and Paige sat down on the sofa. Eli remained on his feet.

"I was having the strangest dream. At first it was pleasant. It was summer and I was sitting out front in the swing seat with Jake sipping iced tea, then the next second it all turned gray and dark and he was telling me to wake up. I kept saying I am awake but…" She shook her head. "The next thing I knew I was alone on the porch and making a dash for the door but I kept hearing his voice saying I had to get out of the house. Then I woke up and heard someone inside." Paige shivered.

"How many were there?"

"Two, I think. I only heard two voices."

"Male?"

Paige nodded.

"You didn't recognize them, did you?"

"I thought..."

He frowned into her eyes. "You thought what?"

She sighed. "I thought one voice sounded a lot like Craig, but I can't be certain. I was in a panic."

"You've heard his voice before, Paige. Was it him or not?"

She frowned and thought about it then shook her head. "I'm sorry, I'm not sure." The townspeople hadn't been very welcoming and she'd only spoken to the realtors, the woman in the grocery store, and the guy at the gas station. "Do you think it could've been him?"

"I don't know, Paige. I just want to cover all the bases."

"You were gone a long time…"

"Yeah, I'm sorry about that. We had a meeting." Only Craig hadn't shown up.

"It's an odd time to have a meeting, isn't it?" She frowned.

"It happens on occasion, especially when we don't get the time to do it during the day." He wasn't about to tell her the meeting was at the church with his pack and others who adhered to the Lycan philosophy and way of life, and that it was about what had taken place since she arrived in Moon Grove. He hoped he'd never have to tell her. But that could all change if they didn't find the black wolf.

TWENTY

Paige was at the small transit center at the end of town waiting to meet her best friend, Stephanie. She was so looking forward to catching up and spending time with her and it would be nice to have someone else in the house. Eli couldn't remain there indefinitely, even though she loved having him around. It was after one o'clock in the afternoon and the bus was due any minute.

The day was overcast with light snowflakes drifting from the low-lying, gray nimbostratus clouds hanging overhead and the chilly wind had picked up. The carnival would indeed be a winter wonderland as Paige had predicted. It would be fun going with Stephanie as she always knew how to make any outing an enjoyable one. She had a terrific sense of humor and loved trying new things.

Her eyes roamed the sidewalk on both sides of the main street. For some reason she had that disconcerting tingle between her shoulder blades, the one Wendy Ellis had mentioned to her the day she'd... the day she'd died. Paige ran her gaze around the few people out and about but didn't recognize anyone, not that she knew too many people in Moon Grove anyhow.

The rumble of the Greyhound bus pulled her attention away from her discomforting thoughts and a smile spread across her face. Her friend was here at last. The blue and gray bus hissed to a stop, the front door sprang open, and the driver climbed out first to open the luggage compartment.

Paige craned her neck, peering in the windows looking for Stephanie. She spotted her friend at the rear of the bus and gave her a huge smile and an excited wave. Stephanie did the same.

Once off the bus, both women wrapped their arms around each other in a happy bear hug. "It's so good to see you," Paige said, stepping backwards.

"It's so good to finally be here." Stephanie walked over to collect her luggage. Paige followed. Her friend had three large cases. "I wasn't sure what to bring so I brought as much as I could," Stephanie told her. Neither one of them knew how long she'd be staying at this point.

Paige grimaced. "I can see that." She grabbed the handle of one overstuffed suitcase and wheeled it over to her car.

Stephanie took hold of the other two cases and tugged them over to the trunk of Paige's sedan. "I don't think they're all going to fit in there."

"That's ok. We'll stuff one on the back seat. All good."

After wrangling with the last suitcase to get it in the medium-sized car and shoving the door closed on it, the women climbed inside and headed to Paige's house. When they arrived, Eli was waiting on the porch.

Stephanie's designing gaze moved to the tall, dark,

handsome stranger on the front steps. "Is that the sheriff?"

Paige wished he'd waited until later to make an appearance. "Uh, yes, that's him."

"Wow! He is cute."

Eli crossed the lawn and tipped his sheriff's hat. "Ladies."

Paige rounded the back of the car and opened the trunk while Stephanie joined them. "Eli, this is Stephanie Harris, my best friend. Stephanie, this is Sheriff Eli Blackwood."

Her friend pushed her hand toward him. "Nice to know there's someone like you looking out for Paige." She gave him a flirtatious smile and roamed his tall, muscular, sexy frame.

For the first time, Paige noticed Eli was blushing.

"Thanks. All in a day's work." Eli's eyes met Paige's then returned to her friend. To move the topic of conversation, which was him, to something else he changed the subject. "Let me help you get those into the house." He pointed to the heavy suitcases in the trunk.

"Thank you, Sheriff," Stephanie said, stepping back and watching him. He had a cute butt.

Paige opened the back passenger door. "There's one in here, too."

Eli dropped the two suitcases onto the porch then returned for the third bag.

When Paige opened the front door and swung it back Eli motioned for her friend to step in ahead of him and then proceeded to lug the burgeoning suitcases into the entry hall. "Where do you want these?"

"Upstairs. First on the left." Paige closed the front door.

Stephanie stood in the entry and gazed around. "So this is your uncle's place. Nice."

"Yes, I'm still finding it difficult calling it mine, even though it is."

Her friend rested a hand on her arm. "That's understandable. Give it time."

"Come on, I'll show you your room." Paige climbed the stairs, Stephanie right behind her.

Later, in the kitchen, the trio sat around the small table drinking coffee and chatting. Eli liked that Paige's friend was only too happy to tell him things about Paige that he didn't already know, to her discontent. There had been a lot of missed years, and he wanted to catch them up. Stephanie and Paige had been friends since college so there were lots of things she could fill him in on.

When three o'clock rolled around, Eli stood up and said he'd better get going but that it had been a pleasure meeting Stephanie. Paige walked him to the front door.

"Thanks for helping with the luggage. I wasn't sure how we were going to get those jumbo-sized suitcases up the stairs. I hope you know I appreciate it."

"Yeah. I know." He sighed. "Well, I guess you don't need me staying over now."

"You being here made me feel very safe. Thank you." She wanted to touch his arm but didn't.

"If you need me you know where I am." Eli stepped onto the porch.

"I'll see you around town some time? Or at the carnival, won't I?"

"Absolutely. I'm glad you're going." He gave her one of those heart-melting smiles then turned around and headed for the street.

Paige sighed as she watched him drive away.

Stephanie came up beside her. "I can see why you like him. He's scrumptious."

TWENTY ONE

The carnival was fast approaching as was the day Paige would open her practice for business. She had decided to wait until the carnival ended, which ran for several days leading up to Christmas Eve, before opening. She wondered if anyone would make an appointment after the holidays. Had she made the right decision starting a practice in Moon Grove? All she could do was wait and see. Stephanie was impressed with the space and furnishings. It was welcoming, comfortable and stylish, but then she knew Paige had good taste when it came to setting up her business. She was going to enjoy working with her again.

"The preparations for the Christmas carnival are coming along nicely, don't you think? I'm really looking forward to it," Stephanie said, sitting behind the reception desk to get a feel for her new workspace.

"Yes, it's looking quite magical with all the twinkling lights and decorated Christmas trees and the colorful stalls being set up." Paige was hanging the last of the artwork around the walls.

Stephanie watched her. "It's such a small town. Intimate is the word I'd use. Have you made any new friends here yet, apart from the delicious sheriff?"

"Not really. I've met a couple of people I was friends with as a child but no one seems to want to get to know me. I've talked to people at the local grocery store and gas station, but it's always surface stuff. A quick how are you, not that they really want to know how you are, the weather's getting much colder, that kind of thing."

Her friend frowned. "I guess after everything that's happened maybe people are scared."

Paige turned around and frowned back at her. "Of me, you mean?"

Stephanie stood up and crossed the office. "Not you so much, but the situation. These places have extensive grapevines and news travels fast. Maybe they're afraid that if they get to know you they'll be in the line of fire."

"What about you? Are you worried about that?"

Her friend sighed and hugged her. "I wouldn't be here if I was. Small towns are cliquey too. Everyone knows everyone… and you're new."

"I'm not new. I was born here."

"You know what I mean." Stephanie walked over to the window, folded her arms and gazed out at the main street. "There's a kind of code in small towns when it comes to outsiders. And they obviously consider you an outsider."

Paige gave a disgruntled groan and joined her friend. "Well let's hope mingling with people at the carnival will change that to some degree."

Later that evening, after dinner, Paige and Stephanie sat in the living room playing a game of scrabble. They drank some wine, talked, and enjoyed each other's company. It was good to not feel anxious for once.

"So, what do you plan to do with mister sexy cop?" Stephanie asked, concentrating on her letters and sorting them for her next move.

"He's a friend, Steph."

Stephanie's eyes moved to her bestie. "Oh, come on, hon, he's more than that. Didn't you notice the way he looks at you?"

Paige was well aware of the attraction between them but didn't want to get into it with her friend. She knew how Steph's mind worked. "What way?"

Stephanie chuckled. "Like a love sick school boy."

"He does not," Paige scoffed.

"He certainly does."

"It's all in your head. He's just watching out for me because it's his job."

Stephanie raised her hands. "Ok, have it your way, but I know you're wrong. Hey, if you don't want him…"

"Don't even think about it, Steph."

"See. You do like him."

"Of course I like him. Right now he's my only ally in Moon Grove." Paige checked her phone. It was almost midnight. "Well, this has been a lot of fun, but I think we should get some sleep, don't you?"

"Yeah, I'm exhausted. We can finish this game another time." Stephanie downed the last of her Merlot, stood up and smoothed the wrinkles out of her tight-fitting skirt. "What's the plan for tomorrow?"

"I thought we might have lunch at the Moon Grove Inn. Rebecca, the woman I told you about, works there and said I could drop by any time for a meal."

"Sounds great." She hugged Paige then headed for the stairs. "Nighty night, hon. Sleep well."

"You too." Paige cleared away the wine glasses and empty cookie plate before heading up to bed. With all the crazy things going on in her life, it was great having someone around who really knew her. She sighed as she climbed the stairs and turned off the light on the landing. It felt good to be at peace for once.

…The thundering footsteps were gaining on her, the ground trembling beneath her feet as the monster got closer. Paige pushed every ounce of strength she could into her aching legs and thrust herself forward through the legion of eerie trees, peering over her shoulder into the pursuing darkness, her blood whooshing in her ears.

Her heaving chest tightened as she forced mouthfuls of air into her lungs to keep the oxygen flowing through her body so she could continue to run. To flee for her life from – she wasn't sure what – all she knew was the creature was enormous.

Oh, my God! It's gaining on me. I can't go any faster!

Tears stung Paige's eyes and the back of her throat burned as she rocketed through the gloom. She tripped and stumbled forward, fumbling to keep her balance. It didn't work and she landed hard on her knees. She attempted to scramble to her feet, the soles of her running shoes slipping on the wet leaves. She needed to get some traction. She had to run! A huge clawed hand reached out of the dark and as she opened her mouth to scream the monstrous palm slid across her face, smothering the sound before she could make it.

Paige was awakened by a shrill scream. Hers. Her breathing came in shallow bursts and she couldn't take a breath. She clawed at her throat feeling as though she were suffocating.

Her bedroom light flashed on, blinding her for a moment, and Stephanie rushed across the room. "What's wrong, honey? Are you all right?" She eased herself down onto the side of the bed, an anxious look of concern on her sleepy face.

Paige attempted to answer her but couldn't speak. Her heart thumped against her ribs and swelled in her throat.

Stephanie picked up the glass on her friend's night table and passed it to her. "Here, hon, drink some of this, it'll help."

Paige took hold of the glass with trembling fingers and raised it to her lips. "Thank you," she said, her voice a shaky whisper.

"It was the dream again, wasn't it? Want to talk about it?"

Paige shook her head and passed the glass back.

"Want me to stay with you?"

Paige nodded.

Stephanie sat the glass on the night table then walked around the queen-sized bed, climbed in next to her friend and wrapped an arm around her. "Try to go back to sleep. The sun'll be up soon."

Paige wasn't sure she could sleep. That particular dream always scared the living daylights out of her, and reminded her of the incident in the woods with the big black wolf that no one believes she saw.

TWENTY TWO

The next afternoon, Paige drove Stephanie into town for lunch and as she pulled into the curb outside the Moon Grove Inn and climbed out of the car she saw Eli step out of the front door and plant a kiss on Rebecca's cheek. When he turned to leave he spotted the two women standing on the sidewalk.

"So, it appears he has someone else in his sights," Stephanie deduced.

Paige pasted a pleasant smile on her face as he came toward them and said to her friend through tight lips, "They've been friends for years."

Stephanie shrugged. "Doesn't mean they're not friends with benefits."

Eli walked up to them. "Hello, ladies, here for lunch?"

"Yes. Paige tells me the food here is wonderful. I could use some home cooking." Stephanie gave him a broad grin.

"Well, she's right. The food is really good here. You're going to enjoy it. Betty Rogers is the owner and chef and she's a great cook. Her desserts are the best."

"Good to know." Stephanie's gaze moved from Eli to

her friend, then back to Eli. He was hot! But he only had eyes for Paige and nothing would change that.

"Can I talk to you for a minute?" he asked Paige.

"Oh, you two go right ahead. I'll just sit on the porch and wait." Stephanie headed along the path bordered with evergreen shrubs, climbed the two front steps and sat in a white wicker chair by the front door.

Eli wanted to reach out and touch Paige's arm but didn't because of her friend and other prying eyes he knew were watching them. "How are you? You look tired."

She knew he was concerned about her and wasn't telling her she looked like crap. "I'm not sleeping very well. I had that nightmare again the one I told you about. It frightens me every time but now even more so since the encounter in the woods with the wolf."

"We don't know if it was a wolf." Yes, he did, even though he couldn't admit it to her.

"I do." She folded her arms. "Why won't you believe me?"

"It's not that I don't believe you, Paige, it's just... maybe because you were so afraid that night you thought it was a wolf."

Paige's voice tightened. "I know what I saw, Eli."

"Ok." He wanted to hold her in his arms and comfort her. He thought having her friend around was a good thing after all. It made staying away that much easier. And he knew he had to keep his distance. For Paige's sake. "Well, enjoy your lunch. I'd better get back to the station."

"Thanks, I'm sure we will." She wanted to ask him when she'd see him again but thought it best not to, especially while Stephanie was in town. Her friend had been known to pilfer first dates right out from under her nose in the past and she didn't want that happening this time. If anyone was going to be with Eli it would be her. But right now that was the last thing she had on her mind.

She watched Eli climb into his Jeep and drive away before walking up the path to the front porch of the inn. Her heart felt heavy for not seeing him as often as before and she hoped she wasn't falling in love with him.

Stephanie stood up and gazed at the closed, multi-panel glass and wood door with credit card stickers pasted in one pane. "Ready to eat? I'm starved." She pushed open the door and stepped into the warmth of a large, open fireplace in the dining room to their left.

Paige followed her in realizing she'd lost her appetite and wasn't feeling the least bit hungry now.

After lunch the pair wandered around town to do a bit of retail therapy, which didn't take up too much time as the business center was less than half a mile long. Then, after stowing their bags in the trunk, they headed over to the carnival location to see how the set up was coming along. All of the stalls were up and the vendors were decorating and stocking them for the coming weekend start. Christmas day was so close.

The rides were the part Stephanie loved the most and Paige knew she wouldn't let her get away with not riding the Ghost Train with her. The Ferris wheel was about her limit but she'd do it for her friend. A miniature, Santa steam train track encircled the entire carnival district which the kids would absolutely love. There was also a merry-go-round, jumping castle, dodgem cars, a fun house and a hall of mirrors. It was going to be so much fun.

Paige had heard there would be a parade down the main

street on Saturday morning to kick off the carnival, with the Snow Princess taking center stage on a beautiful, crystal palace float. A small marching band would play popular carols, and other Christmas character floats would follow, including Santa's North Pole cabin and his elves. There would even be fireworks on the first and last nights. Moon Grove really did go all out for their winter carnivals and Paige was looking forward to going. She hoped she'd bump into Eli there.

As the women were leaving to walk back to the car, Paige noticed a patrol car cruise by and frowned when she realized it was Craig and that he was watching them. A shiver ran the length of her body and she wondered if he had been involved in the break in attempts. She thought the second voice that night was his and Eli seemed to think so too. Was the deputy part of it?

Stephanie noticed the car. "Who's that?"

"One of the town's deputies, Craig Campbell. He's... not a terribly friendly fellow. He seems to have a chip on his shoulder."

"Really?"

"Mm. When I was almost attacked in the woods that night he was so aggressive with me and I didn't understand why because he didn't even know me."

"Sounds like a real jerk to me." Stephanie's gaze followed the cruising patrol car.

Paige grinned. "My sentiments exactly." She rubbed her friend's arm. "I am so glad you're here. I needed this."

Stephanie smiled. "That makes two of us. Let's get home and make some hot chocolate. It's freezing out here. Got marshmallows?"

"Yep, sure do."

The two women continued along the main street to Paige's car unaware they were still being watched... But, this time, by someone else.

TWENTY THREE

Eli had been requested to attend a meeting with the Mayor at city hall. When he stepped into the unassuming brick building and climbed the stairs to the second floor he knew why he'd been summoned. The hierarchy of the town wanted an update on the incidents related to Paige. He'd been given a warning and had chosen to ignore it. Stay away from her. At first, he didn't want to but now he knew he had to. For her own safety.

The receptionist, who he'd known since high school, Linda, stepped out of Mayor Ross Redmond's office and smiled. "You can go in."

His gaze fell on the open door then to her. "Thanks, Lin." He gave her a thin smile and walked in.

"Close the door, Eli, this is official business," Redmond ordered. "We don't want everyone privy to what we're about to discuss." He motioned for the sheriff to take a seat. "Sit down, relax. This should be relatively painless."

Yeah, as long as I do what you want. Eli moved around one of the two chairs situated front and center, took a seat and crossed one leg over the other, resting his ankle on the opposite knee. He waited for the Mayor to continue before he spoke. He knew the routine.

"Any word on the break and enter attempts? How many have there been now… two?"

"Actually, there have been three. One in broad daylight."

The Mayor's severe gaze rested on Eli. "Do you have any suspects or leads?"

"Not yet. But we know there were two males involved."

"That's all you have?" Ross gave Eli an incredulous frown.

"For the moment, yes. We got nothing back on the forensic testing. They're very good at covering their tracks." Eli's thoughts went elsewhere and his eyes moved to the Mayor's desk for a brief moment then back to him. "Makes me wonder if…"

Redmond's left eyebrow arched. "If what?"

"Nothing. Just thinking out loud."

"Well you need to get this situation under control. The townspeople are concerned. Not only for the wellbeing of the young woman but also for the reputation of Moon Grove. What do you think would happen if Miss O'Connell decided to make an official complaint?"

"She won't. I've made sure of that. She trusts me."

"Glad to hear it, Sheriff. It's good to know you have the interests of the people of this town at heart."

"Always." He did have certain people's interests at heart, but the arrogant, self-serving Mayor wasn't one of them. Eli disliked agreeing with the man. He hated that he had to play it low-key with him. But he was his superior what choice did he have? If Paige decided to make a formal complaint he'd be behind her one hundred percent. He knew what came next and waited to be dismissed.

"Keep me informed of your progress." The Mayor's gaze shifted to some papers on his desk. "You may go."

Eli stalked across the room, flung open the door and barged out of the office. If he had his way, Ross Redmond wouldn't be part of his town. Eli detested the smug, mightier than thou attitude of the man and knew one day there would be serious repercussions. Until that day, he'd continue to keep the town safe and do his job to the best of his ability. Both as sheriff and Alpha.

He was about to climb into his four wheel drive when he heard his name and turned around. Linda crossed the sidewalk and came over to him. "Redmond is up to something. Be careful."

He frowned into her eyes. "What do you mean?"

"He had Craig in his office earlier…"

"Craig! Why?"

"I don't know. But my guess is he's pushing him to challenge your position as Alpha. You're a good soul, Eli, and the Mayor needs someone he can manipulate. That isn't you."

"Someone like Craig you mean?"

Linda nodded. "I'd better get back." She turned around then looked over her shoulder at him. "I think he knows who broke into Paige's house. But you didn't hear it from me."

"You know I would never say anything."

She gave him an assured smile then disappeared through the open doorway.

That's what he thought. Redmond was a dog in the sense that he'd do the council's bidding to keep Moon

Grove isolated from the rest of the US. Their tourist trade had all but dried up. Eli knew Ross Redmond liked being the human in the driver's seat of the small community and having knowledge of what took place behind the scenes gave Redmond a sense of power. He'd threatened Eli once before about revealing what he was to those who weren't aware. That's why he pandered to the power-hungry Mayor and the council. He couldn't have anyone telling Paige, not now.

As Eli opened the car door he glanced along the street and saw Paige's car heading out of town. Once they were along the road, a fair way a dark truck turned out of a side street and headed in their direction. Was it following the women? Eli climbed into his four wheel drive, started the engine and pursued the unfamiliar vehicle at a distance.

When Paige pulled into her driveway, the truck cruised past her house and kept going. Eli continued to follow it.

Stephanie stepped out of the car and turned to face the street. "Was that the sheriff?"

Paige closed her door and came around the trunk to her friend. "Probably. He does work here, you know."

"I know, but…" She frowned. "It looked like he was following that truck."

"Maybe it was speeding."

"Maybe." Stephanie rubbed her freezing hands together. "Let's get that hot chocolate with marshmallows on the go. It's so cold." She shivered and breathed warm air into her cupped hands.

The pair crossed the lawn, climbed the front steps and entered the house.

What they weren't aware of was that prying eyes were watching them from a neighboring home.

Eli tailed the truck for some distance before it turned onto the highway heading out of Moon Grove. Was he being paranoid or had it been following Paige and her friend? He'd taken down the interstate plate and would check it out once he was back at the station.

He was about to do a U-turn and head back past Paige's when a call came through on the radio. He had to get back to the station, pronto. Eli swung his vehicle around, switched on the siren, and rocketed along the highway.

When he reached the station, his Jeep screamed into the gravel parking lot spraying dirt and stones everywhere. He leaped from the car and raced inside. "How'd you find him?"

Craig's face beamed. "He was hiding in a shed out back of the gas station. I was filling the tank on the cruiser and needed to take a leak and that's how I found him. I could smell his stinking scent."

Eli pushed the brown wood door open, walked along the narrow corridor and turned left heading to the small cell block. When he opened the door and stepped into the concrete holding bay he was relieved to see the black wolf, in human form, locked in the first cell. He turned to look at Craig. Bobby had followed them in. "Good work. At least now we know Paige is safe."

"From the wolf, yeah, but what about the burglars?" Bobby asked.

"One win at a time, my friend."

TWENTY FOUR

"You have such a wonderful fireplace here, Paige, why don't we make a cozy fire? Wouldn't that be nice? We can sit and enjoy our hot chocolate and be snug as bugs in a rug." Stephanie gave her friend a huge grin then crossed the room and started placing logs into the grate.

"Sounds like plan. Let me help you with that. We need to put some newspaper in first so it will catch alight and set the wood on fire." Paige joined her friend and they each scrunched the pages to wedge between the logs.

Stephanie was about to strike a match when Paige stopped her. "Wait. I'd better check to make sure the flue is open otherwise we'll get smoked out."

Her friend stepped back. "Oh, ok. I didn't know you had to do that."

"Yeah, you do." Paige leaned in under the mantel to check the chimney and when she pressed her hand against a brick behind the grate it wobbled and she fell forward onto the logs. "Ouch!"

"Are you ok?" Stephanie grabbed Paige's arm and helped her to her feet.

"There's a loose brick in there."

Stephanie frowned. "Why would there be a loose brick in the fireplace?"

"I don't know but I'm going to find out." Paige unstacked the logs from the grate and laid them on the hearth.

"Do you think there's something behind it?" Stephanie asked.

Paige gave her a serious stare. "Maybe. Could be why I've been broken into so many times since I moved here."

"Yeah, but what would your uncle want to hide?"

"I don't know. Only one way to find out." She knelt down on the hearth, removed the grate, leaned into the fireplace and wriggled the brick to see if she could loosen it further. After several minutes of trying, without success, Stephanie said, "Let me try."

Paige scooted to one side so her friend could crawl into the space. Stephanie struggled with the brick using both her hands and after a couple of minutes she tugged it out of the wall. "Oh, wow, I did it!" She laid the brick on the floor of the fireplace.

"Feel around in the hole. Maybe there's something in there." Paige was anxious to see what her uncle had hidden in such an obscure place. He obviously didn't want anyone to find it.

Stephanie screwed up her nose. "I don't want to stick my hand in there. What if there's a spider or rat or something?"

Paige pushed her friend. "Oh, move over then, you baby. I'll do it." She leaned in and poked her hand into the gap between the bricks and at first couldn't feel anything. She prodded around with her fingers and felt something soft. "I think I found it! Paige leaned back on her haunches and studied the small, black velvet bag for a moment before opening the strings and turning the pouch upside down. A silver ring with a translucent white stone dropped into her palm.

"Oh, wow, that looks old," Stephanie said.

"Yes, it does." Paige studied it. "I wonder why Jake hid this in there."

"Obviously for safekeeping, although that doesn't make a whole lot of sense."

Paige frowned at her friend. "Nothing about Moon Grove makes sense."

"Maybe your Eli will know something about it. Didn't you say he was your uncle's friend?"

Paige couldn't take her eyes off the piece of jewelry sitting in her hand. She was drawn to it for some reason. "Yes... he... he was." She slipped the ring back into the bag and stood up. "I'll ask him the next time I see him."

"Wouldn't it be wiser to find out sooner rather than later, in case those guys that broke in come back? If that's what they're looking for."

A shiver ran the length of Paige's spine. The thought of someone coming back again frightened her. "Perhaps the ring is valuable."

"Could be. Maybe that's why they want it so badly."

Paige picked up her cell phone from off the coffee table and was about to press Eli's number but stopped herself. Every time she heard the sound of his voice the more her heart wanted to be with him and that wasn't a good thing right now. "I shouldn't disturb him tonight. He could be asleep already. It can wait until the morning."

Stephanie gave her an uncertain gaze. "Are you sure?"

"Yes, I'm sure. Let's put the brick back in place, make that fire and have our hot chocolate. The ring isn't going anywhere and I know just the place to hide it."

Eli walked through the front door of his house, hung his sheriff hat and jacket on the coat rail and dropped his keys into the wooden bowl on the small table standing by the door. He gave a heavy sigh and headed to the kitchen. He'd picked up some takeout on the way home and was looking forward to a quiet night in for once. Having the black wolf in custody made his life that much easier, although the guy wouldn't tell them anything, at least Paige was safe from him for now and that's all he cared about. Maybe it was him and another wolf that had broken into Paige's.

What Linda had told him earlier that day ran through his mind. He wouldn't put anything past Ross Redmond. Was he the one who had orchestrated the break in? Was the black wolf involved with him? Eli made a promise to himself to find out, no matter what the cost. The Mayor had stepped over the line this time, if he was the principal player in this dangerous game, and he wasn't about to let Redmond hurt Paige. *What could he possibly want from Jake's house? And why is it so important to him?*

Earlier, when he'd spotted the truck and thought it was tailing Paige he'd been even more worried for her safety. Turned out the guy had just been driving through town on his way home for Christmas and had taken a wrong turn. He hadn't thought to use his phone's GPS to get back on the right road and had followed Paige's car in the hope it would lead him out of Moon Grove. Once he'd made it to the highway he knew where he was heading.

Eli pulled the containers of Chicken Chow Mein and steamed rice out of the bag, snapped the chopsticks in two and sat on a stool at the kitchen counter to eat. He hoped they'd never find whatever it was they were looking for. A knock on his front door pulled his thoughts back to the present and he laid his chopsticks on top of the container, crossed the room and opened the door. "What brings you here, Wil?" It was after seven o'clock.

"Your young woman has found what the others are looking for."

Eli moved aside and the older man stepped into the room. "She's not my 'young woman.' And how do you know that?" He frowned at Wil as he closed the door and motioned for him to take a seat on the sofa.

"I had a call from *the woman*."

"You mean Clarissa?"

The older man nodded. "You know she knows things. She told me Paige found the ring."

"The Alpha moonstone ring?"

"What other ring do you think I'm talking about?"

Eli's frown deepened. "It's been missing for a decade."

"And with good reason. If anyone unscrupulous gets their hands on it all hell could break loose here in Moon Grove. You know the power it contains."

"Yes, I do." Eli remained on his feet and folded his arms.

"Anyhow, the ring is rightfully yours. You're the Alpha now."

"It's more trouble than it's worth. Its powers have made previous Alphas do crazy things." Eli paced. "I heard that one Alpha killed his whole pack because of that ring."

"That's very true. You were just a twinkle in your father's eye back then, but Jack Foster went berserk and slaughtered his entire pack on his own. He didn't need any help. The ring turned him into an overpowering homicidal maniac."

Eli stopped, turned around and raised an eyebrow. "And you think I should wear it?"

"You're a different kettle of fish, Eli. It wouldn't affect you in the same way. You're a good soul."

"Linda said those exact same words to me today. Am I that transparent?"

"Would I be here if you weren't?" Wil gave Eli an assured smirk.

"Is Paige safe with that ring in her house?" Eli was worried about the supernatural implications associated with it.

"As long as she doesn't put it on she should be."

"So the legends are true. The ring's powers can affect anyone who wears it."

"Yeah. And because Paige has wolf blood who knows what could happen if she does."

A look of concern washed over Eli's face. "Thank God she's a woman, if not she'd have already turned on her eighteenth birthday."

Wil gave him a serious stare. "Have you given any thought to why someone's trying to kill her?"

"Of course I have. That's all I can think about. Why, do you know something?"

"Well, maybe they don't want you two getting together romantically. If you know what I mean."

"Why would someone want to kill Paige to prevent us from having a relationship? What could anyone gain from that? "

The old man gave Eli an incredulous frown. "Are you serious?"

Eli stood with hands on hips. "What do you mean?"

"You and Paige... She's your female Alpha."

The sheriff's eyebrows rose. "What?"

"How much plainer can I say it?"

"But she's not a wolf."

"She has potent Lycan blood in her veins and once you consummate your relationship she will be."

Eli paced and ran his hand down the back of his neck. "I had no idea."

"Don't you remember saying one day you were going to marry her when you were a kid?"

"Well, yeah, but..."

"That's because you're destined to be together."

"Then we'd better do something about preventing her from putting on that ring. Maybe Clarissa should introduce herself to Paige. Can you give her a call back and arrange it? She seems to take your direction better than mine."

"Consider it done." Wil stood up and walked across to the front door. Raising his hand to stop Eli from following him over he said, "Don't bother, I can let myself out."

"You'll call her tonight, right?"

"She'll pay the young lady a visit as soon as I get in the car and pick up my phone."

"Thanks, Wil."

"It's the least I can do after what happened to her family."

Eli frowned at the closed door. Did the old man know more about that night than he was letting on?

TWENTY FIVE

I t was odd. When Paige lived in Washington DC she always had the television on, mainly to listen to the news while she did chores around her apartment. Since she'd moved to Moon Grove she had hardly turned the TV on at all. Tonight was a good example. She and Stephanie were sitting in front of the fire, sipping hot chocolate and chatting, and it felt great. Not much went on in the town, apart from the scary incidents she'd been involved in, and she assumed that was the reason why she no longer bothered with the television. What news could there be? A stray bear ran through the town or there was a bake sale at the local school?

She sat her mug on the coffee table, picked up her cell phone and checked the time. It was almost eight o'clock. That old saying, 'time flies when you're having fun,' popped into her head and she realized it was true. Stephanie had gone into the hall to find a pack of cards to play poker for pennies and just as she came back into the living room a knock on the front door echoed into the entry hall.

"I wonder who that could be," Stephanie said, glancing

over her shoulder at the curtained, white front door.

Paige got up off the floor from in front of the fire and walked across to the living room entrance. "I don't know. I wasn't expecting anyone."

"Maybe it's your hunky sheriff come to pay you a visit." Stephanie winked and grinned. "I think if he had the chance he'd be here every day." Her grin widened.

Paige shook her head and went to the door. Before opening it she took a peek through the curtain, just to be safe. An elderly woman stood outside. She swung the door back. "Hello, can I help you with something?"

The woman was dressed in 1960s, bright colorful clothing, had streaks of purple and pink through her wavy, long gray hair and wore black eyeliner. Chains and beads hung from her neck and she had a ring on every finger of each hand. She reminded Paige of mature-aged hippy. And she reeked of Patchouli oil. "Hello, dear, I'm Clarissa Baker. I live across the street." She pointed in the direction of her house.

"Nice to meet you, Clarissa. Is there something I can do for you?"

Stephanie stood behind Paige and studied the woman.

Clarissa shook her head, smiled and said, "No, but there is something I can do for you."

Paige's right eyebrow arched. "Oh, and what's that?"

"Warn you. You have something in your possession that is…" she fumbled for the right word. There wasn't one. "…dangerous. May I come in?"

Paige gave her friend a sideward glance over her shoulder then returned her gaze to the woman standing on her welcome mat. "What do you mean?"

"The ring, dear. The moonstone ring."

Eli ran his eyes over the documents spread out across the kitchen counter. What was he missing in the reports on Paige's parents' disappearance? He made a mental note to go out to Wil's place the next morning to try to get him to open up about that night. Why wouldn't he? Had someone threatened him? Paid him off?

He glanced at the wall clock over the refrigerator. 8.21 PM. He hoped Clarissa would be talking to Paige and explaining what she could about the ring. He wished he could have been the one to tell her, but knew it was better coming from her. He would have to talk to Paige at some point and ask for the ring, not that he wanted to wear it, he didn't, but it did belong to the pack. How had Jake come into possession of it?

Eli shuffled the papers together, slid them into the manila folder and closed it. If Paige's parents weren't dead, as Wil had insinuated, then where were they? And why hadn't they taken Paige with them all those years ago? Too many questions remained unanswered and it was time to get to the bottom of the mystery.

His cell phone vibrated across the breakfast bar and he snatched it up. It was Bobby. "Hey, Bobby, what's up?"

"You need to get down here right now."

"What's going on?"

"Three of the Mayor's goons are outside. They want the guy in the cell. What do you want me to do, boss?"

So the black wolf and Redmond were involved with each other somehow.

"Tell them to wait until I get there."

"I don't think that's gonna happen. Do you want me to…?"

"I'm on my way. No wolf stuff, all right? Just try to hold them off I'll be there in less than ten minutes." Eli rang off, crossed the room, threw on his jacket and hat and headed out the door. He knew Ross Redmond had something to do with what was going on in Moon Grove. His intuition had been spot on.

Paige invited the woman in and she and Stephanie followed her into the living room. How could she know they'd found the ring? Clarissa perched on the edge of the middle cushion on the sofa and rested her hands in her lap. Paige and Stephanie sat in the opposite armchairs on the other side of the coffee table.

"May I see it?" Clarissa asked, her face invigorated with curiosity.

"How did you know I found it?" Paige's eyes roamed the room and she wondered if someone had planted a bug of some kind.

"I have the gift." Clarissa gave a thin smile.

"What gift?" Paige frowned. "I don't understand."

"There are things I'm unable to explain to you, my dear, for your own safety. But what I can tell you is that I've had the ability to see things before they happen all of my life, and that's how I knew."

Paige and Stephanie glanced at each other sideways. Was the woman crazy? Had Paige let a crazy person into her home? "Ok. You said the ring is dangerous. How?"

"The moonstone ring has certain… *abilities*…"

Paige raised her hand to stop Clarissa from continuing. "Wait. What? Are you saying the ring is magical?"

The woman shook her head emphatically. "Oh, no, dear, definitely not magical."

"Then I'm not sure I get what you mean." Paige placed her hand on the hip pocket of her jeans where the small pouch was concealed.

Clarissa sighed. "It's difficult to explain. I'm not at liberty to divulge too much information right now."

"Is the ring dangerous or not?" Paige could hear the tightness in her voice and tried to relax, but the woman was exasperating.

"Yes."

"How?"

"I can't tell you that."

"Why not?"

"Because I was asked not to."

"By whom?" Paige was becoming more and more frustrated and her tone took on a sharp timbre.

"Uh… a mutual acquaintance."

Paige's eyebrows shot up. "A mutual acquaintance of ours?" She pointed back and forth.

"No, dear, of… Eli's."

Paige folded her arms and huffed out an agitated breath. So Eli knew about the ring too. How? She knew that news traveled fast in small towns but this was ridiculous. She'd only just discovered it. "How does the sheriff know about the ring?"

"He was told by our mutual friend."

Paige popped up out of the armchair and paced. *This is crazy!* "How did this mutual friend find out?"

"I told him, dear."

"And he told Eli?"

"Well, yes." Clarissa gave Paige a curious frown. "Isn't that what I just said?"

"Ok. Yes, I guess. Is there anything else I need to know?"

Clarissa gazed down at her hands and thought about what she could or should tell the young woman. She didn't want to frighten her any more than she already had been. The town's secrets had to be protected but it had become more and more difficult with what had taken place. "You need to give the ring to Eli. It's rightfully his."

"Why is it rightfully his? Do you know how my uncle came to have it?"

"The ring is an heirloom, it belongs to Eli because…" She stopped herself. "I don't know how your uncle came into possession of it. It's been missing for a decade."

Paige didn't ask anything more about the ring. She realized as an heirloom it did belong to Eli. But why was it dangerous? And would he be in danger if she gave it to him?

The four wheel drive screeched to halt on the street, headlights shining two, bright overlapping paths along the road as Eli flew out of the car, leaving the door open, and rounded the vehicle. Bobby was on the front porch standing at the top of the stairs with a shotgun in his hands. The three goons sent by the Mayor stood, arms folded, by the black van they'd arrived in. It's a miracle all hell hadn't already broken loose.

"Ok, I'm here now. What is it you want?"

"We have orders to collect the prisoner and contain him elsewhere," one of the three told him. Each man's bulky frame was chiseled and at least Eli's height and weight, so if a fight ensued it would be sheer strength and will that would win the battle.

"The safest place for him is here in the cells. We all know that." Eli walked up to them and stood with hands on hips.

"We have our orders not to return without him so hand him over or we'll go in and take him." Something shimmered across the guy's eyes and confirmed what Eli had already sensed. Werewolves. Was the guy in the cell part of this pack or was he a liability to it and the Mayor?

Another car screeched to a stop at the curb under the trees and Craig flew up the path and stood beside Eli. Before long another car pulled in behind Eli's and a bulky guy made his way over to the group. Ryan Hollis, the town mechanic, was also one of Eli's pack. He took up position on the other side of his Alpha.

"I hope we can come to some kind of agreement gentlemen otherwise this could get ugly," Eli offered.

Another car screamed into the parking lot throwing up gravel and dirt and a woman climbed out. Rebecca. She marched across the lawn and stood beside Craig.

A fourth car made a screeching stop next to Rebecca's sedan and Paul stepped out and came up to the group.

The trio of muscle gave each other a disturbed frown then the one doing the talking turned back and locked his intense gaze onto Eli. "Ok. You win. *For now.*" They climbed into the black van with tinted windows, spun the wheels on the lawn and hurtled out of the yard.

Bobby came down the steps. "Phew. I wasn't sure how

long I could hold them off on my own. They were getting kinda antsy."

Eli gripped his shoulder. "Thanks for calling in backup. It could've gotten pretty messy out here."

"Yeah. And hard to explain."

The group entered the station and followed Eli into the cell block to talk to their prisoner. He needed answers.

Her parents' house stood before her, dark and foreboding in the gloomy night. The cream colored full moon lay heavy in the blue black sky surrounded by drifting gray clouds above her, but still gave off enough light to see that the door was open. Paige's stomach squeezed into a tight ball as she moved closer to the porch, and when she approached the front steps a shadow darted out of the doorway.

Paige jumped backwards, sucking in a sharp, anxious breath. Her eyes roamed the broken window panes, the dilapidated porch and the lopsided, open front door. "Hello?" she called, her voice quivering. "Who's there?"

No one answered.

Had she imagined it? No, someone was inside. She could feel it.

"Who's there," she asked again, her voice even thinner than before. "I know you're in there so show yourself."

A figure filled the open space. "It's me."

Eli?

Relieved, Paige let out the breath she'd been holding and moved to the bottom of the steps. "What are you doing here?"

"I came to help you." He stepped onto the porch and as he came toward her something shimmered across his eyes. Was it the moonlight?

How did Eli know I'd be here? Paige backed away from him. Her instincts were telling her to run but she didn't.

"What's wrong?" Eli kept moving toward her, down the steps and along the path.

"Nothing. I – I don't even know what I'm doing here."

"You want answers you'll never understand." He stepped up to her and gripped both her arms preventing her from moving away from him.

"What do you mean?"

"There are things about Moon Grove you don't know."

Paige frowned up at him, her stomach tightening even more. "What things?" Did she really want to find out?

"I can't tell you right now." He gave her a peculiar look and that shimmer returned. It wasn't the moonlight.

"Why not?" Paige's heartbeat kicked up another notch. She was afraid of him for the first time.

He pulled her toward the front door. "Why don't we go get those answers?"

"Eli, stop, you're hurting me!"

When he turned his head to look at her she saw that shimmer across his honey colored eyes again and they seemed to glow in the dark. "Come on, Paige. If you want to know the truth you'll have to go inside."

As he tugged her along the path several, huge upright creatures appeared from out of the legion of dark trees. What were they? And why were they coming toward them?

Paige gasped and sprang up off her pillow, her eyes

darting around the shadows in her room, her shallow breathing choppy. What had she dreamed? She frowned and forced her sleepy brain to remember. *Come on, come on, what did I just see?* She sucked in a sharp, shocked breath. Eli! It was a dream she'd never had before, a dream that frightened her more than the one of the wolf chasing her in the dark woods. And Eli's eyes. What did it mean?

Her confused thoughts tugged at the archives of her memory trying to pull the images back into focus in her mind's eye. What had she seen? *Think. Think!* Her parents' house. Eli had been inside. Why? And why had he hidden from her when she'd called out? Was there some kind of meaning to that? Or was it because she and Eli had been friends as children?

She remembered the creatures and her body shivered, goosebumps spreading up her arms. What were they and why were they in her dream? They had walked upright on two legs instead of four but they were beasts of some kind. Paige shook her head. Nothing about what she'd dreamed made any sense. Maybe her subconscious was reminding her of the men that had shot at her and Eli when they were out at the house. But there had only been two, Eli had said. Was she making too much out of this new nightmare? Or was there more to Eli Blackwood and the town of Moon Grove?

TWENTY SIX

The wolf in the cell wouldn't tell him anything and Eli sensed that he was afraid of someone. Was it Ross Redmond? Those thugs that showed up at the station last night? Who was he, why was he in Moon Grove, and why did the Mayor want him so badly? As he drove along the bumpy country road heading to Wil Wallace's property he hoped the old man would finally open up and tell him what he needed to know. People's lives depended on finding out who was behind the recent incidents and who had *killed* Paige's parents. Eli believed they were dead, otherwise where were they now, and why hadn't they come back for their five year old daughter?

When he pulled the four wheel drive up behind Wil's powder blue Chevrolet LUV he noticed the front door of the house was wide open. Unusual for the old man to leave his doors that way as he always had both the screen door and the front door locked every time Eli had been out to his place. He climbed out of the Jeep, rounded the hood, his wolf hackles up, and headed to the porch. "Wil?" he called. "You in there?"

No answer.

Eli pulled his Ruger LC9 from its holster and stepped up onto the decking without making a sound. Was the old man inside? He couldn't sense him. Was he dead? The sheriff eased his body against the wall then raised his weapon and stepped into the open doorway. No one. He used his Alpha senses: hearing, smell and sight as he entered the house.

"Wil?"

Gun raised, he cleared every room. Wil wasn't there. After going through the whole cabin, checking the barn and the grounds outside, Eli began working the scene. No sign of a struggle. No blood anywhere. But he knew in his gut that Wil hadn't left his home voluntarily. There was Lycan scent in the property. Redmond's goons most likely.

He used his shoulder mic. "Rosemarie, do you copy?"

She checked the time before responding. 11:25 AM. "Why, good mornin', Eli, what can I do for you on this wonderful chilly day?"

"Is Bobby around?"

"He sure is, Darlin'. Want me to put him on?"

"Thanks, Rosy."

Bobby was on his feet and across the room in a flash. He could hear the strain in Eli's voice even though Rosemarie hadn't detected it. "Hey, boss, everything ok?"

"I'm out at Wil Wallace's place. Looks like he's been taken against his will."

"Want me to send Paul out to you?"

"Yeah, and do me a favor, don't tell Craig."

"That won't be difficult 'cause he's not here."

Eli scowled. "Where is he?"

"Don't know. He hasn't checked in yet."

Eli paced with one hand on his hip and the phone

pressed to his ear. "Well when he does you tell him I want to talk to him and he'd better be in the office by the time I get back."

"Will do. I'll get onto Paul right now. He should be out there in the next half hour. Need anything else?"

"Not at this stage. Thanks, Bob." Eli rang off. Did Craig have something to do with Wil's disappearance? He hoped not because if he did that meant he couldn't be trusted, which Eli already suspected.

The snow was really coming down and when Paige opened the police station door and stepped into its warmth she shivered as a blast of freezing air blew up the back of her jacket. She hoped the snow would let up enough for the carnival to go ahead. She was really looking forward to some fun. At least it would take her mind off everything else for a while.

Rosemarie smiled at her from behind her desk. "Good mornin', Miss O'Connell, how can I help you today?"

"Please, call me Paige. I came to talk to Eli. Is he here?" Her eyes moved to the windowed office. He wasn't at his desk.

"Not at the moment, hon. Maybe I can help you with your enquiry." The receptionist clasped her hands on the blotter, her professional visage in place.

Paige shook her head and smiled. "That's ok. It's something I really need to speak to him about."

"I'm not sure how long he'll be. He's on official business out of town."

"Oh. Ok, thanks." Paige started to leave but turned

back. She had to talk to him about the ring and her strange dream. He knew more than he was telling her and she needed answers. "Would you ask him to give me a call when he gets back? It's important."

Rosemarie's smile widened and she picked up a pen and scribbled down a note for herself. "I sure will. You have a nice day now. Stay warm."

"Thank you. You too." Paige opened the door and headed to the parking lot around the side of the building.

Bobby McBride was just pulling in and gave Paige a wave as he parked the police patrol alongside her sedan. She wondered if she should wait and say hello or just get into her car a leave. She decided to wait.

"How're you doing?" Bobby asked, coming around her car from the trunk with a bakery bag in his hand. She figured it was morning tea.

"I'm doing ok. You?" Small talk wasn't her forte but she didn't want to appear rude. He'd been a childhood friend and she had to get used to the familiarity of the people in Moon Grove who had known her as a little girl.

He nodded. "Good. Getting colder, isn't it?" He glanced up from under the rim of his wide-brimmed hat. "And the snow's really coming down right now."

"Yes, it is." Paige pushed her gloved hands into the pockets of her coat. "I'm looking forward to the carnival. I can't believe it's almost Christmas already."

"Me neither. My kids are like bees in a hive. They can't wait to see what Santa brought 'em. Only another week and a bit."

"It's a wonderful time of year for kids." Paige glanced upward. "Well, I'd better let you get inside before you turn into a snowman." She gave him a broad grin.

"I guess I'll see you at the carnival, if we don't get snowed in." Bobby tipped his police issue, fawn colored Stetson and headed for the path.

Paige shivered as she opened her car door and climbed in. She started the engine and cranked up the heat to melt the snowflakes sprinkled across her shoulders and wool cap, then backed out of the drive onto the street and headed for home. Stephanie was still asleep when she'd left but should be well awake by now as it was close to midday. Paige wanted to go back into town later to put some finishing touches to her new office before the grand opening. She hoped she'd made the right decision starting her practice in Moon Grove. Would she have any clients? Would any of the townsfolk trust her with their private thoughts and emotions? Only time would tell, she guessed.

TWENTY SEVEN

After doing a thorough sweep of the inside and outside of Wil Wallace's home for finger prints and DNA, Paul and Eli stepped out onto the porch and tacked a strip of yellow crime scene tape across the front door. What had happened here last night? Was Wil still alive?

Eli figured he'd been getting too close to the truth and the only way to prevent him from finding the answers was to remove Wil, his only reliable eye witness and source of information, from the equation. As he watched Paul leave, he stood with his hands buried deep in his jacket pockets and did a 360 degree turn, taking in the whole scene. No tire tracks except for Wil's, his and Paul's. How had they gotten the old man off the property and where had they taken him? It couldn't have been far.

He realized Paige's parents' house was only a short distance from Wil's and decided to take a drive over there before returning to the station. Why? He wasn't sure. He just had a gut feeling he should go there. Was it related to Wil's disappearance? He didn't think so. Nothing made sense, not even to him. Since Paige had moved to Moon

Grove things had gotten out of control and it was time to return them to their natural order, the way they had been before she arrived. There were still some people in the town who knew nothing about the supernatural element of the place, including Paige, and he wanted to keep it that way. For everyone's peace of mind.

Starting the engine, he was about to turn his Jeep around when a black sedan pulled in behind him and blocked his path. Eli turned off the engine and stepped out of the vehicle. He knew right away who it was.

Ross Redmond exited the car via the right hand, back passenger door and strutted up to him.

"What are you doing here?" The sheriff asked, wondering how the Mayor had found out about the abduction in such a short space of time, although he shouldn't have been surprised. The man had his eyes and ears on everyone and everything in Moon Grove.

"I saw Paul's car leaving here and asked my driver to drive up. What's going on?"

"You shouldn't be here. It's a crime scene."

The Mayor's dark eyebrows rose. "A crime scene? What happened here?" His eyes shot to the taped up front door. "Where's the old man?"

Eli's serious gaze ran over Redmond's anxious face. Either the man was an expert liar or he had no idea what had happened here. That meant he had nothing to do with Wil's disappearance. "I came out here earlier to talk to him and found the property open and unattended."

Redmond frowned into the sheriff's face. "What do mean by unattended?"

"Wil's missing at this point, but I think he was taken against his will."

"Taken?" The Mayor's eyes roamed the property. "How and by whom?"

"That's what I'm going to find out."

"Make sure you do. Wil Wallace was a fine officer of the law for a lot of years, if something's happened to him..." he said, returning his gaze to Eli, "I want to know about it."

This put a whole new spin on Eli's theory. If Redmond wasn't involved in Wil's disappearance and what had happened to Paige then who was?

"While I've got you here why do you want the guy in my cell?"

"I believe he's a renegade wolf from a rival pack and he shouldn't be here. I wanted to have a face to face with him and make him aware that he needs to stay out of Moon Grove."

Eli gave him an incredulous stare and folded his arms. "And then what?"

The Mayor folded his arms across his expensive, dark blue suit. "Nothing."

"Were you planning to let him leave or..."

"Of course I intended to let him leave. In fact, my men were going to escort him out of town. Just to be sure he took my advice seriously." The hint of a smirk slid across the Mayor's face.

"Right. You do realize that if he disappears they'll come looking for him, don't you?"

"I meant what I said. I just wanted to make it clear that he wasn't welcome here and not to return."

Eli doubted that. He sighed. "Do you have any intel on whether or not he's one of the men who broke into Paige's house?"

The Mayor's expression darkened. "Why would I? You're the law enforcement of our fine town. You need to find out the answers." A glimmer of something ominous ran across Redmond's eyes and Eli picked up on it. "Do you think he has someone else with him?"

"Maybe. I also think he's the wolf that scared Paige that night in the woods."

Redmond scoffed. "Big black wolf? Had to be him."

Eli's dubious gaze remained on Redmond. "How do you know he belongs to a rival pack?"

"I assumed he did because there's only one nearby. At least that I'm aware of. Where else do you think he came from?"

"That's what I'm asking you."

The Mayor redirected the conversation. He didn't appreciate where the sheriff was going with it. "What do you plan to do with him?"

"Not sure yet. He hasn't given me any answers to my questions and I can't hold him for much longer. It's a violation of his rights."

"Then let me take him off your hands. I'll question him and make sure he doesn't return."

"Thanks for the offer but I think I can handle it."

Redmond knew he could order his men to walk into the police station and take the man by force, but he didn't want a major incident on his hands. He turned on his heel and headed back to the chauffeur driven, luxury sedan, then turned around. "Keep me up-to-date on Wil's situation, will you? I'd hate for anything to happen to him. He deserves to live out the rest of his days in peace."

Eli was surprised at the concern of the Mayor for the old man. "Sure."

Redmond's serious gaze met his. "Thank you." He climbed into the car and the driver backed down the dirt drive.

That was a first. Ross Redmond seldom said thank you to anyone.

Once again, Eli climbed into his wagon and started the engine. There was something about Paige's parents' house that beckoned him since he'd been there the other night and he needed to find out what it was. He did a U-turn and headed down the dirt track to the main highway. It would take about ten minutes to get over there.

When he pulled the Jeep off the road under a clump of snow-laden trees, Eli's gut tightened. He sat and stared out of the windshield at the old house. Even in the early evening twilight it had a foreboding aura to it. He pulled the keys from the ignition, slipped them into his pocket and trudged through the tall, wet grass to the front porch. His senses piqued and he stood and listened to the surrounding woods.

What had brought him all the way out here today? What was the date? He reached into the inside pocket of his coat and slid his cell phone out. December 17th. The day Paige's parents disappeared.

Eli's eyes roamed the gloomy stretch of unkempt land. The heavy snowfall and the ominous gray clouds hanging overhead gave the place a creepy vibe. Was there something or someone lurking nearby? If so, they were keeping off his Lycan radar. He checked his pistol and shoved it back into its holster, then continued along the path to the front steps. Who were the two men that had been here that night? Had they murdered and disposed of

Paige's parents? Eli thought that was a distinct possibility as the couple had never been seen or heard from again. What parent would vanish and leave their young child behind?

He climbed the weathered treads and stepped onto the porch. The decaying boards groaned under his weight and he jumped across to the threshold before the decking gave way beneath him. The old house should have been demolished years ago, but it belonged to Paige, whether she knew it or not, and he assumed not, so it was her decision to make.

His gaze shifted around the damp, musty interior before he climbed the creaking stairs to the second floor. He'd felt bad about Paige seeing the blood soaked mattress. Not a good memory to have of her parents, whether she remembered them or not. What did Wil mean when he'd said, 'Assuming they *were* killed.'? He wished the old man had told him what he knew; now he may never get the chance to.

A sound downstairs caused Eli to swing around and leap over the banister. If he didn't hold his weight he'd go right through the floor. He landed on all fours, the boards distorting beneath him, and was on his feet in a split second. Where had the noise come from? He whipped through the dilapidated house. No one. But he was sure he'd heard something. Lowering his heart rate and breathing, so he could hear a pin drop, he did another search of the down stair rooms. It was then that he noticed the cellar door ajar underneath the staircase. It would be pitch black down there but his acute nocturnal vision would enable him to see in the dark recesses of the cellar. He pulled his pistol, eased the door back so that it wouldn't creak and stepped inside.

Someone was here. He could smell their scent.

Luckily, the cellar had concrete stairs, not the open wooden kind most underground storage rooms had, which allowed him some cover from being attacked between the treads. When he reached the bottom of the staircase he used his wolf vision to scan the sodden, overgrown subterranean cavity. Some old crates stood in the far corner and that's where the smell emanated from. "You might as well show yourself. I know you're down here." Eli crossed the room, gun drawn. "I said show yourself."

He moved closer to the rotting wooden boxes. He couldn't hear a heartbeat. Was it another wolf? If so, then why hadn't he sensed it? He shoved the top box forward but no one jumped clear. When he moved around the mound of disintegrating wood he found a hole in the wall big enough for someone to crawl through. Whoever had been in the house had gotten out.

Eli flew up the stairs and into the entry hall then leaped across the porch onto the path. His eyes scanned every inch of the property. No one was there.

TWENTY EIGHT

On the way back to the station, Eli received a call on his two-way. Rosemarie informed him that Paige O'Connell had been into the station to see him and asked if she could pass on a message. As the sheriff had taken much longer than expected she thought it best to let him know. He cruised along the main street, past the police station, and headed over to Paige's. It was a good excuse to see her again. He missed spending time with her, even though it was in her best interest that he remained at a distance.

When he arrived, he pulled in behind her car, got out and crossed the lawn. The door opened as he climbed the front steps and Paige greeted him with a serious expression. After the dream she'd had she wanted to know the truth.

"Something the matter?" Eli stepped onto the porch.

Paige came outside and pulled the door closed behind her. "We need to talk."

Eli gave her a curious frown. Whenever a woman said those four words a man knew trouble was brewing. "Ok."

He shoved his hands into the pockets of his jacket and followed her along to the swing seat. He sat, she remained on her feet.

"Mind telling me what's going on?" Eli asked. He could see she was upset about something and figured it had to be related to Clarissa's visit the night before.

"I have something that belongs to you." She tugged the small, black velvet pouch out of her coat pocket and passed it to him.

Eli knew immediately what was inside. "Thanks. It's been missing for ten years."

"Do you think Jake had it all that time?"

He glanced at the small bag in the palm of his hand then returned his gaze to Paige. "Hard to say. Quite possibly."

"Last night Clarissa came over and told me the ring was dangerous. She wouldn't elaborate and said you'd told her through a mutual acquaintance not to say anything. Why?"

Eli sighed. He had to think of a plausible excuse to placate Paige as he couldn't tell her the truth. "I asked her not to so that I could tell you myself." What else could he say?

Paige eased her tense body onto the swing seat beside him. "Ok. That's fair, considering the ring is an heirloom and belongs to your family."

"Yes, it does." It was an important talisman to his wolf pack family. "Look, there are things about Moon Grove I can't tell you about right now. I hope you'll trust me enough to be patient."

Paige's frown deepened. *That's partly what he'd said to me in my dream.* "I think you'll want to confide in me after I tell you about the dream I had last night.

His right eyebrow arched. "What do you mean?"

She pressed her spine against the seat, clasped her gloved hands together in her lap and sighed. "In the dream I was out at my parents' house. I wasn't sure why I was there but something had drawn me to it."

Eli frowned. He'd had the same feeling today.

"When I reached the porch I saw a shadow dart out of the doorway so I called out. Of course no one answered at first and that made me even more afraid. I stepped away from the porch and called out again. This time someone did appear."

Eli shifted his muscular frame around in the seat so he was facing her. "Who was it?"

"You."

He inhaled a deep breath. "Go on."

"As you came toward me something shimmered across your eyes. At first, I thought it was the light from the full moon, but when you came closer it happened again."

Eli remained silent.

Paige eyed him sideways. What was he hiding? He'd have to tell her sooner or later. "I stepped backwards away from you but you grabbed my arm and tugged me toward the front door."

"Then what happened?" He folded his arms.

"You said something about I wouldn't like the answers once I found them. Then a group of creatures came out of the trees heading toward us." Paige's frown turned to a questioning scowl. "But they were on two feet." She shook her head. "It didn't make any sense. I was so afraid I couldn't breathe and when I woke up I was still unable to catch my breath."

Eli sat in quiet contemplation. *Paige had that dream because of her connection to me. But how did her subconscious mind know about the werewolves? She hadn't been in Moon Grove long enough to become aware of the supernatural aspect of the town yet. And her aunt knew nothing about it either. Her father's blood has to be the reason. She may wake up one morning and remember everything... know about everything.*

Paige turned to him a concerned frown on her face. "Eli?" She touched his arm. "Eli?"

His intense gaze moved to her and his voice was tight. "What?"

She snatched her hand away.

"I'm sorry. I was just trying to get my head around your wild dream."

"Wild dream? Is that what you think it is?" Her expression turned to hurt. He hadn't thought her other dream was 'wild.'

"Well it doesn't make a lot of sense, does it?" He stood up and leaned against the porch rail. "You saw me hiding in your parents' old house. Why would I be there? And then you saw creatures that walked upright like human beings?"

Paige sighed. "I know how it sounds. It sounds crazy even to me but that's what I saw. And your eyes frightened me, Eli. Something about them really frightened me."

He reached for her and pulled her from the swing seat with more force than he'd intended. He had to keep his Lupine sensitivities in check. "Look into my eyes now. Do I scare you?" He couldn't have her figuring it out. He had to dissuade her. To keep her safe.

She stared into those honey colored pools that she'd

grown to love gazing into and shook her head. "No. But in the dream…"

"That's all it was, Paige – a dream. With everything that's happened to you since you moved here it's a wonder you're not having far worse nightmares." His heart felt heavy in his chest. He hated having to lie to her. Well, not tell her the truth anyhow. He knew he would have to eventually, but not now.

Paige's gaze remained on his. Was he right? Was that all it was?

"You've known me only a few weeks, but I'm sure you've summed up the kind of man you think I am. Do you believe there's anything about me to be afraid of?"

"Of course not, you're a good man, Eli. I know that, but I think my mind is trying to jog something out of my memory that's been suppressed since I was a child. The information may be jumbled right now, but I'm sure it will straighten itself out over time."

That's what he was afraid of. "Maybe we should both go see Doc Taylor."

Paige scowled and stepped away from him. "You think I need a shrink?"

"I think we both need to figure out what our dreams are trying to tell us." He hoped that while under hypnosis the doctor could make her forget what her mind was attempting to dislodge, at least for a while longer. It was worth a shot.

"I'm a psychologist, Eli. I know what I'm doing and I don't need another doctor to tell me what I already know."

"Well I'm going to make an appointment to see him. I need to find out why I've started having that dream again. I thought I was over it." He wasn't about to tell her she was in it too and that she disappears, leaving behind a blood trail.

"Why don't you let *me* help you?" She smiled up at him. "You could be my first client." She didn't like using the word *patient* even though that's what her clients were.

"Thanks. I think I'll pass."

"But why?"

"Men's business."

Her eyebrows rose. "Oh, come on. Seriously?"

Eli gave a sharp nod. "You bet."

She sighed. "All right, if you must."

He touched her arm. "I must."

Paige shook her head. "I'll never understand the fraternity thing that men seem to have. It's like the Freemasons; a religious fraternity with secrets." She frowned up at him. "What church is supposed to have secrets?"

"Apparently quite a few these days," Eli replied. Paige would be horrified to discover just what kind of secret fraternity Moon Grove had in the large white church on the hill?

She arched her left eyebrow and said, "Mm."

"I have to go." Eli walked to the front steps. "Want to meet me at the carnival Saturday?"

Paige's eyes moved to the closed door. "I would but…"

"Your friend?"

She nodded. "I don't want her to feel like the third wheel."

"Ok. Well, I hope I see you there." He stepped off the porch, crossed the lawn to his car and gave her a wave before getting in.

"You will." Paige waved goodbye. She would've loved

to have gone with him. Hopefully another time. She opened the door and stepped into the lit entry hall.

"You gave it to him?" Stephanie asked as she came down the stairs.

"Yep. And I'm glad to have it out of the house. Maybe now whoever is looking for it will find out Eli has it and leave me alone."

Eli thought it would be a good idea to swing by the station before he drove home. He knew he couldn't hold the young man for much longer but decided to give questioning him one last shot before releasing him the next morning. Why wouldn't he at least give his name? And where had he come from? The wipers on his Jeep were doing an inadequate job of clearing the heavily falling snow from the windshield, and as he slowed down to pull into the parking lot beside the station house he almost hit something.

"What the hell!" He eased his foot down on the break so as not to slide across the road and came to a stop under the trees out front. He threw open the door and jerked his large frame out of the driver's seat, his wolf eyes roaming the surrounding street and closed shops. No one. He gave a heavy sigh, got back into his four wheel drive, backed up and pulled into the lot.

Climbing out of his car, he scanned the street again. What had he nearly hit? A stray dog? His heart thudded in his chest as the realization hit him and he raced around to the front porch. The door stood wide open. Eli pulled his pistol and eased his body along the external wall.

"Bobby?" he called into the dark office. No answer. He whipped his cell phone out of his jacket pocket and speed dialed his deputy. He could hear the phone chiming *It's Beginning To Look A lot Like Christmas* from inside the building. "Bobby?"

Eli moved through the open doorway into the reception area with caution, keeping his wolf senses on high alert. Why were the lights out? He continued sweeping the room, checking behind desks and the partition at the front counter. No one. The door to the cell block was open and a solid weight sank into the pit of his gut. He pressed his back against the wall beside the open doorway and peered around the frame. "Bobby?" he whispered loudly.

Where was he?

Without a sound Eli eased his large frame along the corridor leading to the cells. As a Lycan it was easy for him to remain unheard. When he reached the closed, heavy blue metal door he waited a beat before pulling it open and stepping into the cell block, gun raised.

Bobby was lying unconscious on the floor of the locked cell the wolf had occupied.

Eli rushed over, grabbed the barred door and wrenched it from its hinges, then knelt down beside Bobby and pressed his fingers against his friend's carotid artery. He felt a beat. *Thank God!* Eli checked him for injuries and his hand came away from the back of his deputy's head smeared with blood. How had the guy managed to catch him off guard?

He lifted Bobby onto the cot and called for an ambulance.

The *someone* he'd almost hit had been their prisoner. Now he'd never get the answers he was looking for.

TWENTY NINE

The snow had eased up by the time Saturday came around and when Paige glanced out of the living room window she could see it was shaping up to be a beautiful winter day. She and Stephanie would be leaving any minute to drive into town for the parade. It was hard to believe Christmas was only a week away. With everything that had happened, she hadn't made time to do any Christmas shopping or prepare for the holidays. She'd have to make a point of finding time during the coming week.

Stephanie came down the stairs dressed in a red wool, knee length jacket, red knit hat with a white pompom on top and a green scarf. She also had on a pair of black jeans and black knee high boots to finish off the Christmas look. "What do you think?" she asked, doing a twirl at the bottom of the staircase.

"Very holiday-ish," Paige told her, a smile spreading across her face.

Her friend always loved dressing up for all of the holidays: Easter, Halloween, Thanksgiving and Christmas. It had become a Stephanie Harris tradition.

"Why aren't you getting into the holiday spirit?"

Paige sighed. "I will. It's just... I'm still trying to get over everything that's happened since I arrived here." She shrugged into her gray jacket, burgundy cap and white scarf.

"Oh, here." Stephanie whipped her green scarf from around her neck and replaced Paige's white one with hers. She then wrapped Paige's scarf around her neck. "There. A little bit of Christmas color to brighten your mood. Shall we get going? We want to find a great spot for the parade, don't we?"

"Yes, we do." Paige opened the front door and waited until Stephanie stepped onto the porch then followed her out and locked the door behind her. She wondered why she even bothered when people kept breaking into her house.

After the women drove away, Clarissa crossed the road, walked up to Paige's front porch and ran her eyes around the street to make sure no one was watching, then climbed the steps. She pulled a wicker chair from the right hand corner of the porch, placed it in front of the door and climbed onto it. Reaching up, she stuck a small, dry garland of Wolfsbane to the outer jamb then climbed off the chair. *Now for the back door.*

Clarissa lugged the heavy chair around to the side gate, unlatched it and continued around to the backyard. She opened the screen door then hauled the chair up the steps and into the alcove. She climbed onto it and stuck a sprig of Wolfsbane above the back door, too. *That should keep her safe from the intruders.* The one thing she hadn't considered was now Eli wouldn't be able to enter the house either.

The floats, music, Christmas characters and the Snow Princess couldn't help but put a smile on Paige's face and get her in the holiday spirit. She snapped photos on her cell phone, laughed and waved as the pageant continued past them. Once the parade was over the crowd dispersed, making its way to the carnival grounds for a fun day of rides, food and games.

Stephanie and Paige returned to her car and drove down the main street to find parking closer to the event. Once they located a spot nearby they climbed out of the car and were about to head over when someone called out to Paige. She swung around and saw Rebecca approaching dressed in similar colors to Stephanie.

"Hi, how are you?" she asked, eyeing Stephanie as she caught up to them.

"Oh, hi, Rebecca, I'm good. How are you?"

"I love this time of year. Brings out the best in people, don't you think?" Her eyes remained on Paige's friend.

"Uh, yes, it seems to." Paige gave Stephanie a sideward glance. "This is my friend, Stephanie. She's staying with me for a while."

The young woman gave Stephanie a forced smile and held out her hand. "Nice to meet you."

Stephanie shook it. "You too."

Rebecca looped her arm through Paige's and walked with her. "So how is your office coming along?"

"It's finished and ready to open. I'm just going to wait until after the holidays."

"Oh. Sounds great. Have you met Doc Taylor yet? I'm

sure you'd both have a lot in common, being doctors of the mind and all."

"No, I haven't, but Eli thought I should, too." Only in a different capacity to Rebecca's suggestion.

"He should be at the carnival later. I'll introduce you if I see him." Rebecca gave her a broad grin.

Paige felt awful that Stephanie was walking behind them but what could she do? She didn't want to seem unsociable.

When they reached the carnival grounds Rebecca unhooked her arm from Paige's and said, "I'll try to catch up with you later," and dashed away.

Paige breathed a relieved sigh and turned around to her friend. "I am so sorry about that. Because we were friends when we were kids she seems to think that bond is still there."

"Don't worry about it. It's all good. Let's go have some fun!" She looped her arm through Paige's the way Rebecca had done, gave her friend an indulgent grin and led her straight to the Ghost Train.

The dark, claustrophobic atmosphere made Paige's stomach shrink and the muscles in her shoulders and solar plexus tighten. The air felt thick around her and she couldn't take a deep breath. She hated the Ghost Train but didn't want to disappoint her friend who had come all the way from Washington to help her out. It was the least she could do. As the car meandered through the maze of doors, dark caverns, overhead spider webs, and ghoulish figures popping out at them, Paige had the overwhelming urge to jump out of the train and run back to the entrance. Shrill screams and manic laughter echoed into the eerie atmosphere around them through crackling speakers in the ceiling, and as the car continued onward to the creepy sound of warped horror movie music it took a sharp left turn through a double set of doors and came to an abrupt stop.

"Well that can't be good," Stephanie said, her eyes roaming the gloom.

"No, it can't." Paige fumbled in the dark for her jacket pocket, tugged her phone out of it and pressed the flashlight app. "We're closed off from the rest of the ride. I wonder what happened."

"Maybe we'd better get out and walk back."

"Do you think we should?" Paige's breathing had shallowed and small beads of perspiration dotted her forehead. She felt dizzy too.

Stephanie took the phone from Paige's hand and pointed it at her. Her friend's face was as white as a sheet. "Yes, I think we definitely should."

The pair climbed out of the train and walked back to the doors their car had come through. They were locked. Stephanie tugged on the handle of one door then the other. Neither would budge. "That doesn't make any sense. We just came through these doors."

"They're electronic. They probably lock automatically until the next car approaches." Paige didn't have another answer and hoped she was right otherwise someone had deliberately locked them in.

Stephanie shone the light behind them. The track continued. "Ok, then I guess we'll go that way."

They could hear other cars travelling past the locked doors but no one would hear them over the eerie music, screams and creepy laughter if they called out. Their best option was to work their way back through the ride to the entrance or a maintenance exit, whichever they came upon first.

Stephanie could tell Paige was in a panic. "We'll be out of here in no time. The ride isn't that long."

"I'm sure you're right," Paige said, her voice shaking.

As the pair continued forward the light on her cell phone dimmed. Paige snatched it from Stephanie's hand and frowned at the display. The battery was almost flat. "Oh, no! I forgot to charge my phone this morning."

"That's ok. I've got mine so we should be fine." Stephanie reached into her pocket. Nothing. She tried the other pocket. "Dammit, I must've left it on my bed."

Paige's throat constricted and the light died on her phone, leaving them lost in the dark.

THIRTY

Eli roamed the carnival looking for Paige. He remembered her saying that she and Stephanie were going to the parade and straight on to the carnival afterward when he spoke to her on the phone. He'd wandered just about every ride, game stand and food vendor and no sign of her. His eyes surveyed the grounds and the people walking around it. Where was she?

Bobby spotted him and threaded his way through the crowd with his wife and two kids in tow. "Hey, Eli, enjoying the carnival?"

"Eli smiled at Barbara and the kids. "Yeah, it's pretty special this year with the Snow Princess granting Christmas wishes for good boys and girls."

Bobby's two kids, a boy and a girl, glanced up at their parents and the boy said, "Can we go see her? Please!"

"Ok. But make sure we can see you," Bobby told them.

Both heads bobbed with enthusiasm and the siblings raced off across the grounds to the crystal palace float.

"Paige not here?" Bobby asked, gazing around at the people passing by and standing around the game stalls and other vendors.

"I haven't seen her. Maybe they got held up or something."

Barbara shook her head. "No, we saw them at the parade. They were standing in front of the inn." She turned to look at her husband. "Weren't they, hon?"

"Yeah, that's right they were."

Eli frowned and ran his eyes over the people moving through the carnival. "Then I wonder where they are?"

Paige could feel her breathing getting shallower as she and Stephanie, now holding hands, trudged through the dark Ghost Train. They were wandering blindly with no idea how to get out. Why hadn't she said no? She wondered why this section of the ride was here if it wasn't being used. Her eyes had adjusted to the gloom and she could just make out the narrow track on the floor and the occasional, dusty shaft of light piercing the seams of the canvas ceiling, but nothing else. How had they ended up here? Did someone do this on purpose or was it a technical glitch in the ride's mechanism?

Stephanie came to an abrupt halt, gasping in a nervous breath. "Did you see that?" she whispered.

Paige's heart rate cranked up several notches and she couldn't take a breath. "No. What?" Her whispered words were breathy, uneven.

"I thought I saw something move in the shadows up ahead."

"Are you sure?" A cold shiver ran the length of Paige's spine and her bladder tightened – she needed to pee. "Could it be… a… a mannequin… or something?"

"Yes, I'm sure. And I don't know what it was. It could be a mannequin." Stephanie's voice had an anxious edge to it.

The two women continued moving ahead with caution.

"Why haven't we found a way out yet?" Paige couldn't understand how they were still trapped inside.

"I wish I knew. The ride didn't look this extensive from the front."

Paige gripped her friend's hand and pulled her to a stop. "I don't think we're alone in here," she whispered.

"See, I told you." Stephanie squeezed Paige's hand. "Let's turn around and go back the way we came."

The pair spun on their heels and hurried through the ride, keeping to the right side of the track. Paige hoped she'd only imagined a shadow dart out of the way not far from where they'd been standing.

A metal clang echoed around the pitch black space. "What was that?" Stephanie blurted.

"Keep moving, Steph, keep moving. We have to get out of here now!"

After leaving Bobby and his wife, Eli walked the entire venue again. No sign of Paige or her friend. Something was off. She said she'd be at the carnival so where was she? He checked with some of the game vendors but they hadn't seen the women. He wandered the rides and asked at the Ferris wheel, the Dodgem cars and the Christmas train. Then he remembered Paige telling him her friend would be sure to make her go on the Ghost Train with her and that she hated it. He made a beeline for the ride.

When he got there the Ghost Train was closed with a 'Back in 5 minutes' sign posted on the entry podium. Perhaps the guy needed a toilet break. Eli decided to wait around until he got back. He leaned against the spooky wall decorated with skeletons, spider webs and creepy gothic mansion, and folded his arms. The wall vibrated and an empty car whipped through the exit doors. Eli turned around and frowned at it. *What the hell?* His gut told him something was wrong. Where was the vendor if the ride was operating?

Eli whipped his cell phone out of his jeans pocket and pressed speed dial for Paige's number. Straight to voicemail. "Hey, Paige, would you mind giving me a call when you get this. I'm outside the Ghost Train. Looking forward to seeing you. Thanks."

It wasn't like her not to answer her phone. Something was definitely off.

Another empty car came through the exit. *What's going on?*

Eli stalked over to the Merry-go-round. "Hey, do you know where the guy is that's operating the Ghost Train?"

"Uh, yeah, that would be me," he replied, pointing to himself. "Can't be in two places at once, pal."

"Fair enough. Did two women get on the ride? One with short red hair and the other…"

The guy nodded. "Yeah, yeah, about fifteen minutes ago. They'd be long gone by now. The ride runs for less than five minutes."

"Did you see them get off the ride?" Eli's gut tightened. His Lycan instincts were certain Paige was in danger.

"Well, no, like I said, I can't be in two places at once. Sorry."

"Mind if I get on?"

"No problem." The guy left the Merry-go-round and followed Eli back to the Ghost Train.

Just as he was about to climb into a car an ear-splitting scream echoed out from inside the ride. "Call 911 now!" Eli burst through the double doors and into the dark on foot.

"Paige? Paige where are you?" His nocturnal vision scanned the ride as he whisked along the track. "Paige, answer me!"

Eli stopped and used his Lycan hearing. There.

He continued through the ride until he came to pair of doors painted like a mouth with bloody razor sharp teeth and pressed his hand against one door. Locked. He tried the other. Locked too.

"Paige, are you in there?"

His hearing picked up hysterical sobbing.

Eli raised his booted foot, kicked the doors open in one swift movement and followed the sound.

Paige was on her knees on the floor, Stephanie cradled in her arms with blood running from the corner of her mouth.

Eli raced up to them. "Paige, are you all right?"

She gazed up at him, her eyes dazed. "Stephanie's hurt… is she… is she dead?"

He could hear a faint heartbeat. "No, she's alive. We'll get an ambulance here as fast as we can." He was on his phone to Bobby. "I need an ambulance at the Ghost Train now." His deputy told him one was already on its way. Eli rang off. "It's going to take a while. The ambulance has to come from the next town." He crouched beside Paige. "Let me take a look at her."

"It was meant for me, wasn't it?" Tears rolled down her face. "Whoever locked us in here was trying to kill *me*. Why?"

"I wish I knew, Paige." He leaned in to take a closer look. Three deep stab wounds to the chest and abdomen, whoever did this wanted the outcome to be permanent.

THIRTY ONE

Eli stayed with Paige at the medical center until Stephanie was out of surgery. The doctor told them she would make a full recovery as long as her condition didn't change, but nothing was certain. She'd sustained some serious injuries. They'd had to remove her spleen and repair other organs. She was lucky the knife hadn't punctured her heart. The next couple of days were critical. He told the pair to go home and get some rest. It had been a long afternoon of waiting around and she wouldn't wake up for another few hours. Staff would let them know if there was any change.

Paige was reluctant to leave but, after some persuasion from Eli, decided to do what the doctor had suggested. She needed her strength to keep her going otherwise she'd fall into a heap. Too much had happened over the past few weeks and it was finally taking its toll. If anything happened to her best friend because of her she'd never be able to live with it. She wished she'd never asked Stephanie to come to Moon Grove.

It was an awful thing to think, but Eli was relieved that

it wasn't Paige lying in recovery. He hoped Stephanie made it because he knew if she didn't it would be Paige's undoing. She was only holding on by a thread and the death of her friend would tip her over the edge. He glanced at her sideways as he drove toward the town. What was she thinking? "Paige?"

She'd been gazing out of the passenger window vacantly and realized someone had said her name. She turned her head. It was Eli. "Yes?"

"I don't think you should be alone right now. Do you want to come to my place?"

Her jumbled thoughts couldn't comprehend the question. "What?"

Eli could see she was out of it. "I said do you want to come over to my place for a while?"

She nodded but he could tell she still hadn't taken in what he'd said.

"Paige?"

"Yes?" She frowned at him.

"Did you hear what I said?"

"I... think so." Tears stung the backs of her eyes and she blinked to prevent them from spilling down her face.

"Do you want to repeat what I just asked you?"

"Um, you said..." Paige gave him a blank look. "What did you ask me?"

She was definitely in shock.

"Never mind. It's ok." He decided he'd just take her to his place anyway. Safer than being at her house alone right now.

When he reached the boundary of Moon Grove he made a right and continued on to his property. He lived in a single story, brown wood clad home on a few acres. It had been left to him by his mother and he'd lived there his entire life. He loved the memories of his mom and still missed her every day. No one ever gets over losing a loved one they just learn to live with it.

Eli pulled the four wheel drive up to the front steps, turned off the engine and sat for a moment. A lot had happened in the last six hours. Who was trying to kill Paige? And why? Nothing made any sense. He stepped out of the car, walked around to the passenger door and opened it. "Come on, let's get you inside."

Paige took his hand and climbed out of the vehicle. She was exhausted and needed to sleep.

Once inside, Eli sat her down on the sofa and went to make up the spare room which had once been his childhood bedroom. When he returned to the living room Paige was curled up in the fetal position sound asleep. He grabbed a checked throw rug off the backrest and tucked it around her. She'd most likely sleep for a few hours.

He stood watching her, his heart beating just that little bit faster. It would be wonderful waking up to that lovely face every morning but he knew that could never be. His past wouldn't allow him to be involved with someone else, even though he had feelings for Paige. He'd lost his wife because of what he was and he wouldn't let that happen to anyone else he cared about. His eyes moved to the gold framed photo of him and Michelle on their wedding day sitting on the bureau and he walked over, picked it up, and ran his eyes over her beautiful face. His heart still ached for his dead wife but there was nothing he could do about that. He tucked the photo upside down inside the top drawer and closed it. He didn't need Paige seeing it and asking questions he was unable to answer.

He'd been out with the pack tracking a renegade wolf that had turned up in town and had killed two of the residents when it happened. While they'd been searching, the monster had doubled back and headed for Eli's house. Michelle had been asleep when he broke in and never knew what was coming. When Eli arrived home he found her dead in the bedroom, her throat slashed open and a message scrawled in her blood on the wall above the bed: *Come and get me. If you can!* The members of his pack had gone berserk. They hunted the woods day and night until they located the wolf, then tore him limb from limb and burned the remains. He wouldn't get the chance to murder anyone else. That had been seven years ago.

Eli gave a heavy sigh, blinked back the tears he couldn't shed, and wandered into the kitchen to make some coffee. He needed to eat otherwise his wolf would attempt to emerge and he couldn't allow Paige to see the shimmer in his eyes that she'd witnessed in her dream. He pulled open the refrigerator door and his eyes roamed the contents. A sandwich would have to suffice. He took out the bread and other ingredients and laid them on the kitchen counter before returning to the fridge for the milk.

As he closed the door he looked up to see Paige standing in the doorway. "Hey." He sat the milk carton on the counter and walked over to her. "Feel like something to eat?"

She shook her head. "I got a text message from Stephanie's parents." A tear slid down her cheek. "They asked me to stay away from the medical center. That they didn't think it was safe for me to visit their daughter." She burst into tears and Eli couldn't help but pull her into his arms. He hated to see her cry.

"They're just concerned about her, that's all. Give it time. They'll come around."

"She's my best friend. I love her."

"I know. But it might be the best thing for the both of you right now."

Paige looked up at him, tears streaking her face. "You're right." She swiped at a lone tear sliding down her cheek. "It's too dangerous. I should never have brought her here in the first place."

"Hey." Eli wiped away the rest of her tears with his thumbs. "Didn't you say she wouldn't take no for an answer?"

She sniffed back the urge to cry again and her chin quivered. "Yes. She said safety in numbers. But look how that turned out."

He slid his arms around her. "You can't go blaming yourself. Whoever attacked her in the Ghost Train thought she was you. You had nothing to do with that." Looking into her tear-filled eyes made Eli want to lean in and kiss her but he wouldn't – for so many reasons – the most important being that she was vulnerable right now. Before the thought had left his mind, Paige stretched up and pressed her lips to his.

Realizing what she'd done, she darted backwards and raised her hand to her mouth. "I – I'm sorry, Eli, I shouldn't have done that." Her cheeks flushed and another tear slid from the corner of her left eye.

"Don't give it a second thought. It was just a reaction to the situation."

It wasn't.

Paige had wanted to kiss Eli for the longest time and because of her distraught emotions she'd done what she promised herself she wouldn't do. She couldn't think about a relationship with anyone, not with everything that had happened and could still happen. "Thank you for understanding."

"I do, Paige. I understand completely." He rubbed her arm, knowing how difficult it was not to give in to his desires. "Want some coffee?"

She nodded. "Thanks."

Eli wandered over to an overhead cupboard, took two mugs from the shelf and sat them on the counter. "What about something to eat? You need to keep up your strength, you know." He eyed her sideways.

Paige shook her head. "I'm not hungry. But thanks for the offer."

Eli brought the mugs over to the table and set them down. Paige crossed the room, pulled out a chair, and sat down. She felt exhausted and hoped the caffeine would kick in and give her a lift.

"Do you need anything from your place? I can go grab some things for you, if you like."

"I'd like to come along, if that's ok? A change of clothes would be nice and a pair of pajamas, and my make up too."

"Ok. Just let me eat and then we can go."

Eli pulled the Jeep up behind Paige's car. Bobby had driven it back for her and his wife and kids had followed him. He'd left the keys in a flower pot on the front steps and had messaged Eli to tell him where to find them.

As he climbed out of the car, Clarissa called his name.

He wandered across the street to her. "Hey, Clary, what's up?"

"I wanted to let you know that I added some protection to Paige's house. I've tacked Wolfsbane to the front and back doors and connected them with a spell so that no Lycan can intrude."

Eli gave her an incredulous frown. "What about me? How am I supposed to go in there now?"

She waved the comment off. "Oh, silly boy, you have the ring." She reached out and raised his left hand to look at the moonstone but Eli wasn't wearing it. "Where is it, dear?"

"It's here." He reached into his jacket pocket and retrieved the small black bag.

"Well put it on. It's the only way you're going to be able to enter Paige's house."

Eli sighed. He hadn't made a decision about whether or not he wanted to wear the ring. As Alpha he knew he should but he wasn't sure he wanted the responsibility of its power. "I'm not... I don't know if I want to wear it."

"You have to, Eli, you're the Alpha."

Right at that moment, Paige walked up to them. "Hello, Clarissa, how are you?"

The older woman reached out and touched Paige's arm. "What's more important is how you are, my dear? You've been through quite an ordeal."

Tears stung the back of Paige's eyes and she did her best to hold it together. "Yes. I'm... ok, I think."

"Well you're in good hands with Eli. He'll look after you." She glanced sideways at him and grinned. "When you're finished over at Paige's could you come back? I need to talk to you about something."

"Sure. We shouldn't be too long." Eli took Paige's arm and walked her down the path to the sidewalk. "You go on in and I'll wait out front." They crossed the street and walked up to the porch.

Paige gave him a curious frown. "Don't you want to come in? What if someone's inside?"

Eli climbed the steps with her and stood with his hands in his pockets while she unlocked the door. "I think you'll be fine."

"Ok." Her frown deepened. "Are you sure you won't come in?"

"I'm good. Just don't take too long."

She nodded and climbed the stairs.

Eli's eyes roamed the street and the neighboring houses. All seemed pretty quiet. Everyone was at the carnival. Clarissa was still out front of her house so he crossed the road and walked up to her. "What did you want to talk to me about?"

"Wil."

"What about him?" Eli's serious gaze rested on the old woman.

"He isn't missing, dear."

"Where is he?"

Clarissa glanced over her shoulder to her open front door. "He's here."

THIRTY TWO

After Eli drove Paige back to his property and settled her in for the night he told her he had to go out for a while on police business but wouldn't be too long. He made sure the house was secure and told her to keep the front door locked and not to open it to anyone but him. Not Bobby, Craig or anyone else. She understood. Paige said she'd take a shower, watch some television and wait for him to get back. She knew she wouldn't sleep in a strange house with no one there.

By the time Eli drove away from his place it was after five o'clock. It would be dark soon and he didn't want to leave Paige alone for too long once night set in. No one knew she was at his house but he still didn't like the idea of her being on her own for any longer than she had to be.

Traveling back toward town, Eli noticed a set of headlights coming up behind him. Nothing unusual about that, except that his hackles went up not long after it appeared and his gut told him he was being followed. He continued along the dark road and when he reached the turn off leading into Moon Grove he drove past it. The vehicle turned the corner, heading for town.

Eli did a U-turn about twenty feet along the road, drove back to the turn off and headed toward the main street. The vehicle, a dark colored truck, was now in front of him. He whipped his cell phone out of his pocket and took a shot of the license plate. It wasn't the same truck he'd followed past Paige's place, so who was it. He plugged his phone into the console and ran the number through the DMV database. It belonged to Moon Grove Town Council. One of Redmond's goons no doubt. Had he followed him and Paige out to his house?

He spun the wheels, did a sharp turn, cutting off a car on the opposite side of the road, and sped off toward his property. He snatched his phone from the console and pressed speed dial for Paige. It went to voicemail. Maybe she was taking that shower she mentioned and couldn't hear her cell ring. He hoped that was the reason. He pressed the accelerator to the floor and his four wheel drive hurtled along the road. Making a hard right he skidded around the corner on a slick piece of road, fish-tailed, straightened the Jeep and continued at break neck speed to get to his house as fast as he could. His driveway came up quickly and he almost overshot it.

Eli tried her number again. Still no answer.

He screeched the car to a halt, turned off the engine and dashed out of the vehicle onto the front porch. He pounded on the door. "Paige?" He darted to the window and peered in through the sheer curtains. She wasn't in the living room. Everything seemed quiet and he didn't want to spook her by shouldering the door, as he knew Paige would have secured all the locks and he wouldn't be able to use his keys to get inside. He walked to the end of the porch, down the side steps, and wandered around back.

The light was on in the bathroom and he could hear the shower running. Eli breathed a relieved sigh and headed back to the front door. He'd wait until she was finished and take her with him. Better to be safe than sorry.

Ten minutes later, Paige wandered into the living room towel drying her hair dressed in pajamas and robe. She felt fresher and more awake than earlier. Eli knocked when he saw her through the window and she crossed the room to the door. "Eli?"

"Yeah, it's me." He heard the multiple locks click back.

She greeted him with a smile and stepped back to let him in. "That was fast."

"I think it'd be a good idea if you came with me."

Paige gave him an uncertain stare. "Why? I thought I was safe here." Her eyes moved to the window and the darkness beyond it.

"I'd feel better if you weren't here alone. I should've thought of it before I left."

Her eyes widened. "What happened to make you change your mind?"

"Like your friend said safety in numbers." He gave her a thin smile. "Why don't you go get dressed?" He glanced at the time on his phone. 6:00. "Can you be quick?"

She nodded and dashed down the hallway.

Eli pulled up outside Clarissa's at around six thirty. He wasn't sure what he was going to tell Paige about Wil being there, he'd have to figure it out as he went along. The more he tried to keep things from her to keep her safe the more she was thrown into situations that required explanation. When they reached the front door, it swung open. "Come in, come in, my dears. It's freezing out there. I've got brownies and coffee ready."

"Thanks." Eli motioned for Paige to go in ahead of him and followed her inside. His eyes roamed the living room, dining room and part of the kitchen he could see through the door under the upstairs landing.

Clarissa waved them in. "Come on through."

They followed her into the kitchen.

"Have a seat." She picked up the plate of cakes from off the counter and set it down in the center of the table, then brought over the coffee pot. Three mugs were already in front of them.

Paige gave Eli a surreptitious sideward glance and she wondered how having coffee and brownies was police business.

Clarissa poured two mugs and slid one across the knotted wooden table to Paige, along with the plate of scrumptious looking treats. "Here, dear, try one." She turned her gaze to Eli. "Why don't you head upstairs? My guest is in the second room on the left.

Eli scraped back his chair and stood up. "Thanks." He glanced at Paige. "I won't be long."

Paige watched him head to the entry hall before turning to Clarissa. "What's that about?"

"Police business, dear." She gave Paige a wry smile. "Eat up. Do you have cream or sugar in your coffee?"

Eli knocked before opening the door and waited to be invited in. He wondered how the old man had escaped whoever had been out at his property that night, and how he'd managed to get himself here. As Clarissa chose not to drive these days, he was curious about who had helped him.

"Come on in, Eli. Don't stand out in the hallway all night," the gruff voice said.

Eli stepped into the room and closed the door. "Thanks."

Wil didn't have a scratch on him. He'd managed to elude whoever had broken into his home. "I guess you're wondering how I got outta the house the other night."

"Yeah, as a matter of fact I was." Eli sat down on the twin single bed opposite the old man.

"I have certain escape routes set up in my place. I used the trap door in the hall closet. They didn't look in there."

"You mean you were still in the house when they came in?"

"I don't move as fast as I used to, you know. When I heard them on the front porch I knew I had to get outta sight. Once they were inside, I opened up the door in the floor and crawled under the house. I stayed there until they left."

"How'd you get back here?"

"Clarissa. She had Ryan pick me up at the end of my drive and bring me here."

Eli gave Wil a stern frown. "You knew they were Lycan?"

"Sure I did. And I got a feeling it was Redmond's men."

The sheriff remembered the concern the Mayor had shown for Wil. "I don't think so. He seemed sincerely concerned about your disappearance and wellbeing."

"Ha! Appearances can be deceiving. Don't take anything he says as Gospel." Wil gave Eli a knowing glance then pulled an old notebook out from under his pillow. "You'll want to read this. It'll give you some of the answers you've been looking for." He pushed the battered, dark green book with black triangular corners across the space between them. "And don't trust the Mayor. He knows a lot more than he's telling you."

Eli ran his gaze over the old A4 sized notebook. "These your recollections of what happened that night?"

Wil chuckled. "Not only what happened then but what's been going on in this town for years. Make sure you keep it safe. Wouldn't want it falling into the wrong hands."

"I will. Thank you. Do you know what happened to Paige's parents?"

Wil gave a heavy sigh and pointed to the book. "I'm tired of talking. It's all in there. Read it."

"Do you need me to do anything for you? Want a patrol car to come by on the hour?"

"Nah, what would be the point? You know Clarissa has this place stitched up so no one can get in. How else do you think she's lived this long with the things she knows? Besides, certain people would get suspicious if the police came by here regularly. I'd prefer to remain incognito... as they say."

"Ok." Eli gave him a nod and stood up. "If you need anything let me know." He extended his hand. The old man shook it. "And thank you for this." He raised the notebook.

"Help the girl before something permanent happens to her. How's her friend doing?"

"She's recovering. Her parents are taking her back to Washington in a couple of weeks."

The old man nodded. "Best place for her. Pity you couldn't talk the O'Connell girl into going with them."

Eli gave him a serious stare. Should he try to talk Paige into leaving Moon Grove? Did he want her to? He crossed the room and opened the door. "Thanks again for the notebook, Wil. I appreciate it."

Clarissa poured coffee into the third mug when Eli entered the kitchen. It smelt good. His stomach growled as he took his seat beside Paige and both women chuckled. The older woman pushed the plate across the table. "Here, have some of these before your stomach eats your backbone."

Paige noticed the book in his hand. "What's that?"

"Police business. I can't discuss it with anyone."

"Oh, ok." Paige picked up her mug and sipped her coffee. There was always something she couldn't know about. Moon Grove seemed to have a lot of secrets.

Eli munched on a brownie. "These are delicious, Clary." He frowned at the cake in his hand. "And they taste familiar."

"They should. They're your mom's recipe." She beamed, resting her elbows on the tabletop.

Eli stopped chewing and thought about it. Yes, they were his mom's recipe. He remembered how much he loved her chocolate fudge brownies. "Thank you for baking them. It's been a long time."

"My pleasure, dear, I knew you'd like them. I'll give you some to take with you."

Once Eli had devoured a couple more he stood up. "We'd better go, it's getting late."

Clarissa took a plastic zip lock bag out of a drawer and returned to the table. "Here, take these with you. You can have them with some hot chocolate when you get home."

"Thanks." Eli kissed the woman's cheek then turned to Paige. "Ready to go?"

She nodded and stood up. "Thank you for the coffee and sweets... and the conversation. It was nice."

"Anytime, dear." Clarissa walked them to the door. "Safe travels home, dears. The roads are dark and slippery."

"We'll be careful." Eli passed the brownies to Paige and they headed down the path to his car.

"Do you want me to take that for you?" Paige asked, pointing to the old notebook in his hand.

"No need. I'll just drop it on the back seat."

Paige wondered what was so important about the book that he wouldn't let her hold it for him.

THIRTY THREE

"**S**he's out at the sheriff's place. What do you want me to do?" the deep, gravelly voice said into the receiver. He was freezing his nuts off at a pay phone outside the town's only gas station operated by another werewolf. He'd been tailing the pair at a distance and hid the truck off road, waiting. When the sheriff left the property he'd thought the woman was with him but she wasn't. Stupid move. He could've had her and the deed would be a done deal. Once he realized she wasn't in the Jeep and he'd been spotted he turned off the road and headed for Moon Grove.

"Nothing for the moment. At least we know where she is."

"Then I'm heading home. It's friggin' freezing out here. Call if you want me to go out there."

"We need to find Wil Wallace. Any word on him?"

"Nope. It's like he's vanished into thin air. He was long gone by the time we got inside his place. We searched the barn and the surrounding property but there was no sign of him."

"All right. If you find out anything about his

whereabouts let me know immediately. Understand?"

"Sure thing, boss." He rang off. The situation was out of control. The only guy who knew everything about the town and its inhabitants was missing and the woman who could ruin everything was shacked up with the sheriff.

If she found out the truth about her parents it would mean disaster for Moon Grove.

After Eli made sure Paige was asleep he went out to his four wheel drive and grabbed the notebook from off the back seat. What would he find out about Paige's parents and, as Wil had indicated, other things that had occurred in the town over the years? He stepped inside, closed the heavy screen door and locked it then closed the front door and locked the two deadlocks. No one would get inside without effort. He'd made sure to implement security measures for his own safety because there were people in the town that wanted the werewolf population extricated. Now that Paige was at his house it was twice as important.

Eli shrugged out of his jacket and dumped his large frame into an armchair, giving a heavy sigh. He hoped he'd have some answers for Paige by the time she woke up in the morning. He flipped through the two hundred or so paper leaves then turned to the first page and began to read.

As far as Wil knew Paige's parents were dead. The blood at the scene had been a clear indication that both her mother and father had been exsanguinated before the bodies were removed. There had been no tracks to follow and the house had been wiped clean of prints – all prints. So what Paige had remembered was correct. Someone had shot them in the bedroom then disposed of the bodies.

The old man had a lot of dirt on the Mayor and had discovered that his goons were wolves. The previous Mayor had been Alpha of the Moon Grove pack and had stepped down because Ross Redmond threatened to expose him. Eli had been elected Alpha by the pack members after Greg Harrison disappeared from his home and never returned. Wil believed Mayor Redmond had something to do with his demise but could never find any evidence to prove it. And Eli had been moved into a position the Mayor had believed would help his and the council's cause. He'd thought the sheriff would be easy to manipulate. Eli wasn't a puppet.

Wendy Ellis had been warned off by Redmond on more than one occasion and was told that if she didn't stop sticking her journalist nose where it didn't belong there would be serious consequences. Wil believed he was the one who had ordered her death but had no proof to back up his assumptions. Would the Mayor really have someone killed because they had discovered the secrets of Moon Grove? Eli knew Redmond was an opportunist and would do anything to keep his status, but murdering Wendy Ellis? It seemed more likely the council had something to do with it.

By the time the sun came up, Eli had finished reading all of Wil's entries and had looked over the newspaper clippings and other stuff tucked inside the book. The old man had his suspicions about a lot of people in the town, some Eli suspected himself, including Craig. He knew Craig Campbell was one to be concerned about for a lot of reasons. He'd make sure no one knew Wil's or Paige's whereabouts. He had no idea who could be trusted and their lives depended on it.

Was his best friend, Bobby, involved? He hoped not. They'd been friends since they were kids and Eli hated to think the Mayor had his deputies, who were also his pack, in his proverbial pocket. Craig he could believe, but not Bobby. Even so, he would keep what he knew to himself. He'd been aware of certain underlying factors about Moon Grove and the members of the council, but Wil's notebook had opened his eyes to so much more. There had been many murders and cover ups over the years and it didn't sit well with him. Sooner or later someone would have to pay the piper. He hid the notebook in the floor safe under his nightstand and decided to take a quick shower and change into some fresh clothes before Paige woke up. He dropped two coffee pods into his espresso machine, ready to make two cups when he finished, and headed to the bathroom.

The hot water massaged the tension from Eli's neck and shoulder blades and his body relaxed under the prickling spray. He'd take Paige over to Clarissa's before heading into work. That was the safest place for her right now while he performed his official duties. Once he got through the morning routine he'd tell Rosemarie he'd be taking the afternoon off and head over to Doc Taylor's. He had done what he said he'd do and scheduled an appointment to see him. He needed to get to the bottom of why the dreams had returned. He knew it had something to do with Paige moving back to Moon Grove, but what was the connection?

He wiped the condensation off the bathroom mirror and stared at his reflection. His eyes shimmered and he knew he had to be careful while Paige was in the house. He wrapped a large, navy blue towel around his waist and as he pulled open the door she came out of the spare bedroom opposite.

"Oh!" Her face flushed at the sight of Eli almost naked in front of her. He had an amazing body: Broad shoulders, muscled chest, and six pack abs that tapered to a slim waist. Her stomach tightened and that familiar tingle awoke her female core and she wondered what it would be like making love to him. She felt her cheeks blaze and averted her eyes.

"Sorry. I thought I'd be done in here before you woke up." He gazed into her lovely, blue eyes and something stirred inside him. He wanted to pull her face to his and kiss her. Hard. "Well, I'd better get dressed. I'll make us some breakfast when I'm done. The coffee machine is ready to go if you want to press the button." He sidled past her in the hall, his eyes remaining on her for longer than they should have, then turned around and hurried along the hallway to his room. How long could he deny the growing feelings he had for her?

Around lunch time, Eli gave Paige a quick call to ask her to stay inside the house and not to go across to hers for any reason. It was far too dangerous. He'd be there by three to pick her up. Paige promised she wouldn't leave the house and told him she was making dinner for them to take home, courtesy of Clarissa, who was teaching her how to make Osso Bucco. She was feeling quite domesticated as she used to eat out most nights back in Washington and never cooked at home.

Eli told her he'd look forward to dinner and rang off

when he reached the doctor's office. He parked on the opposite side of the street a few cars down and as he was about to get out of the Jeep he saw Rebecca coming out of Doc Taylor's. Why had she been to see him? Being one of his pack she should have mentioned it. He waited until she drove away before crossing the street. The Doc worked from home and had converted his garage into a private office for his patients.

The sheriff walked down the drive to the cream colored, timber clad building and opened the door. Doc Taylor didn't have a receptionist. Eli picked up the school ma'am type bell on the counter and shook it. The thin, metal tinkle echoed around him and he set the bell down in its place.

The second door opened. "Hi, Eli, come on through." The doctor moved aside and the sheriff stepped into the comfortable, bright consultation space. He never liked lying on a sofa to discuss his personal issues and John Taylor never asked him to. He usually sat and made notes while Eli paced. It had been a few years since he'd paid the doctor a visit and before beginning the session they got reacquainted while John poured them both a mug of coffee. "How have you been, Eli? It's been a while since you've been here. Something happen?"

Eli gave him a sheepish glance. "Yeah, I know. I haven't really needed to talk. Until now, that is." He removed his police issue, fawn Stetson and set it down on the foot of the sofa.

"I would have thought, as the Alpha, there would be a lot to deal with." John crossed the room and handed Eli a mug with 'Healthy Mind Happy Life' printed on the outside. "Careful, it's hot."

"Thanks." Eli blew into the black brew. "Yeah, but nothing I can't handle."

"So what's been happening in your life these days?" The doctor's left eyebrow arched. "Dating anyone?"

"You'd know if I was. It'd be all over Moon Grove, wouldn't it?" Eli gave him a thin smile. "Anyway, I'm too busy with…"

"You mean you're still not over losing Michelle."

He sighed. "Yeah, something like that I guess."

"I hear you're spending a lot of time with Paige O'Connell."

Eli's serious gaze met his. "*Official* time."

"Is that all it is?"

"Yes." The grapevine had been spreading more gossip. *Was that the reason why Rebecca had been here? To tell John about Paige and him?*

"So what brings you here now?" John sat down, set his coffee on a small round table beside his chair and picked up his iPad and stylus.

Eli ran his free hand through his wavy hair. "The dreams are back."

THIRTY FOUR

While the women worked in the kitchen, Paige thought it would be a good time to see if she could coerce Clarissa into opening up and telling her about Eli. Although he seemed to be an open book there was something she knew he wasn't being honest about with her. The day had been an enjoyable one and Paige felt less stressed for the first time in a while. After cooking the Osso Bucco, Clarissa helped her make a pumpkin pie, another of Eli's favorites. The pair sat at the kitchen table drinking coffee and nibbling cookies while they waited for the pie to bake.

"Clarissa?"

The older woman set her mug of coffee down on the table and moved her perceptive gaze to Paige. "Yes, dear?"

"Have you known Eli for a long time?" Paige bit into a homemade oatmeal cookie. It was moist, chewy, and delicious.

"Oh, yes, dear, his whole life. Why do you ask?" She smiled. Clarissa thought she should let Eli tell Paige she was his maternal grandmother.

"So you could tell me about when we were children?"

"You went to the same kindergarten. You, Eli, Bobby and Becky used to play together all the time. In fact, you all used to have regular sleepovers at each other's houses."

"We did? I wish I could remember." Paige sipped her coffee.

Clarissa chuckled. "Eli used to say one day he was going to marry you." She reached across and patted Paige's hand. "He *was* only six years old at the time."

"What was his mom like?"

The older woman let out a wistful sigh. "She was a dear, sweet thing. Would do anything to help anyone. She had a hard life working two jobs just to make sure Eli never wanted for anything. Mind you, they weren't well off but he had all the love a child could need. His mother tried to compensate for his father running off and leaving them."

Paige nodded. "Yes, Eli told me a little bit about that."

"Good for nothing…" Her eyes met Paige's. "Sorry, dear, but when I think about him it makes my blood boil. At least Eli grew into a fine man."

"Yes, he is. He's certainly taken good care of me during everything that's happened."

"And he'll continue to do so until whoever has been doing those dreadful things is caught and put where they belong."

"He doesn't tell me much about himself. Is there anything you can share?"

Clarissa's left eyebrow arched. "What do you want to know?"

"I don't know, maybe just something about his life before I came to Moon Grove. Has he dated anyone?"

A smile spread across the older woman's face. "You like him, don't you?"

Paige shrugged. "I'm curious, that's all."

Clarissa gave her a knowing stare.

Paige gave a resigned sigh. "Is it that obvious?"

"Probably not to Eli, he's too busy trying to keep you safe. But, yes, to me it is."

Paige's cheeks flushed. "I wasn't looking for romance at all, but I *do* like him."

"He's had a hard time with losing his mother and then…" She stopped herself before she said something she couldn't take back. Something she knew Eli wouldn't want her to share.

Paige straightened in her seat. "And then?"

"Nothing, dear, just an old woman rambling." She saw that Paige's mug was almost empty and wanted to change the subject. "More coffee? That pie should be ready soon."

Paige knew there was something in Eli's past that he wouldn't share with her and she wondered how terrible it could be.

"We could try hypnosis again. It seemed to work the last time," Doc Taylor suggested. "Maybe it will open your subconscious and tell us more."

"As I said, there was more to the dream this time than there has been before but it still doesn't lead me anywhere."

"Do you want to give it a try?"

Eli sighed. "I don't know. Do you really think it could unlock something hidden in my head?"

"There's only one way to find out." John stood up and walked over to the shelves behind his desk to retrieve the metronome. "You're going to have to lie down for this." He gave Eli a thin smile.

The sheriff blew out a noisy breath, shifted his Stetson from off the sofa to the table beside it and laid down, clasping his hands across his abdomen. "You know I'm not comfortable with this. Never was."

"Yes, I know. But it's the only way you're going to get answers." He set the metronome in motion: Tick, tick, tick, tick. "Close your eyes, take deep breaths, and listen to the sound of my voice. I'm going to count back from ten and by the time I reach one you'll be fully asleep. Nod if you understand."

Eli nodded.

"Ten. Nine. Eight. Seven. Six. Five. Four. Three. Two. One." John waited a beat. "Eli, can you hear me?"

"Yes," he answered.

"Good." The doctor took his seat, picked up his iPad and activated the voice recording. "I want you to go into the woods to where you find the blood trail."

Eli's eyes began to move rapidly beneath his heavy, closed lids and his breathing quickened.

"Relax, Eli. You're safe. Nothing can hurt you. What do you see?"

"I – I see blood. There's a trail leading further into the dark trees. I don't want to follow it but…" Eli's breathing came in shallow bursts.

"But what?"

"If I don't go Paige could be hurt."

The doctor's right eyebrow arched. "Is Paige with you?"

"She ran ahead and disappeared. I can't find her."

"Do you think the blood is hers?"

"I don't know." Eli's voice was anxious, sharp, his six feet four inch frame tight.

"Take a deep breath in and let it out slowly."

The sheriff did as he was instructed and the tension drained from his body.

"Now, follow the trail. You're safe. Nothing can happen to you."

"I don't want to. I don't want to see what's in there."

"You have to, Eli. You have to help Paige."

His head bobbed on the pillow and he let out a long sigh. "All right. I'll go."

"You have a protective vibration around you, nothing can harm you. Keep moving into the trees. What do you see?"

"It's dark. There's a lot more blood now." Eli's breaths were short, anxious bursts. "I can't breathe. The air is thick and the trees are denser here."

"Just remember you're all right, Eli. You're safe."

Eli's face screwed up. "I see... I see Paige's parents' house at the end of the trees."

"Keep moving toward it."

"The blood trail leads into the house. The front door is open." Eli's eyes moved rapidly beneath his lids again. "I don't want to go in there."

"Is Paige in there?"

"I don't know."

"Then you have to go in to find out."

Eli panted. "No." He shook his head. "I can't."

"It's all right, Eli. You can do this. Go on."

"No!" Eli sprang off the pillow and woke up. He turned

to Doc Taylor. "What was that? What just happened?"

"We had a breakthrough." John smiled and turned off the voice recorder on his iPad.

"I was at Paige's old house, wasn't I?" He frowned.

John nodded. "Yes, you were."

"I don't understand. Why was I there?"

"I don't know. Only your mind can answer that question. Maybe we can do another session in a couple of days. See if we can make further progress. What do you think?"

Eli launched himself up off the sofa. "I don't know. I don't like where this is going."

"Don't you want to know where the dream is taking you? And why?"

The sheriff paced. "I did, but… now I'm not so sure."

"You know you're going to continue having those dreams until you get to the bottom of why you're having them, don't you?"

Eli snatched his Stetson from off the table, pushed it on his head and headed for the door. "I'll think about it."

THIRTY FIVE

Eli pulled into the curb outside Clarissa's house, turned off the engine and sat for a moment. What had the hypnosis proved? Why had the trail of blood taken him to Paige's parents' house? What couldn't he remember? He glanced out of the passenger window and saw Paige waiting at the front door.

He pulled the keys from the ignition, climbed out of the vehicle and walked up the path to the porch. He didn't want her to see he was disturbed by what had occurred at Doc Taylor's so when he reached her he gave her a huge smile. "Something sure smells good." The sweet aroma of fresh baked, pumpkin pie drifted into his nostrils from inside the house. He'd know that smell anywhere.

"I baked a pumpkin pie for dessert," Paige said, smiling back.

"I'm starved." Eli stepped into the entry hall. He hadn't eaten since breakfast and that wasn't a good thing for his inner Lycan.

"Good. Then you'll enjoy the dinner we prepared."

"I can't wait." He shoved his hands into the pockets of his jacket and followed Paige into the kitchen.

"Hello, dear," Clarissa greeted him. "How was your day?"

"Busy. I'm looking forward to dinner and a quiet night."

Clarissa passed the casserole dish to Paige and the plastic container to Eli. "Well, then, you'd better get home and eat these goodies. Just heat the Osso Bucco for ten to fifteen minutes and it should be fine."

"I will. Thank you for today, Clarissa," Paige said. "I've had a wonderful time."

"My pleasure, dear." She motioned for the pair to move ahead of her to the front door. "Take care on the road and have a lovely evening you two."

Eli opened the door and Paige stepped onto the porch and headed down the path to the sidewalk. The sheriff leaned in and kissed Clarissa's cheek before following Paige. "Thanks for taking good care of her, Clary, and for keeping Wil out of sight." His grandmother had always been a free spirit and didn't like the constraints associated with the name Gran or Grandma.

"Always, dear boy, on both accounts." She smiled and gave him a conspiratorial wink.

Eli tipped his hat and headed down the path to the car. He pressed the remote, took the casserole dish from Paige, waited until she was in her seat, then sat both the container and dish on her lap. "Let's get home fast. I'm starved and that smells wonderful."

Paige's smile widened. She was glad Eli appreciated the effort she put into making a home cooked meal for them. And it would be nice to sit down and eat it together. Her heart did a little kerthump and she realized she liked staying at his house with him.

It took thirty minutes to get to Eli's and once inside, Paige popped the casserole straight into the oven to reheat and sat the pumpkin pie on the kitchen counter. She opened the container and breathed a relieved sigh when she saw that Clarissa had remembered to put the bowl of whipped cream in for the pie. Everything was perfect.

While Eli showered, Paige set their places. She noticed a few bottles of red wine sitting in a small wine rack in the living room and placed a bottle on the table along with two wine glasses. The aroma of the Osso Bucco filled the kitchen and Paige's stomach growled. She was hungry too.

Eli came into the room dressed in a pair of black sports pants and a white T-shirt. He looked fresh and smelt good too. The cologne he'd chosen sent a distinct message to her female core and she busied herself with dinner preparations so as not to allow the heady emotion to envelop to her. She couldn't allow her feelings to influence her better judgement, especially with what was going on right now. They needed to find out who wanted her dead. And why. Romance would just get in the way.

"Dinner smells amazing. You didn't mention you could cook." Eli crossed the room, picked up the bottle of wine, uncorked it and poured a small amount into each glass.

"I have a confession to make," Paige said, eyeing him sideways. "I used to eat out most nights or get delivery when I didn't. Clarissa is the cook. She guided me through every step of the recipes."

"But you still cooked it." Eli gave her one of his heart-stopping smiles.

Paige's forehead wrinkled. "I guess that's true."

Eli sat down and took a sip of wine.

"I hope it was ok choosing a bottle to go with dinner."

Paige glanced over her shoulder as she set the casserole dish down on the chopping board on the counter.

"Absolutely. They've been sitting around here for far too long collecting dust, may as well make use of them." He sipped more of the Pinot Noir. "And you have good taste. This is a perfect match for the Osso Bucco."

Paige's left eyebrow arched. "So you know something about wine?"

"I know a little about a lot of things. Gotta keep the gray matter motivated." He prodded his right temple with his index finger and smiled.

"Yes, you do." His smile made her heart quiver. She brought the casserole dish over to the table. "Dig in. It's nice and hot." She offered him the serving spoon.

"Thanks." Their fingers touched as Eli took the utensil from Paige's hand and his heart thumped against his ribs. As much as he tried to avoid it he knew he was falling in love with her.

Paige's face flushed and she snatched her hand away. "Let's eat." She moved to her chair, sat down and sucked in a large mouthful of wine. How long could she dance around her growing feelings for Eli?

The sexual tension in the room was palpable. Paige ate looking at her plate and Eli refilled his wine glass a couple of times before going into the living room to retrieve another bottle.

Paige pushed back her chair, stood up and cleared the plates from the table. "Ready for dessert? We have whipped cream to go with the pie."

"Sounds great."

Paige cut the pie and placed a wedge on each plate then spooned on the whipped cream. She carried the desserts over to the table and set one down in front of Eli. Before she could move away he stood up, pulled her into his arms and kissed her hard on the mouth. She was so taken aback by the moment that she almost dropped her dessert on the floor and only just managed to slide the plate onto the table before wrapping her arms around his waist. The heated kiss continued.

THIRTY SIX

"What did you find out?" the voice on the other end of the line asked. Now that Eli Blackwood had returned to the psychiatrist they would finally learn what he remembered in his dreams. He knew something about the night Paige's parents disappeared because he'd been sleeping over. They were camped out in the living room under a sheet tent Paige's mom had secured to the coffee table and the sofa.

When Paige's parents were shot, she'd been upstairs. She had gone up to her room to get a board game to play with Eli. The men who had entered the house were not there to harm the children, only the parents. The plan had been to remove Abbey and Devlin from the house and deal with them elsewhere, but things had gone wrong when Devlin tried to grab the gun to protect his wife and himself and had been shot and killed. The mother? What were they supposed to do with her? They'd both been removed from the house by the kitchen door and loaded into the waiting F100 and the kids had been left alone.

"He's remembering more about that night. His dream is disorienting but it's still leading him to Paige's parents' house. It hadn't done that before. It has to be because she's so close to him now."

"If he remembers more he'll figure out who was in the house. Can you do your mumbo jumbo and make him forget?"

John Taylor sighed. It was unethical to erase parts of someone's memory and the mind didn't always fair well afterward, but he had no choice. "I can try."

"Don't try. Do it!"

"He's a strong man. It may not work at all." The doctor paced, hand to his forehead. He didn't want to be a part of all this.

"Make sure you wipe that particular memory. He can't remember who was in the house that night. Understand?"

"Yes, I understand."

"Good. Otherwise there'll be unpleasant consequences."

"Don't threaten me…"

"Then *do* what you're told."

"I said I'll try. That's the best I can do. The mind is a tricky mechanism and as I already told you it may not work."

"Make it work." The line went dead.

John took a seat at his desk and breathed a heavy sigh. It was after eight o'clock and he was tired, tired of being manipulated by unscrupulous people. How had he allowed himself to get involved in all of this? He hated having to deal with Eli in a dishonest manner. He'd always liked the sheriff and found him to be a good, honest man. Now he had no choice but to hypnotize him and attempt to erase his memory of being at Paige's house the night her parents were killed. The doctor knew her father was Lycan but had no idea about the mother. He'd always thought she was human and wondered when Devlin had turned her. He didn't understand the point behind their deaths. What could they possibly have known that got them murdered?

His thoughts moved to the recent events: The break in at Paige's, the near miss in the woods, and the attempt on her life at the carnival. Those incidents were something he definitely didn't want to be implicated in. Attempted murder would see his license revoked and him in jail, even though he had nothing to do with any of it. His association with the wrong people would be enough to give him a criminal record. He wouldn't be able to practice anywhere. He picked up the digital phone and keyed in Eli's number. Voicemail kicked in. "Hi, Eli, it's John. I was wondering if we could meet tomorrow to discuss your next session. I think it's important to get to the bottom of your dream as quickly as possible. Give me a call in the morning to schedule a time." He stopped and frowned at the notes on his iPad for a moment. Would he be able to wipe the memory of Eli being at Paige's parents' house that night? He had no choice. If he didn't and everything unraveled he'd be arrested. "Ok. See you soon."

Would Eli want to make another appointment? He'd been upset by what had been released from the dark recesses of his mind. The doctor knew the sheriff was on a quest to find out the truth of what had happened to Paige's parents, but would he want to delve into his dreams and his mind further after what he discovered?

His wife appeared at the door. "Dinner's ready, dear." She frowned at him. "Something the matter?"
John gave her a thin smile. "Nothing I can't handle." He crossed the room, wrapped his arm around her shoulders

and walked her back into the house. He hoped she would never find out what he'd done – sold his soul to the devil... almost.

Paige pulled herself out of Eli's embrace and stepped away from him. "I can't, I'm sorry." She raised a hand to her mouth, savoring his taste on her lips. She knew she wanted him as much as he wanted her. The intense emotion exuded from every fiber of her body and she was finding it difficult to control. She wanted to know what it would feel like to lay beneath him and allow him to become part of her. But she couldn't. Not now.

Eli moved toward her. "Paige, it was a kiss. I'm not asking for anything more." He couldn't because if he did it would unlock the Alpha gene inside her and right now he didn't want that.

Her eyes remained downcast. "But it could be if we let it." She couldn't look into his beautiful, honey colored eyes for fear her resolve would dissolve.

"Yes, it could, but now isn't the right time. I know that. There is too much going on to contemplate taking how we feel further."

Her gaze shot up to his. "You feel the same?"

He smiled and her heart almost stopped. "Of course I do. Why do you think I kissed you like that?"

Paige wanted to run into his arms and stay cocooned inside his safe, loving embrace and it took every ounce of self-control not to. "Maybe when this is all over?"

"Yeah." His sexy smile widened. "In the meantime, it's ok to hug, you know. I won't bite."

"Ok, if you say so." She wanted to be held by him. Feel his strong arms around her. "Thank you."

"For what?" He frowned into her eyes.

"For understanding. It would be easy to…"

He shook his head. "No, it wouldn't. You're vulnerable right now and I couldn't take advantage of that. When the time's right we'll be together."

Paige stepped up to him, stood on tip toes, and kissed him gently on the lips. "You're amazing. Any other guy would do just that – take advantage of the situation and me."

He brushed her cheek with gentle fingers. "I'm not any other man, Paige." Wasn't that the truth? He was Lycan, and so was she only she wasn't aware of it yet. His idea of having Doc Taylor wipe her memory was out of the question now. She had to know the truth about her parents, her past, and him. What would happen when she did?

THIRTY SEVEN

The next morning, Paige asked Eli to drop her at her office so she could tidy up and collect the tools and other items left in the kitchen. He told her he'd have Bobby cruise by again just to make sure she was all right and that he'd come by later to drive her back to his place. He was the sheriff, after all, and could afford some time off. Time devoted to keeping Paige safe.

Eli got out of his Jeep, walked around the hood to the passenger door and opened it for her. She always felt special when he did that. He was a true gentleman and it was one of the things that had drawn her to him. He'd been raised well by his mother and Paige appreciated it.

"I'll be here at three to pick you up."

"You don't have to do that. I'll be fine here until you finish work." She took his hand and climbed out of the four wheel drive.

"It's no bother. We need to talk anyhow."

Paige frowned. "What about?"

"Now's not the time. I have to go, but we'll talk tonight."

"Do you want me to go home? If you need some space

it's ok." She gazed into his beautiful eyes. They drew her in even further each time their eyes met.

"Of course not. You're welcome to stay as long as you like."

"Then what?"

"We'll talk later. Ok?" He reached out and rested a reassuring hand on her arm. "Don't worry about it, it's fine."

Paige sighed. "If you say so."

Eli took the keys from her hand, walked over to the front door of her office and opened it for her. Once inside, he handed the keys back. "Make sure you keep all the doors and windows locked while you're here. And don't let anyone in."

"Don't worry, I won't." She dropped the keychain into her purse.

He checked his watch. "Good. I'd better get going." Eli crossed the office to the door. "See you later."

"See you. Have a good day. And say hi to Rosemarie for me."

"I will." He gave her another of his heart-stopping smiles and stepped outside.

Paige locked the door and stood at the window with the gray vertical blind pushed back to watch him drive away before wandering down the short hall into the kitchen. She still had some unpacking to do. She'd purchased a dinner set and wanted to store it in the cupboard along with some unperishable groceries: sugar, cookies, Parmalat milk and some spreads for sandwiches. Once that was done she packed the tools, string, tape measure and other bits and pieces into the box and sat it by the front door ready to take with her later. Now all she had to do was find a capable receptionist and she'd be ready to start work.

By the time she'd finished it was midday and she was famished. She headed into the kitchen to the refrigerator. She'd packed herself some leftovers from the previous night and planned to heat them up in the microwave. A knock on the door made her jump and she wondered who would know she was there. Eli had made her promise not to let anyone in so she pushed the kitchen door closed and sat down at the table to wait for her lunch to reheat. The knocking continued.

Paige fossicked in her purse for her cell phone and pressed Eli's number.

He picked up on the first ring. "Everything all right?"

"There's someone knocking on the door. They've been out there for a while now."

"Ignore it. They'll get the message and move on."

"It wouldn't be Bobby checking in, would it?" She bit her bottom lip and frowned.

"I didn't ask him to, so, no, it shouldn't be him."

Paige shivered.

"Do you want me to come over?"

"No…" The microwave dinged and Paige almost jumped out of her skin. She spun around and frowned at it. "You can't drop everything and come running every time I call. I'll be fine." She hoped she would, anyhow.

"If it'd make you feel better I can be there in less than ten minutes." He was on his feet and out of his office. "I'm on my way." He told Rosemarie he was going out for a while and hurried across reception to the door.

"Eli, don't. I'll be ok."

"Too late. I'm already out the front door and heading to my car. I'll see you soon." He rang off.

Paige felt like a scared little girl and it didn't feel good. She hated bothering Eli while he was at work, but who else could she turn to?

The knocking continued.

Go away! Please go away. She cupped her hands over her ears. Who was out front and why were they still there after so long?

The knocking stopped.

Paige gave a relieved sigh. *Thank goodness.*

She got up from the table, opened the door and peered along the hall. No one appeared to be outside now. Why had they been so persistent?

When Paige turned around a man in black clothes and ski mask was right behind her.

Eli pulled up outside Paige's office and before getting out of the car he gave her a call to let her know he was there. The phone rang for longer than it should have and then switched to voicemail. He took the phone from his ear and frowned at the screen. Why wasn't she picking up? He rang off and tried again. His voice was tight as he climbed out of the car and left her a voicemail message. "Hey, Paige, I'm here. Want to open the door?" He thought that by the time he crossed the sidewalk she'd be standing in the open doorway. She wasn't.

He peered through the plate glass window. No sign of her in the office. He tried her number again. "Pick up, Paige. Pick up." Still no answer. Her voice on her answering machine sounded happy and carefree. It must have been something she'd recorded before moving to Moon Grove. Eli pushed his cell phone into his jacket pocket, stalked along the sidewalk, turned the corner and headed behind the row of stores. When he came to the rear entrance of the office he found the door wide open. His heart dropped into his stomach and he flew inside.

Paige was unconscious on the floor, the contents of her purse and the cupboards strewn around the small room. He knew what they were after. Why did they think Paige was in possession of the moonstone ring?

Eli fell to his knees and scooped her into his arms. "Paige, can you hear me?"

She had a bump on her forehead which was already turning a deep shade of pinkish purple. He peeled back an eyelid to check her pupil. Dilated. She'd have a concussion for sure with the size of the lump. He eased her out of his arms, ripped off his jacket, folded it and placed it under her head then called 911.

He sat down on the floor beside her, wrapped his fingers around her wrist and checked her pulse. Rapid but ok. "Help's on the way, Paige. Hang in there. They'll be here soon."

Doctor Thomas Hoskins moonlighted at the next town's medical center three days a week and was glad to be there to help when he saw Eli Blackwood rushing into the ER with the paramedics and a young, red haired woman on the trolley. He recognized her right away. Paige O'Connell. He hurried through the double doors and followed the group into a cubicle. "Eli, what happened?"

"Hey, Doc, someone attacked Paige at her office. When I got there she was unconscious and the place had been ransacked." His eyes moved from the doctor to the paramedics as they lifted Paige off the trolley and onto a hospital gurney.

The doctor rested a comforting hand on the sheriff's arm. "Let me take a look at her and then we can go from there. Any idea how long she's been out?"

"Uh, yeah, maybe forty minutes give or take." I spoke to her just before I left the station and it took about eight minutes to get to her office. The ride here took around thirty so…"

"Ok. Have a seat in the waiting area and I'll come out to you when I'm done in here."

Eli's gaze moved from the doctor to Paige then back to Doc Hoskins. "Can't I stay here? I'm the investigating officer."

"It wouldn't matter if you were the President himself. You can't be in here while I examine my patient." He pointed to the door. "I promise I'll take good care of her. It won't take long."

Eli gave a heavy sigh. "All right. But you'll let me know how she is as soon as you find out anything, right?"

"Yes. Now go on." He pointed to the doorway. "Let me get on with my job."

Eli stalked across the small emergency room and out the door. He hated leaving Paige alone with strangers… strangers to her, anyhow.

As he sat down on a chair closest to the ER entrance his cell rang. He snatched it from the pocket of his jacket. "Sheriff Blackwood speaking."

"Eli, it's me," Bobby said on the other end of the line. "How's Paige doing?"

"She's unconscious. Doc Hoskins is with her."

Rosemarie snatched the phone out of Bobby's hand and pressed it to her ear. "You make sure that young lady is ok, you hear me?" She sounded anxious and breathy.

"I will, Rosy. I promise."

"What a terrible thing to happen. Who would do such a thing?"

"I don't know, but I'll make sure I find out. This has to stop."

"Do you think it was the same person who broke into her house?"

"Yeah, I do. They went through her purse and the cupboards at her office. The place will need cleaning up before Paige can go back there."

"I can go. I don't mind." Rosemarie wanted to feel useful, given the circumstances. "It's quiet here at the moment and Bobby's in attendance."

"No, Rosy, I don't want you going there alone. Not while whoever hurt Paige is still out there."

"I guess you're right." She sighed into the phone. "Well, just let me know when and I'll take Bobby with me. Craig can do some work for a change."

"Don't worry, ok? I'll give you a call later on to let you know how Paige is doing."

"Thank you, Eli, I appreciate that." She handed the phone back to her companion.

"We need to find out who did this as soon as we can," Bobby said. "Who knows who'll be next?"

"Agreed. Just make sure Rosy doesn't leave the station alone. I don't want her going to Paige's office to clean up unless someone's with her."

"Will do."

"Ok. I'll call you later. Doc Hoskins is coming over to me." He rang off.

THIRTY EIGHT

Clarissa hung up the phone and turned to Wil. "That was Rosemarie. Paige is in the hospital. Someone attacked her at her office. They must still think she knows about the ring, maybe they think she has it." She walked back to the table and sat down. "When will this end? That young woman won't want to stay here if this keeps happening."

Wil reached across the table and patted her hand. "She'll stay. She's in love with Eli, even if she doesn't want to admit it to herself, and he's in love with her. They're meant to be together."

Clarissa's left eyebrow arched. "Since when did you become such an old romantic?"

His forehead wrinkled. "Who said I'm a romantic? It's a fact. She's his Alpha female."

"Oh, I thought you'd become a bit of a softy in your old age." She grinned and gave him a wink.

"Bah humbug." He waved her comment off and folded his arms, his cheeks flushing slightly.

"Come on, now, don't be a Scrooge."

"Eli thinks I am."

"Well, that's because you're always gruff with him. Try a little honey instead of cactus juice."

"What?"

"Never mind." She batted her right hand at him and changed the subject. "Something has to be done about whoever is trying to hurt Paige."

"Agreed. But what? We don't even know who's been doing it."

"What about the Mayor? He's an odd man and he has those wolves working for him."

"Eli doesn't think he has anything to do with it. But, like I said, you can't trust him. He's out for himself and no one else."

"If not him then who?"

"Don't ask me, I'm none the wiser." He picked up his coffee mug and took a sip. "Argh, it's cold."

Clarissa pushed back her chair and stood up. "Want a fresh cup?"

Wil looked at her and smiled. "Sure. If you're offering."

She crossed the kitchen to the coffee pot. "I was thinking about Elijah the other day. I sometimes wonder where he went."

"Don't bother wondering about that no good son of a gun. Eli's better off without the likes of him around."

Clarissa came back to the table, set Wil's mug down in front of him and took her seat. "Yes, I know you're right. He has his name but that's about all. Thank goodness he's more like Katie than his father."

Wil's expression softened. "You miss her still, don't ya?"

"Every day." A sad smile crossed her weathered face

and she rested her chin in her hand. "And I'm sure Eli does too. You never get over losing a loved one. The pain just gets buried inside you and you keep going. What other choice do we have?"

Will nodded. "Sad but true.

Clarissa sighed and looked into his eyes. She cared for Wil and had the sneaking suspicion he felt the same for her. It was nice having a man around the house. It had been a long time.

Eli stood up as Doc Hoskins approached. "How's she doing?"

"She's awake but she has a concussion and is a little woozy." He motioned for Eli to take a seat and joined him.

"When can I talk to her? I need to find out if she saw her attacker."

The doctor rested a hand on Eli's shoulder. "Just give her a bit of time to come out of it properly and then talk to her. You may not get much sense out of her right now."

"Did she ask for me?"

Doc Hoskins nodded. "Yes, but I told her she needed to rest for a while first. I've given her something for the pain and I think she'll sleep for an hour or two."

"Why would you do that? We need to get on this now, not in a couple of hours."

"And I have to think about the welfare of my patient. Paige has been through a frightening ordeal, one of several I believe and she needs to rest right now. The questions will have to wait."

Eli huffed out a frustrated breath. "And while we're

waiting whoever did this could be long gone." He pulled himself out of his seat. "I need to do something. I'll come back in a couple of hours and speak to Paige." He stalked along the corridor and out the exit.

Heading over to his car he heard his name and turned around.

Rebecca crossed the parking lot. "How is she? Is there anything I can do?" she asked as she approached Eli and gave him a hug.

He eased out of her embrace. "Not at the moment. They've given her a sedative and she'll be out of it for the next couple of hours."

"Oh, ok. Do you need anything?" She gave him a concerned frown.

"I'm ok. But thanks." He opened the car door. "Can I ask you something?"

"Sure. Anything." Rebecca had always had a thing for Eli even when they were teenagers. She had hoped that one day he'd feel the same about her but that never happened. She knew he thought of her like a kid sister and sometimes it hurt, but there was nothing she could do about it. She knew he had feelings for Paige.

"Why were you at Doc Taylor's the other day? And why didn't you tell me? I need to know these things as your..." his eyes roamed the parking lot making sure no one could hear him, "Alpha."

Rebecca gave him a disgruntled frown. "How'd you know about that?" She folded her arms.

"I was outside. I was there to see him myself."

"So you're seeing Doc Taylor? Are you having those dreams again?"

"Don't change the subject, Bec. Why were you there?"

"It's personal. All you need to know is I'm not crazy and I can do what I have to when I have to."

"That's not what I'm asking. Are you ok?"

Her scowl softened. "Yeah, I am."

"If you need to talk…"

She waved the comment off. "It's all good. Where are you heading?"

"Back to the station. I want to talk to Bobby and Craig about what happened today. We need to get a handle on who's doing this."

"Yeah, we do before someone else gets killed." Her serious gaze met his. Wendy Ellis shouldn't have been murdered and it didn't sit well with the pack. "We're meant to protect the people of this town, but how can we when an unknown assailant is out there?"

"It has to be someone we know. They've been looking for…" Eli stopped himself, remembering he wasn't sure who he could truly trust right now.

Rebecca's eyebrows shot up. "They've been looking for what?"

"Nothing, just theorizing out loud. When I have something to share with the rest of the pack I'll call a meeting."

"Don't keep us in the dark, Eli. We can't help if we don't know what's going on." She turned and strutted across the lot to her car.

Later that afternoon, when Eli entered the ER he was pleased to see Paige propped up on the gurney. She was still pale and had a gauze bandage around her head but she was back in the land of the living and that's all that mattered. He crossed the room and came over to the foot of the bed. "How're you feeling? You had me worried there for a while."

Her face lit up. "I'm so glad you're here. I don't know anyone and it feels unnerving. Doctor Hoskins has been checking in on me and he said I could be released once you arrived, so please let's get out of here."

"Let me go find him and see what has to be done before you can go. You'll probably have to sign a release form and medical insurance form."

"I already did so there shouldn't be anything else." She threw back the white sheet covering her and swung her legs over the side of the gurney.

"Hey, wait a minute. Let me help you." He gripped her waist and eased her onto the floor.

"Thanks." Paige stepped into her shoes. If she hadn't been so eager to get out of the medical center she would have indulged in the closeness of Eli for a while longer.

As they were about to leave, Doc Hoskins came into the ER. "All ready to go?"

"Yes. Thank you for looking after me today."

"It's been a pleasure, Paige." He shook her hand. "Remember what I said. If you experience any dizziness or headaches you need to come back, pronto. All right?"

"Absolutely." She smiled.

"Ok. Take care of yourself and come see me next week at my office in Moon Grove. Just to be sure everything's fine."

"Is that necessary?" Paige hadn't seen a doctor in years and didn't think she needed to follow up. She felt a little worse for wear but other than that she was fine. "I feel ok."

"With any kind of head injury, yes, it's necessary." He

handed her a business card. "Give my receptionist a call tomorrow and schedule an appointment."

Eli took the card from her hand. "We will."

"All right, then, you're all set to leave."

The four wheel drive was parked in a POLICE parking zone right outside the medical center entrance. Eli escorted Paige over to it and opened the door for her. She gave him a sour scowl as she climbed in and he wondered what he'd done to deserve it. He handed her the seatbelt then closed the passenger door, walked around the rear of the vehicle and climbed in. "Everything ok?"

She turned to look at him, her arms folded. "No, everything isn't ok. I didn't want to go see Doctor Hoskins next week. I'm fine. I'm a doctor too, you know, and I know how I feel."

"Ok, fair enough, but with a head injury you can't be too careful."

"I understand how worried you must've been when you found me, but I'll be fine. I don't need to go see the doctor."

Eli let out a deep sigh. "I'd appreciate it if you did. Just to be safe."

Paige sighed. "Oh, all right. If I must."

Eli started the Jeep. "Thank you."

"Could we go by my place? I'd like to pick up some clean clothes."

"Sure." He backed out of the parking space and headed for the highway. He wanted to see Wil about his notebook. He needed clarification about something he'd read.

THIRTY NINE

By the time Eli pulled the Jeep in behind Paige's car it was after four o'clock. Paige opened the door and climbed out. He knew she was still upset about him making the decision for her to see Doc Hoskins next week. He walked up to the front porch with her and waited for her to open the door.

She turned to look at him. "Coming in?"

"I need to see Clarissa for a few minutes. Will you be ok to grab your things and come over when you're done?"

Paige nodded. "Ok, sure."

"Good. See you in a bit." He pushed his hands into the deep pockets of his jacket, strutted down the path and crossed the street.

Paige stood in the open doorway watching him. She knew he had something on his mind, hence the conversation they were supposed to have had that afternoon, except she'd been attacked, so what was it? She'd felt closer to him since they'd been sharing his house and sometimes it worried her. Were they getting too involved too quickly? She locked the door and wandered through the house to make sure it was secure before heading upstairs. She wasn't about to take any chances.

As she packed some fresh clothes into a small travel bag she realized that since she'd been staying at Eli's she hadn't had the horrible nightmares she'd been having before. Why? Had Eli still been having his dream? She made a mental note to ask him. Picking up the bag from off her bed, Paige crossed the room and headed downstairs.

Her cell jingled, breaking the silence in the house, and caused Paige to lurch forward on the stairs and almost lose her balance. She pulled her phone out of her coat pocket and checked the screen. Stephanie? She pressed the answer button. "Hey, Steph, how are you? It's so good to hear your voice. I've been so worried about you. When can I come see you?"

Her friend didn't sound like herself and it immediately set off alarm bells.

"I'm just calling to tell you I can't be friends with you anymore."

Tears stung the backs of Paige's eyes and her voice became quiet. "Why?"

"You're asking me why after what happened at the Christmas carnival?"

Paige could understand her friend being traumatized about *almost dying,* who wouldn't be, she had been traumatized too, but never dreamed Stephanie would end their longstanding friendship. "It wasn't my fault, Steph."

"Maybe not directly, but indirectly it was. Someone was after you and got me instead."

"I asked you not to come but you insisted."

"Oh, so now it's my fault I got stabbed and nearly died."

Paige held in the burning sob threatening to escape, the aching lump in her throat almost choking her. "That's not what I said."

"It doesn't matter. I just wanted to tell you in person, well as *in person* as I could under the circumstances. I didn't want to text you because that would've been awful."

"And you think calling me makes it any easier? Do your parents have something to do with your decision?"

Silence.

Of course they did.

"Steph?"

"What?"

"I'll miss you." She pressed the button to end the call and burst into tears.

When Paige hadn't shown up Eli got worried. He left Clarissa's, crossed the street, marched up the path, knocked and waited. Paige came to the door with puffy red eyes and he couldn't stop himself from reaching for her and pulling her into his arms. "What's wrong?"

"Steph – anie called. She ended our friendship." Paige sobbed against Eli's firm chest.

He stroked her silky, red hair. "I'm so sorry, Paige. That's hard."

She spoke into his jacket, her words muffled. "We've been best friends since college. What am I going to do without her?"

Eli slipped a finger under her chin and raised her face up to meet his gaze. "Eventually you'll make new friends. I know it hurts right now, but it will get easier."

Paige continued to sob, her heart breaking for the loss.

The drive back to Eli's was quiet. Paige hadn't said a word since they'd climbed into the Jeep and headed out of

Moon Grove. He knew she was devastated at the loss of her best friend and wondered what he could do to cheer her up. Nothing, most likely. She needed time to grieve and he had to give her that time. He hated seeing her so unhappy.

"I was thinking I'd make my world famous mushroom omelet for dinner. How does that sound?" Eli attempted to lighten the heavy mood.

"Sounds delicious," Paige said, her voice almost a whisper.

"But I'll need your assistance. Think you're up for it?" He gave her a quick glance and one of his heart melting smiles.

Paige's heart rate ticked up a notch or two despite how she felt. Eli was a sexy man and she was attracted to him, there was no denying it anymore. "I think I can handle it."

"Great." He pressed the accelerator down and headed for home.

When Eli pulled up in front of his house Craig was standing on the front porch, hands in pockets and a scowl on his face. Eli gave a heavy sigh. "Wait here for a minute while I find out what he wants."

He'd get no argument from her. Paige didn't like Craig and the further away from him she could stay the better.

Eli strutted up to the front steps and stood with hands on hips. "What are you doing here, Craig?"

"I want to talk to you about something."

"Ok. What?"

His deputy's eyes moved to the car and Paige sitting in the passenger seat. "Not here."

Eli glanced over his shoulder. "Why not? Paige can't hear us."

Craig descended the steps and stopped in front of him. "It's about her mother."

Eli's left eyebrow arched. "What about her?"

"That's what I want to talk to you about. Somewhere private."

"Ok, you've got my attention. When and where?" He folded his arms.

"Be at the church in an hour."

Eli locked his gaze onto Craig. His gut warned him something was off about this whole situation but he needed answers, so did Paige. "All right. I'll be there."

Craig gave him a satisfied smirk, pushed his hands into the pockets of his jacket and stalked across the yard to his car.

Once he'd driven off Eli's property, the sheriff walked over and opened the door for Paige.

"What did he want?" she asked, stepping down out of the four wheel drive and gazing along the dark, tree covered drive.

"Police stuff, that's all." He closed the door and walked Paige over to the porch. "I have to go out for a while later. I'll take you with me and drop you at Clarissa's on the way."

Paige frowned up at him. "Is everything ok?" She could sense an uneasiness about him.

"Sure, everything's fine. Now let's go inside and make those omelets. I'm starved."

FORTY

Eli parked in the parking lot behind the large, white church on the hill overlooking Moon Grove and walked around to the front entrance. It was dark now and his Lycan instincts had well and truly kicked in. The doors were locked. He raised his fist and pounded on one, golden oak colored door. Was Craig playing games with him? No one else was around. Was this a ruse to get him here to an unpopulated location to attack him and try to usurp his leadership? Eli's hackles went up and he glanced over his shoulder, his eyes roaming the surrounding shadows. *Where is Craig?*

He stepped backwards away from the door, shoved his hands into the pockets of his jacket and waited. No one came to let him in. He tugged his left hand free and checked the time. Ten minutes after eight. He couldn't sense any other wolves. He pulled his phone out of his pocket and keyed in Craig's number. His wolf hearing picked up the jangle of a cell phone coming from inside the church and he knew it was his deputy's.

Eli marched up to the door and pounded on it again.

"Craig, I know you're in there. Open up. What the hell's going on?"

He heard the deadbolt click back and the door swung out of his reach. A man he didn't recognize but somehow knew appeared in the doorway. "Hello, Eli."

The sheriff stepped backwards, a cold fear traveling through his veins. "Why are you here?"

A smirk spread across the man's face. "Is that any way to greet your dear old dad?"

Eli's eyes moved to the interior of the church. "Where's Craig?"

"He's indisposed." Elijah stepped outside. Eli took another step backwards.

"Is he all right?"

Elijah gave his son a faux-concerned frown. "No. I don't believe he is."

"Want do you want?" Everything fell into place as Eli realized it had been his father in the woods the night Paige was almost attacked and that he had instigated the other attacks on Paige and the break-ins at her house.

"I came to get what's rightfully mine."

Eli's eyes locked onto him. "And what would that be exactly?" He knew what his father was talking about but wanted to hear him say it.

"I *want* the moonstone ring," he spat, his hand extended for Eli to hand it over.

"And what makes you think I have it?" Eli stalled while he tried to think of a way out of the life-threatening situation he'd been thrown into. He knew his father wouldn't hesitate to kill him if he thought it would provide him with the power he pursued.

"Well, if you don't have it then your girlfriend must."

"Leave her out of this. She knows nothing about our kind and she doesn't have the ring."

"Oh, come on, Eli, what do you take me for? A fool?" He paced then stopped and turned around. "Her uncle hid it a decade ago so she must know where it is."

"I can guarantee she has no idea about any of this."

Elijah's brooding gaze remained on his son. "Then you have it. Show me your hands."

Eli held both his hands out in front of him. "Satisfied?" He had hidden it in a place no one would find it... a secret place in Clarissa's house protected from supernatural creatures, so he knew the ring would be untouchable.

"Maybe that meddling grandmother of yours has it. The old witch! Or she put some kind of cloaking spell on it."

"Clarissa doesn't have it either."

"Then where is it?" His eyes glowed red, his inner demon wolf agitated, his frustration palpable.

"Why do you want it so badly?"

Elijah gave a haughty chuckle. "Are you serious? I want what it offers. Haven't you craved its power, being the Alpha? Think of what it could do for you."

"It doesn't interest me."

"Then you're a bigger fool than I thought you were. How can you be my son? You have no ambition."

Eli stared into his father's eyes and his own eyes glowed golden. "I wish I wasn't your son. I wish I'd never been born Lycan."

"It's your heritage so get over it. The one thing you will not do is consummate your relationship with that woman. Our blood will not be joined with theirs. I'll make sure of it."

"You won't touch her! I'll kill you before you have the

chance to get near her." Eli's wolf struggled to emerge. Is that what his father wanted? To goad him into turning? A confrontation to the death so he could take the place of Alpha? He stepped back and inhaled a long breath through his nostrils. He wouldn't give Elijah the satisfaction.

"You're weak and pathetic. You call yourself an Alpha?" He gave a humorless chuckle. "I could challenge you and beat you in the blink of an eye. Where's your wolf strength?"

Eli grabbed his father by the front of his black sweater and shoved him inside the church. "Let's see how weak I really am." He picked Elijah up with one hand and tossed him across the huge hall. His father's body flew through the air and crashed into a white marble statue of Moon Grove's first Alpha, shattering it into several large pieces. Eli ran his eyes along the nave and spotted Craig lying dead in front of the first row of pews, his head twisted at an odd angle, his eyes staring, splashes of blood smeared across his jacket where he'd been shot with silver bullets.

Eli stalked across the church to where his father had fallen. He was gone.

As he raced around to his Jeep, Eli whipped his phone out of his pocket and called Clarissa. "Elijah's here. I think he's on his way to you."

"Don't fret, dear, I know exactly what to do." She had always had the feeling that Elijah would return one day to claim his rightful place, so she'd made specific provisions for just such an occasion.

"Thanks, Clary. I'll be there as soon as I can." He jumped into his car, rammed the key into the ignition and started the engine, the tires squealing on the slick, snow-covered grass as he spun the Jeep around and sped down the hill.

He pressed the Bluetooth button on the dash and asked Siri® to call the station. Rosemarie picked up on the second ring. "Hi, hon, what can I do for you?"

"Is Bobby there?" Eli was breathless.

The hair on Rosemarie's neck stood static when she heard Eli's anxious voice. "Let me put you on speaker."

"Bobby, Elijah's here and on his way to Clarissa's. He's after the moonstone ring and Paige and they're both there."

His deputy was on his feet. "I'll round up the others and meet you there."

"Bob, Craig's dead. Elijah killed him. His body's in the church."

"Jesus H Christ!" Bobby's eyes shifted to Rosemarie. "Sorry, Rose." He knew how much she hated blaspheming. "Ok, I'll send out an alert to everyone else. See you there." He was across the room to the coat rack and pulling on his jacket as he stalked out of the office.

"Eli, please be careful," Rosemarie said, her heart pounding. "He's older and stronger than you are, honey."

"I know. I will. Don't worry."

"I always worry when it comes to a maniac wolf like Elijah. No offence."

"Yeah, I know what you mean." He rang off and pressed his foot to the floor. Eli despised his father. After what had happened to his mother he had no qualms about ridding Moon Grove of Elijah's presence.

Clarissa was rummaging in the cellar when Paige wandered down the stairs into the confined, dim space. "Can I help you with whatever it is you're looking for?" she asked, crossing the claustrophobic room to where the older woman was searching.

"Thank you for the offer, dear, but I've found it." She spun around and blew a puff of white powder into Paige's face.

Paige coughed and sneezed. Everything around her distorted into watery waves and before she could ask Clarissa what she'd done she was out cold on the floor.

Wil emerged from the shadows. "Are you sure she won't remember what happened when she wakes up?"

Clarissa's right eyebrow arched. "Have you ever known any of my spells not to work?"

He scratched the back of his head. "Can't say as I have."

"Then let's get her into the panic room. We'll all be safe in there. Elijah won't know where we are despite his Lycan sensitivities."

Will grabbed Paige's shoulders and Clarissa gripped her ankles. They eased her through the small space in the bricks, laid her on a cot stretcher, then pulled the heavy, lead lined metal door with the faux bricks on the outside closed.

Clarissa's front door burst open and Elijah stormed inside. Her parlor tricks no longer had any effect on him; he'd become immune. He raised his head and used his Lycan hearing and olfactory senses to sniff out her hiding place. Inhaling a long draught of the environment around him he recognized hers and two other distinct body scents – Paige O'Connell's and Wil Wallace's. Was that feisty old codger still breathing? Elijah thought he'd died years ago.

He stalked through the house.

No one.

They had to be here somewhere. There hadn't been enough time for them to make a run for it. Besides, if they had he'd be able to follow their scent and catch them off guard in no time. He knew they were still in the house. But where? He moved through the downstairs rooms like a black blur in his dark clothing, then climbed the stairs. Stalking along the hallway, he kicked open each door and stepped into the empty room. Where were they hiding? "Clarissa? Come out, come out, wherever you are," he said in a sing song voice, giving a devious chuckle. "I know you're here somewhere so you may as well make it easy on yourself." He jumped the banister and landed on all fours in front of the open kitchen door. "*Clarissa!*" he yelled, his voice the tremor of an earthquake reverberating through the house. "I will find you and when I do it will not be pleasant."

He gazed over his shoulder, spotted the cellar door and a satisfied smirk spread across his lips. Turning on his heel, he stalked over to the paneled wood door under the stairs and threw it open. He tried the wall switch. No light. Clever, but not clever enough. His nocturnal vision allowed him to see in the dark. He stomped down the wooden stairs to make an impact on their already jangled nerves and chuckled again when he reached the bottom step. "Now, where could you be?" He folded one arm across his abdomen, rested the other elbow on top and tapped his index finger against his stubbled chin. "Eenie, meenie, miney, mo." He raced across the small space and clawed a pile of storage boxes to the floor. No one. He frowned and turned around. They had to be down here, there was nowhere else for them to hide.

Bobby pulled into the curb a couple of houses down from Clarissa's, turned off the headlights and sat in the dark. He didn't want Eli's father getting a whiff of his scent and disappearing. Paul stopped behind him, got out of his car and joined Bobby in the patrol car. "Anything happen?"

"Not yet. But he's in the house."

"Should we go in?"

"Let's wait until the others arrive. We're better as a pack. Elijah is a powerful Lycan without anyone's assistance. You and I wouldn't stand a chance against him on our own."

Paul nodded and folded his arms. "Ok. So we wait."

Ryan Hollis was the next one to show up. He climbed into the back of the patrol car. "What's happening?"

"Elijah's inside," Paul told him, peering over his shoulder.

"And you don't think we should go in?"

Bobby eyed him through the caged partition. "No. We need to wait for Eli. He'll be here any minute."

Rebecca climbed into the back seat beside Ryan. "Where's Eli and Craig?"

"Eli's on his way." He waited a beat, not knowing how to break the news. There was no easy way to say it. "And Craig's dead."

"What?! How?" Rebecca, Paul and Ryan said together.

"Elijah killed him. His body's up at the church. We'll need to do something about that later." Bobby and the others hadn't liked Craig because of his antagonistic attitude toward Eli, but to die the way he had at the hands of a monster wolf was wrong. He was still one of their pack, no matter how they felt about him, and he'd be given a proper Lycan send off.

"Have you seen Eli's dad yet?" Rebecca shrugged out of her jacket. Her wolf was eager to get into the fray and her body temperature was on the rise.

"Eli would hate you calling Elijah his *dad*." Bobby's eyes met hers in the rearview mirror.

"Well he is, regardless of their estranged relationship." She dropped her jacket on the floor.

"Yeah, maybe, just don't let him hear you say it."

"Touchy much?"

"Hey, I agree with him. Elijah's a nutcase, plain and simple. He'd kill you while smiling at you." Bobby turned in his seat and glanced through the cage. "And don't forget that. He's cunning and manipulative, especially where women are concerned. I remember hearing my dad talking about him once when I was a teenager. He said Elijah would kill his own mother to get his hands on the moonstone ring. After a decade you don't think he's gonna to be more obsessed?"

Rebecca scowled at Bobby. "Ok! I get it. He's a monster."

"Yeah, he is so watch your back in there."

"Thanks for the advice but I can take care of myself."

Bobby chuckled. "I don't doubt it. I've seen you in action."

Rebecca was a sweet thing until her wolf emerged.

Eli tapped on the driver's window and Bobby jumped. He pressed the button on the armrest. "Geez, Eli, want to give me a heart attack or somethin'?"

Eli crouched beside the car. "What's happening?"

"All we know is he's inside Clarissa's house. There hasn't been any kind of altercation that we can tell. We were waiting for you to get here."

"Ok. Good. Let's spread out. Bobby, you and Bec circle the house. Make sure you've got silver with you. I'll go in with Ryan and Paul. Once the outside is secured we'll attempt to lure him out of the house into the rear yard and then we can go on the attack. Aim to subdue not kill, unless it's absolutely necessary. "Are we clear?"

Everyone nodded.

"Ok, then, let's go."

FORTY ONE

Clarissa could hear Elijah outside their hiding place and wondered if her spell had worked. What was he doing? And why had he stopped right there? Did he know where they were? She rasped in an anxious breath and Wil wrapped an arm around her shoulders. He could see the worry etched into her face.

He didn't speak, but she knew what he was thinking. It would be all right. Elijah was just testing their resolve, trying to unnerve them into giving themselves away. Paige would only be unconscious for another thirty minutes or so, and Clarissa hoped Eli and the other wolves would arrive any minute to deal with his father before she woke up.

She wondered why she hadn't picked up on him being back in Moon Grove. She was usually very good at that sort of thing. Maybe he had some kind of spell on him to prevent her from homing in on his wolf vibration. He'd been away for so long who knew what he'd done or could do now. He was a formidable force even on his own. Imagine what he could do if he was the Alpha of a pack. Was he? Is that why he was so strong now?

Paige stirred and Clarissa jumped. It seemed she was coming out of it sooner than anticipated. She reached into her pocket, scooped a palm full of the powder into her hand, leaned across and blew it into Paige's face. *That should keep her asleep for a good hour at least.* She couldn't have her waking up now, not with what was happening and where they were. What would she tell her?

"Clarissa? I know you're here. I can smell your scent. Why not come out so we can talk face to face." He strained his wolf ears to listen. No heartbeat, no breathing, nothing. He started to second guess himself. Maybe they had managed to get away after all.

Something caught his attention – a soft creak in the floorboards above.

He flew up the stairs.

Just as he reached the top landing, the door slammed shut in his face and he tumbled down the stairs backwards. Light streamed in from the hallway and Eli raced down the wooden steps, grabbed his father by the scruff of the neck and hauled him back upstairs before he had a chance to react.

Paul and Ryan were about to grip his arms when he regained his dazed senses and threw Eli off. The trio jumped him but he was far stronger than the three of them together. He tossed Paul into the living room, Ryan out onto the front path and Eli up the entry hall staircase without breaking a sweat and raced out the door.

Eli, Paul and Ryan were on their feet and in hot pursuit, Eli calling out for Bobby and Rebecca to follow them. The five whipped along the sidewalk, over front fences, through backyards, keeping on Elijah's trail, but when they reached the next block he'd vanished, along with his scent.

"What now?" Bobby asked, standing with hands on hips, panting.

"We have to find him. Get back to your vehicles and do a thorough sweep of the area. If anyone comes across him let me know. Do not approach him alone. I'll head back to Clarissa's to tell them we've chased him off."

Everyone dashed back to their cars and took off in each direction.

Eli knew where Clarissa had them hidden. He descended the wooden steps, crossed the small underground room and knocked on the bricks. "He's gone. You can come out now."

The brick work shuddered and the door popped open. The lead lining was the reason Elijah couldn't sense or smell them.

"Thank you, Eli. I was beginning to think my spell hadn't worked. He was standing right where you are now and I thought he'd found us. I was praying for you and the pack to get here. I didn't know what else to do. If I'd faced him he would have killed me, Wil and Paige."

Eli kissed his grandmother's forehead. "It's ok now. He's gone and we'll make sure he doesn't come back."

"He's shrewd, dear, he'll find a way. He came right inside despite the Wolfsbane and other charms I have around the house. He's stronger than any of us could imagine. Who knows what he's learned about the Lupine curse and how to control it while he's been gone. He's obviously discovered a way around Wolfsbane."

"I'm glad you told me, Clary. At least we know not to try any of the regular preventatives on him." Eli wondered if silver would still work.

"Please be careful my darling grandson. I don't want anything to happen to you." She reached up and lovingly touched his face.

"I will. Always. I have too many people who depend on me."

"Yes, you do. Me included." She smiled.

"Especially you, Gran."

"Oh, you." She play slapped him. She disliked those old-fashioned names for grandparents and thought them so outdated.

Eli glanced into the panic room. "Let's get Paige upstairs and on the sofa before she wakes up."

"She won't wake up for a good hour. I had to double dose her."

Eli frowned at her. "She was coming out of it so soon?"

Clarissa nodded. "Must be her father's blood."

"Must be." She was stronger than he thought.

Wil and Eli carried Paige upstairs and eased her down onto the floral sofa sitting in the center of the living room. When she woke up she wouldn't remember anything about what happened. It would appear as though she'd fallen asleep.

Clarissa set Paige's empty coffee mug on the table and an open magazine as a prop. She'd think she was having coffee and dozed off. At least that was the plan.

Eli's cell jingled and he snatched it from his jacket pocket. "Any news?" he asked without checking the caller ID.

"This is far from over, son. Believe that." The line went dead.

Eli ripped the phone from his ear and checked the ID. Blocked number. "Dammit!"

"What did your father say?"

"This isn't over."

"Of course it isn't. It will only be over when he's been put down." She rubbed Eli's arm. "I'm sorry, dear."

"Don't be sorry. You're right. This won't end until he's dead. He'll continue to come after you, me, Paige, and anyone he thinks he can bully or manipulate, like Craig, and nothing will stop him... until I do."

"It's not for you alone, Eli. Your pack can help."

Eli shook his head. "No. I won't put anyone else's life at risk. It has to be between him and me."

Clarissa's stomach shrank and icy fingers of dread roamed her spine. For the first time in a long while she was afraid for her grandson.

FORTY TWO

When Paige woke up it took a few seconds for her to remember where she was. As she gazed around the comfortable space she realized she was lying on Clarissa's sofa. Her eyes met the empty mug and magazine sitting on the coffee table. She must have finished her coffee and dozed off. It wasn't like her, but given the circumstances she guessed her body needed the added rest after the traumatic experience at her office, and the pent up tension of the past few weeks.

Paige turned back the warm, checked blanket Clarissa had draped over her, swung her legs over the side of the couch and stretched. *What time is it?* Her eyes roamed the living room looking for her jacket. Paige's heart bumped against her ribs. Her phone was in the pocket. She stood up and walked to the doorway. Her jacket was on the coat rail by the front door. She breathed a relieved sigh, wandered over to it and plucked her phone from the right hand pocket. It was almost 10 PM. *Wow! I must have been really tired.*

She shook off the dregs of sleep and headed to the kitchen. Eli and Clarissa were sitting at the table talking.

The older woman's eyes moved to her when she appeared in the doorway. "So, you're awake. Feel better?"

"I guess. I didn't even realize I was that tired." She sat down next to Eli.

Clarissa popped up off her chair. "Want a fresh cup of coffee and blueberry scone?"

Paige frowned, her sleepy mind still trying to decipher why she'd fallen asleep. "Um, sure. Thanks." Her gaze moved to Eli. "I'm sorry you had to wait for me. You should've woken me up."

He shrugged. "No big deal. You needed the rest and I had no place to be."

Clarissa sat the coffee and plate in front of Paige. "Eat up, dear."

"Thank you." Paige picked up the scone and took a bite. "You're such a wonderful baker, Clarissa. You'll have to give me the recipe for these too."

"Of course, dear." She took her seat. "I can email it to you."

Paige set her scone down and turned to Eli. "What did you want to talk to me about?"

"It can wait till later. Just sit, relax, have your supper and then we'll head back."

"How did your police business go?"

"Fine. Not much goes on in Moon Grove. It was just a minor issue."

She gave him a curious frown. "Oh, ok." What wasn't he telling her? It always felt as though there was more going on than he cared to admit.

When Paige finished, Eli stood up and eased back her chair. "Ready to go?"

"Mm hm." She got to her feet, brushing the scone

crumbs off her hands onto the plate. "Thank you for your hospitality, Clarissa. I really appreciate it."

The older woman waved the comment off. "Don't mention it, dear. I love the company."

The three walked into the entry hall and Eli helped Paige on with her jacket before shrugging into his.

Clarissa opened the door and a chill blast of frozen air rushed inside. "It's a cold one tonight."

"Yes, it is," Paige said with a shiver.

"Take care driving home and stay warm."

"We will." Eli waited for Paige to step onto the porch and head down the path before he leaned in to kiss his grandmother on the cheek and whisper in her ear. "Make sure you keep this place locked tight. And call me if there's any trouble."

"I will, dear. Goodnight." She waved to Paige who was standing on the path.

On the drive back Paige thought it was the perfect time to ask Eli about whether or not he was still having his dream. "Eli?"

He glanced at her sideways then returned his gaze to the dark, snow covered road. "Yes, Paige?"

"I want to ask you something." She clasped her hands in her lap and bit her bottom lip.

"What is it?"

"Since we've been sharing your house… have you had that dream?"

Eli thought about the question. Had he? He frowned. "I don't think so. Why?"

"Because I haven't either."

"That's strange, isn't it?"

"Yes, it is. I've grown so used to falling asleep and

waking up in fear it's become a nightly ritual." She turned her gaze to him. "What do you think it means?"

He now knew what it meant. Because she was his Alpha female and they were in such close proximity whatever caused the dreams didn't exist when they were together. "I'm not sure. What do you think?"

Paige shrugged. "I have absolutely no idea. Maybe we should sit down and compare our dreams... see if there's any similarities to them."

Eli gave her a sideward glance. "We can if you'd like. Do you really think it'll help?"

"I don't know. But it can't hurt, can it?"

"You're right. It can't hurt." Or could it? Eli knew he couldn't keep the truth from Paige for much longer and wondered how she would react to what he had to tell her.

Clarissa and Wil set about adding a double protection to the house. They tacked extra mistletoe and Wolfsbane around the inside of every door and window and sprinkled dried mountain ash tree powder across the front and back thresholds and in front of the cellar door. Clarissa stood in the entry hall with a white candle in her hand and called to the Goddess of Light for protection against the evil of the werewolf Elijah. If she asked for broader protection from all werewolves then Eli and his pack wouldn't be able to enter the house. Once the spell was cast, she dripped three drops of Wolfsbane oil into the flame to seal the spell and hoped it would hold.

"Do you think it'll work?" Wil asked, a worried frown creasing his weathered features.

"I hope so. It's the best I can do." She took his hand and led him into the kitchen for a cup of hot chocolate laced with verbena – also known in ancient Egyptian times as 'tears of Isis' – which would prevent Elijah from attacking them physically, if he returned tonight. They would need to ingest a lot more for it to work indefinitely though.

Eli came into the living room with two mugs in his hands, set them both down on the coffee table and sat beside Paige on the sofa. He'd redressed her head wound and they were both in their pajamas and robes, warm against the winter chill. Paige was comfortable sitting with Eli dressed ready for bed and realized it didn't feel weird at all. In fact, it felt nice.

"Do you want to tell me about your dream?" she asked, picking up her mug and taking a cautious sip of the black brew.

He gave her a curious frown. "I was hoping you might start. That way I can compare your dream to mine and tell you which parts are the same, if any."

"Oh, ok." She frowned and thought for a moment. Where to begin? "I'm usually running for my life through dense woods and something big is chasing me. I never see it but I know it's there. After a while I stumble and fall and it comes up on me... and that's when I wake up."

Eli considered what Paige had told him. Nothing appeared similar to his dream except the woods. But which woods? "The one component that seems to be the same is the woods."

"Tell me about your dream." She sipped her coffee and her eyes moved to his face, his gorgeous, handsome face and those mesmerizing eyes. Her heart trembled against her breastbone.

Eli realized that telling Paige about his dream and being completely honest with her would change everything. But he had no choice. They had to figure out what the dreams were trying to tell them. He had a feeling he already knew what Paige's dream meant – that his father was in pursuit of her to prevent them from uniting the bloodlines. But the blood trail in his nightmare made no sense at all, except that it led to Paige's parents' house. Did the blood represent what happened to her mom and dad?

"My dream is different. It's in the woods but I'm not being chased. I'm playing a game of chase with a little girl and she disappears into the trees. I feel afraid in the dream and I call after her. Then I hear a shrill scream and I see a blood trail…"

"Oh, my God!" Paige brought her hand up to her mouth, her eyes wide.

"As I follow the trail the blood gets heavier. I'm terrified at that point but feel compelled to follow it."

Paige sat her mug down on the coffee table and reached for Eli's hand. "Do you find out where it leads?"

Eli nodded. "To your parents' house."

Paige gasped and her body tightened. "My parents' house?"

"Yes." He liked the feel of her skin against his and squeezed her hand gently.

"But why?"

Eli shrugged. "I wish I knew."

"None of it makes any sense. I'm being chased by

something and you're chasing someone." Paige stared into his eyes. "Who are you chasing?"

Eli didn't want to answer the question. He wanted things to remain the way they were – Paige having no idea about the supernatural element of Moon Grove and him. He knew there was no other way, he had to tell her. "You, Paige. I'm chasing you."

Paige sat in silence, still holding Eli's hand, and tried to make sense of what he'd just told her. In his dream she was the little girl he was playing chase with. Obviously that stemmed back to their childhood friendship, but why would they be playing alone in the woods? And what about the blood trail? What did it mean?

"Paige?" Eli's voice broke into her thoughts.

She gazed up at him. "Yes?"

"I think I know who's chasing you in your dream." It was time for the truth.

"Who?" She frowned into his soulful, honey colored eyes.

"My father."

"I don't understand. How could it be your father? I always have the feeling that it's an animal of some kind."

"Remember the dream you had about your parents' house and those creatures you saw?"

Paige eased her hand out of his and pressed her spine into the sofa's backrest. Her stomach shrank into a tight knot of nerves and the overwhelming fear that she wasn't going to like what Eli was about to tell her crawled over her.

FORTY THREE

Elijah sped along the highway in his black Chevrolet Corvette, snow dusting the windshield like oversized, white confetti, the rhythmic beat of the wipers whooshing back forth across the glass. He was enraged that he hadn't been able to get the information he wanted about the ring from the old witch or that he was unable to dispatch the woman his son was in love with before he made a fatal, irreversible mistake. Fate. Destiny. Who needed it? When he'd arrived in Moon Grove he had a solid plan – to get his hands on the moonstone ring and vanish. He didn't want to be Alpha of the town he just wanted the power of the ring. He hadn't even considered the possibility that his son would oppose him. Blood was meant to be thicker than water, wasn't it?

Ok, he could understand why his son was angry with him for leaving. That he harbored resentment for him not being around while he was growing up. That he was on his own when his mother died. Elijah felt a sliver of guilt over her death but shrugged it off. Nothing would deter him from doing what he had come to his old hometown to do – get his hands on that ring.

He took the exit ramp heading to a cabin he'd rented in a remote location in the outlining forest miles from the boundary of Moon Grove. It had been his sanctuary for the past couple of months while he developed his scheme to take back what was rightfully his. Once he had the ring he would be unstoppable. The power it possessed was all that he craved. He made a left turn onto the slick, dark road and continued west. The snow fall picked up and he flicked the wipers to full speed, his Lycan vision steadfast on the black void ahead of him, the high beam of the headlights carving twin circles of brightness into the distance.

Something darted across his path and he slammed on the brakes to avoid a collision. The sports car lost traction, slid across the slippery road, skidded off the shoulder and crashed into the large trunk of a tall pine tree.

Eli stared into Paige's eyes uncertain of how to impart what he had to tell her. After everything that had already happened, this would be the insult to injury. But he had no choice now. With his father in town hell bent on ending her life, Eli had to do whatever he could to protect her. Was this the solution to their current situation? He wasn't sure. How could she be his Alpha female? Was it their bond, their connection to the supernatural world that had drawn her back to Moon Grove?

He took her hand in his and she didn't pull back this time. "There are things about Moon Grove that you know nothing about."

There was that unsettling phrase from her dream again.

She swallowed the anxiety lodged in her throat, her heart beating that little bit faster. "What things?"

"Let me ask you a question."

She gave him a dubious stare. "All… right."

"Do you have any belief in the supernatural?"

Paige leaned back and frowned into his eyes. "You mean like spirits and demons and werewolves?"

He nodded.

She shrugged. "No, I don't. Why?"

"There's an underlying current in Moon Grove. It's…"

"Wait. What do you mean by underlying current? Are you saying there are demons here?"

"No. Just listen, ok? The wolf that chased you in the woods that night… *was* my father." There was no way to sugar coat it.

Paige's frown deepened. "That's not funny, Eli. After everything I've been through…"

He squeezed her hand. "Paige, I'm serious."

"I don't believe you. I thought you of all people understood." She pulled her hand free and folded her arms.

"Paige, look at me."

She wouldn't.

He reached out and turned her face to him. The gold shimmer ran across his eyes.

Her heartbeat sped up and she could feel the color drain from her face. "That's what I saw in my dream."

"Because I'm Lycan."

"What's that?"

"I'm a wolf – a werewolf."

When Elijah came to in his wrecked convertible twenty minutes later, he was still in his seatbelt in the driver's seat. The impact had crushed the hood of his car into the dashboard and he was trapped. He'd been traveling way above the speed limit and when he'd braked the car had spun out of control. His left leg was wedged amongst the twisted metal and he couldn't move it. He could smell and feel the warm, wet sensation of blood trickling down his shin and a sharp, jagged bolt of pain shot up his thigh. He was a Lycan Goddammit! He could get out of this.

The realization that in his weakened state he might not be able to free himself sent a nervous quiver through his gut. What could he do? Wait in the freezing cold until a car came by, if a car came by? The area was remote. That's why he'd chosen it. Elijah tried to ease his tall frame back in the seat so he could wrench his leg free from the wreckage, but when he attempted to do it the excruciating trail of pain exploded. His agonized howl echoed around the tall, snowcapped trees, his breath coming in short bursts. He hated pain, especially in his human form.

He summoned his inner wolf.

His eyes shimmered and glowed fiery red, his face elongated, the jawbones cracking and shifting into place, his fingers stretched into clawed talons… and then nothing. Elijah let out a frustrated roar. Why couldn't he turn? He panted. The pain had increased tenfold and was radiating up his left thigh. He had to get free.

A bright light shone into the car from behind and his eyes darted to the rearview mirror. Someone had pulled over. They were coming to help him. His heart felt elated and despite the immense pain a smile slid across his face.

Once he was free he'd devour his aide to gain his strength and make use of their car as soon as he was able to drive.

"Are there more of your kind?" Paige was stunned. As a psychologist she believed in the tangible. She had no idea creatures like Eli and his father existed and she wasn't sure she wanted to know.

Eli could see the fear in her eyes. The way she looked at him now was different. "Yes. I have a pack."

"Who's in your... pack?"

"There are far more important things to discuss than who's in my pack."

"I'd like to know."

Eli gave her a curious frown. Did she want to know for the right reasons? "Ok. Bobby, Rebecca, Paul and Craig whom you've already met." He hadn't had time to tell her about Craig's death yet. "And Ryan Hollis."

Her eyes widened. "The mechanic?"

He nodded.

She inhaled a deep breath and released it slowly. Was any of this real? "What do I have to do with all of this?"

That was going to be more difficult to explain.

Elijah was out of luck. The guy had called the emergency services and they had arrived, red and blue lights pulsing color into the dark atmosphere around them. Dammit! He'd need sustenance once he was free so he could heal.

After half an hour of hacking at the twisted metal his

leg was free. It had already started to heal but wouldn't mend completely without human blood and flesh. The paramedics wanted to take him to the medical center in the next town but he refused. "Just bandage me up and take me home."

"You need to be in the hospital. You've lost a lot of blood and that wound needs to be stitched. And you'll need antibiotics to prevent infection," the pretty, blonde paramedic told him. Bernadette, her white and black name tag displayed.

Mm, she would be a delicious morsel. He could smell her blood and his mouth salivated. He swallowed. "I appreciate your concern but I have other important matters to take care of. I cannot go to the hospital."

She gave him a serious frown. "If infection sets in you could lose your leg. I'm sure you wouldn't want that, would you?"

What a stupid question.

"No, of course not." He gave her a charming smile. "But I can assure you I'll be fine. I'll take good care of it. I just need to get home." He had a supply of blood and raw meat in the refrigerator that would have to suffice, seeing as he couldn't eat fresh meat.

She shook her bobbed, golden locks. "Ok. I'll do what I can but the onus is all yours."

Elijah raised his hand as if swearing on a bible. "I take full responsibility."

How could he explain everything to Paige so she wouldn't freak out? If he told her that once they made love she would turn into a Lycanthrope she would pack up and move back to Washington. And he couldn't blame her. Eli sighed. Why did any of this have to happen now? As far as he was concerned destiny was overrated. The thought crossed his mind: Was he in love with her because of his own feelings or was it because of the bond they shared? He hoped his feelings were real and not preconceived by fate.

"Paige... what I have to tell you is going to be difficult to understand. It's... I didn't even know about it until recently. Wil Wallace told me."

"Told you what, Eli?" They were still holding hands and she eased hers out of his and rested it on top.

"That you and I were destined to be together. That it was predetermined before we were even born." A lightbulb came on in his head and he understood what his dream meant, at least most of it. The blood trail still didn't make sense yet, but he was sure it would soon.

"What do you mean?"

"Your father was..."

Paige jumped up off the sofa. "Don't tell me my dad was Lycan too." Tears stung the backs of her eyes. "Is that why he was killed?"

Eli stood up, came around the coffee table and pulled her into his arms. "I think your parents' deaths had something to do with the moonstone ring. And I think my father was the person your dad was meant to deliver it to, only someone returned it to the pack, then years later, to protect the town, Jake somehow got his hands on it and hid it away so no one would find it."

Paige looked up at him. "How?"

"I don't know. I guess that's a question we'll never have an answer to."

"I can't believe my dad was a... a..."

"Werewolf?"

The sudden epiphany caused Paige's body to tremble. "I have his blood. Am I Lycan too?"

Eli gave her a thin, heartfelt smile. He hated having to tell her. "Yes, Paige, you will be."

"Will be?" She stepped backwards out of his comforting embrace. "What do you mean?" Her heart raced now. What more could she discover about herself that she didn't know? She was a werewolf descendant, her father had been one, and Eli and his father were too. It all seemed like another horrible nightmare. Maybe she'd wake up and it would be just that. She closed her eyes and sighed. Unfortunately, it was real.

Eli held out his hand. "Come and sit down." She took his hand and he led her back to the sofa. How could he tell her that once they made love her whole world would change forever?

The ambulance eased up to the front porch of the wood cabin and stopped. Both paramedics jumped down out of the cab and rounded the back. Opening the double doors of the vehicle, Bernadette climbed up and secured Elijah to the stretcher with safety belts before they lifted him down. "Feeling ok? she asked.

He'd be given a shot of morphine for the pain and was feeling pretty cruisy. He nodded.

"We'll get you inside and settled. Can I have the keys?"

"Door's not locked. Who'd bother way out here?" he answered through the oxygen mask.

"Ok, great. I'll just go open the door and be right back."

Once inside, they settled Elijah on his bed and Bernadette checked the dressings and his vitals. "All set. We've left a pack in the bathroom so you can keep the wound clean and dressed. That has to be done daily. The stiches will need to come out in a week and you'll have to make a trip to the medical center for that. Do you need someone to pick you up?"

"No, I'll get a friend to take me," he lied. By tomorrow the wound would be well healed.

"All right then, take care." She headed for the door.

"Bernadette?" Her blood and flesh were intoxicating and his body was reacting to it. If he didn't let her leave soon he wouldn't be accountable for his actions.

She turned around. "Yes?"

He swallowed the saliva building on his tongue. "Thank you for your help. I appreciate it."

"You're welcome." She smiled and continued out the door.

If only he could've gotten rid of that ambulance. He would have devoured them both.

Ryan was on the phone to Eli the moment he returned home and back to human form. "Eli? It's me. I know where Elijah is and he's incapacitated."

"How do you know that?"

"Because I was the one that incapacitated him."

"How?"

"I was out for a run and I could smell his scent. I spotted the sports car traveling out to that cabin on Old Wolf Ridge Road so I followed it to make sure it was him. Anyways, I raced ahead and got a few hundred feet in front then darted out onto the road. He ran off the shoulder and into a tree."

"And he was injured?"

"Yeah. Pretty bad too. A driver saw the lights and pulled over and called 911. I was hoping Elijah would be dead, but no. Sorry, Eli, I know he's your father and all."

"That has nothing to do with it. Call the others and meet me at the church. We need to plan how we're going to get rid of him while he's weak."

FORTY FOUR

"I'm sorry, Paige, I have to go out for a while. Let's finish this when I get back, ok? In the meantime, you might want to get some sleep. Sun's going to be up in a few hours. He crossed the room and shrugged into his jacket then pressed his police issue Stetson onto his head and opened the front door.

Paige followed him across the living room. "Do you know when you'll be back?"

"Not at the moment, no. I'm sorry our conversation was cut short. I know you want answers."

"Yes, I do, but I understand this is important. Finding your father will ensure our safety."

He smiled and rested his hand on her arm. "Thank you for understanding."

"Just be safe."

"I will." He stepped out onto the porch. "Lock up."

Paige nodded and waited until he drove away before closing the door and turning the keys in the deadbolts. She sighed as she headed for her room. She felt exhausted, and nothing had been resolved between her and Eli. It was difficult getting her mind around him being a supernatural creature – that *she* was a supernatural creature. How could something like this happen in the twenty-first century?

She turned off the light in the hallway and stepped into the room that had once been Eli's childhood bedroom. She hadn't remembered his house or his mom and she felt a pang of guilt. At least the room had a queen-sized bed in it now. Paige wouldn't have been able to sleep in a single bed. She turned back the covers and climbed into the warmth of the electric blanket. Soon her eyes closed and she drifted into another frightening dream…

Paige was racing through the woods only she wasn't on two feet. She seemed to be flying through the trees on all fours, clawing at the underbrush as she sped faster and faster into the dark, everything hurtling past her in a blur. Eli was beside her in wolf form. She knew it was him by his honey colored eyes and fur color. Others were following them. Four more wolves. When they reached the end of the trees they all stood up. Her parents' house was across the field. Why were they here?

They stepped out of the dense forest into the haze of the gloomy day and headed for the house. Paige could feel her body stiffen. She didn't want to go into the decayed remains. She wanted to forget what she couldn't remember. Her mom and dad had died in that house and she wanted it torn down – gone for good.

As they crossed the overgrown yard they turned into human form each standing naked in front of the abandoned building. Eli held out his hand and Paige reached for it. "Let's go inside."

Her stomach tightened, she wanted to remain outside where it was safe.

Eli led her to the porch in all his naked glory and Paige

felt her cheeks flush when he turned to face her. She longed for them to make love again like they had when she'd emerged a wolf.

Paige awoke, her heart thumping against her ribs, her body trembling. If she and Eli made love she would turn into a werewolf!

She threw back the covers and stumbled out of bed. She needed a drink of water. No, this time she needed something stronger. Paige headed to the living room, flicked on the light and walked across to the bureau sitting against the wall beside the sofa. She snapped open the cap on the new bottle of whiskey, turned over a glass and poured half a shot. She downed it in one mouthful and coughed as the heat slid into her belly. She was still shaking.

What should she do? Pack up and leave? How could she after everything she'd learned? And, she realized, she was in love with Eli. Was it the magnetic pull of the werewolf gene or was it actual love? She hoped her feelings were real. She poured herself another shot and spilled it down the side of the glass onto the bureau. A pool of alcohol spread across the top. "Oh, shoot!"

Paige opened one of the bureau doors to see if there was anything inside to wipe up the spill. There wasn't. She opened the bottom drawer, then the middle, then the top drawer and frowned at the upturned photo frame sitting inside. She picked up the picture. Eli was married! Where was his wife?

The pointed corner of a piece of paper peeked out from the back of the frame. Paige eased it out from behind the cover and opened it. Michelle Blackwood's death certificate. Paige felt the prickle of discomfort, as though she were violating Eli's personal life, so she refolded the document, squeezed it back into its hiding place and returned the photo to the drawer. As she walked to the kitchen to grab a cloth to clean up the spill she promised herself never to bring it up. She'd wait until he wanted to tell her. That one line on the certificate surfaced in her mind and she shivered. Cause of death – an animal attack.

Eli and his pack circled the outside of the cabin without a sound. They'd rubbed pine oil all over themselves in the hope that it would help reduce their scent and hide it from Elijah when they turned into wolf form. Bobby had called the medical center and found out that Eli's father had sustained a serious gash to his left leg which had required stitches. He'd been treated at the scene, as he didn't want to go to the center, and was delivered back to his residence afterward. He was on heavy medication for the pain which should see him sleeping until the next morning.

If he was human.

Which room was he in? Eli stepped onto the front porch and peered through the window. No sign of Elijah. Hopefully the meds had done their job and he was asleep. It would make their task of killing him that much easier.

The others turned into wolf form and stood off to the left side of the cabin waiting for Eli's order.

After moving around the entire building, he discovered that his father wasn't in the house. He shouldered the door and rushed inside, checking the bedroom, bathroom, toilet and kitchen. Empty blood bags and remnants of bloody, raw meat lay on the stainless steel sink. His father had rejuvenated and was on his way to Paige. Eli raced out of the cabin. "We need to get back to Moon Grove… now!"

FORTY FIVE

Eli pressed the pedal to the metal as his four wheel drive lurched forward and sped along the highway. He had to get back to Moon Grove before Elijah had a chance to get to Paige. He told his team he needed to face his father alone despite their opposition. "Was he crazy?" Bobby had said. "Did he want to get himself killed?" Rebecca had added. No, he didn't want to get himself killed but he had to do this on his own. He couldn't risk any more lives.

He screeched to a stop outside Clarissa's and stalked up the path to the porch. He'd called to tell her where the moonstone ring was and had asked her to meet him out front with it.

When she opened the door she hesitated before placing the small, black bag in the palm of his hand. "I hope you know what you're doing, Eli. Giving Elijah that ring is a dangerous move."

"I know, but I don't have a choice. I only hope I'm not too late and that he'll agree to spare Paige's life for it."

Eli raced down the path, climbed into the idling Jeep and sped away.

As he drove toward his property his heart thumped against his ribs. What if he was too late? *What if Elijah has already killed Paige?* Tears stung his eyes and he blinked them back. *No, he's too shrewd for that. He'll want to make a trade seeing as he's sure I have the ring.*

The four wheel drive hurtled along the driveway and screamed to a stop outside Eli's front door. When Paige opened it he was shocked.

"Are... are you ok?" he asked, rushing up to her.

"Yes. Why?" She frowned up at him then ran her anxious gaze around the dark yard. "Is everything all right?"

He took her by the arm, led her into the house and closed and bolted both front doors. "My father is on his way here. I thought he would've been here by now. I thought..."

Paige touched his anxious face. "It's ok. I'm fine." She smiled up at him.

"Grab some things. We need to go to Clarissa's."

"Why? Aren't we safe here?"

"We'll be safer there. She has certain precautions in place around the house.

"What kind of precautions?"

"It would take too long to explain right now. Let's just go."

"Ok, give me five minutes."

"Be quick." While Paige was in her room packing Eli rushed down the hallway to his. He threw some clothes into a sports bag and was back in the living room in minutes. "Come on, Paige, we have to go."

"I'm ready." She grabbed her coat and they headed out the door.

Eli pressed the Bluetooth button on the console and called Clarissa's number to let her know they were on their way. No answer. "That's odd. I know she's there." A cold lump of fear sank into the pit of his stomach and he pressed the accelerator to the floor.

He called the station. Bobby picked up on the second ring. "Moon Grove Sheriff's Depart…"

"Bobby. We need to get back to Clarissa's ASAP!"

"Understood. Meet you there."

By the time Eli pulled into his grandmother's driveway the sun was almost up. The sky was a hazy, yellow gray and the snow had turned to a drizzle. Bobby and the others arrived within minutes and they converged on Eli's Jeep.

"Is Elijah inside?" Ryan asked, his eyes roaming the front of the house.

"I'm not sure. All I know is no one is picking up when I call." Eli pushed open the car door and climbed out. "I thought he'd go after Paige but when he didn't the only other person I could think of was my grandmother. I think he knows I have the ring, maybe he realized I hid it here."

"You hid the ring here?" Paul asked. "That wasn't a wise move, Eli. My dad told me it lets off some kind of supernatural vibration. Didn't you know that?"

Eli frowned at him. "No, I didn't." So that meant his father knew the ring was in the house all along. Why hadn't he taken it when he broke in before? Something slithered in Eli's gut and he knew the answer. Because he wanted a reason to come back and finish what he'd started, to kill Clarissa and Wil. "We need to be inside now!"

He told Paige to stay locked in the four wheel drive while he and his pack entered the house. She wasn't about to argue. She had no intention of coming face to face with Elijah.

The front door wasn't locked, which in itself was unusual, and the Wolfsbane above the door was lying on the welcome mat. The spell his grandmother had cast against Elijah had failed. How had he gained more power since he'd been gone? Was he the Alpha of another pack somewhere? That would explain his strength. Eli was stronger, now he was an Alpha, but he still didn't have the power his father had.

Eli swept the Wolfsbane off the mat with the toe of his boot, drew his weapon loaded with silver and eased the front door open. The house had been turned upside down. Furniture and other items were scattered throughout the downstairs rooms. "Clary? Wil?" he called as he and the others stepped into the entry hall. Could they be downstairs in the panic room? He flew down the cellar stairs. The door to the room lay wide open. Where were his grandmother and Wil? He raced back up the stairs. "No one's down there. Check the bedrooms."

Ryan and Paul took the stairs two at a time and disappeared into the hallway. Within seconds Ryan appeared at the top of the railing. "Nothing."

Rebecca headed into the kitchen. "Eli!"

Eli raced through the door and was confronted with Wil lying in a pool of blood on the linoleum floor, his throat ripped out. He gave a heavy sigh. There was no point checking for a pulse, he knew the old man was dead. The chair Clarissa liked to sit on had been knocked over and the back door was wide open.

Elijah had taken her and that meant only one thing. He'd be hearing from his father soon.

As the thought entered his head his cell phone chimed. No Caller ID. He pressed the dot on the screen.

"Don't hurt my grandmother."

"Now why would I do that? She's my guarantee that you'll give me what I want."

"When and where?" Eli had no time to argue he needed to make the trade and get his grandmother back safely.

"The church. Tonight. 8 PM sharp." The line went dead.

"Dammit!"

Rebecca stood with her hands on her hips and gave him a frustrated scowl. "He has her, doesn't he?"

Eli nodded. "Yes."

"So what are we going to do about that?" Bobby asked, arms folded across his muscular chest.

"We're going to play his game with one twist. We'll get there ahead of time and set a trap for him. I wanted to do this alone but now I know I can't. I need your help."

"You've got it," Paul said. "Always."

Eli sighed and his gaze ran around his team. "Thank you."

"No need. That's what we do. We're a pack and you're our Alpha, it's a done deal," Ryan added.

Eli glanced over his shoulder at the dead man lying on the floor. "But first we need to lay Wil to rest and clean up before Clary comes home."

Paul and Bobby went out to the police Jeep and brought in a black tarpaulin, crime scene cleaners and some gloves. They set to work wrapping Wil's body in the tarp and then cleaning the kitchen and rearranging the upturned furniture. Eli, Ryan and Rebecca went through the rest of the house and replaced the photos, ornaments and other paraphernalia before setting the furniture back in place. By the time they finished the house looked as though it had never been disturbed. All the better for Clarissa when she got back. Losing Wil would be difficult enough for her to cope with. Eli knew they cared for each other.

Paige's phone jingled while she waited in the Jeep. She'd offered to help with the cleanup but Eli said it was better for her to remain in the car. She knew why. It was because Wil Wallace's body was in the house. How many more people had to die before Elijah was stopped? She answered the call.

"Hello?"

"Paige O'Connell?"

She frowned. "Yes, who's this?"

"Jackie Gilbert from the Moon Grove Postal Service. I just found a letter with your name on it. It appears it's been sitting here for a few weeks. I don't understand why it wasn't delivered to your address."

"A letter? Do you know who it's from?"

She turned the thick envelope over. "Yes, it's from Wendy Ellis."

Paige's blood ran cold.

FORTY SIX

Paige was out of the car and at the front door in seconds. "Eli? Eli, where are you?" She stepped across Clarissa's threshold into the entry hall, her eyes roaming the living room then the dining room. Eli emerged from the kitchen.

"What's wrong?" He walked up to her blocking her view into the other room.

"Can I borrow your Jeep?" she asked, breathless.

"Why? Where are you going?" He frowned into her eyes.

"I just got a call from the post office in town. There's a letter there for me from Wendy Ellis."

Eli's eyebrows rose. "Wendy? How is that possible?"

"Apparently, it's been there for a few weeks."

"I'm coming with you."

"There's no need, I can go. I'll be in a public place so I'll be fine."

Eli shook his head. Not only did he not want Paige wandering off alone, he was curious about what Wendy had written in her letter. "Let me tell the others and we'll leave."

Paige climbed back into the car and waited.

Three minutes later Eli crossed the lawn and climbed in beside her. "Ok, let's go get that letter."

Redmond placed the receiver into its base and gave a frustrated sigh. Couldn't anyone do what he asked without messing it up? He pushed back his plush, executive office chair and walked over to the window. Gazing down at the main street and the accumulating car and pedestrian traffic he wondered when this whole, inconvenient situation would be resolved. Craig, as it turned out, had been a double agent. Who could've guessed that Elijah Blackwood would return to Moon Grove more deranged than when he'd departed? These new turn of events put the town and its residents in jeopardy and something had to be done about it, which is what he'd been trying to do when one of his men had been killed. He could only assume by Elijah's hand. Who else could it be?

His phone rang and he rushed across the expansive office to answer it. "Hello?"

"Redmond. Long time no see."

A heavy weight sank into the Mayor's gut. "Elijah, what a…"

"Cut the crap, Ross. You and I know there's no love lost between us so don't bother saying it's a pleasant surprise because we both know that would be a lie."

The Mayor swallowed hard. "What do you want?"

A devious chuckled on the other end of the line sent a chill up Ross's spine. "You always were one to get straight to the point."

A bell tinkled above the door as Paige pushed it open and stepped into the tiny post office. No one was behind the high, dark wood desk but another bell sat on counter – the round, domed kind with the button on top. Paige wondered why someone hadn't heard the tinkle when they entered. Her hand hovered over the brass device and she was about to ding it when a woman popped up from the other side. "Oh, hello. I didn't hear you come in." She had a set of white headphones in her ears and plucked one out. "You must be Paige O'Connell." She smiled and held out her hand. "Jackie."

Paige shook it. "Nice to meet you."

Jackie's eyes moved to Eli. "How are things, Sheriff?"

"Good. How are things with you?"

"Can't complain."

Paige cleared her throat. "Uh, you said you had a letter for me?"

Jackie snapped her fingers and rolled her eyes. "Oh, yes, that's right. Let me just go out back and get it for you. Won't be a tick."

Eli and Paige's eyes met but neither spoke. For some reason that she couldn't explain the post office gave Paige a unsettling vibe. It was like stepping back in time, but not in a good way.

Jackie returned with the letter in hand. "I'll need you to sign for it 'cause it's registered mail."

"Do you have any idea why it wasn't delivered?"

Jackie shrugged. "Sorry, no. It was mixed up in a pile of unclaimed mail. Don't know how that happened." She gave an embarrassed smile, swung the ledger around on the counter and pointed to where Paige had to sign. "If you'll put your autograph right there, I can give you your letter."

Paige scribbled her signature onto the line, turned the book back around and held out her hand.

"I also need to see a form of ID with your signature on it."

Paige huffed out a frustrated breath. After the postal service not delivering her registered letter to her they were still prepared to go through the protocol before handing it over. She passed her license to the woman.

Jackie scrutinized the picture, comparing it to Paige, then checked to see if the signatures matched. "Ok. Everything appears to be in order." She passed the envelope to Paige.

"Thank you." Paige ran her eyes over it wondering what the contents would hold. She wasn't about to open the letter in the post office, although she could see that Jackie was keen to find out what was inside. "Can I have my license back, please?"

Jackie glanced down at the counter. "Oh, sure. Sorry." She handed it back. "Have a nice day."

Eli opened the door and they stepped outside. "Want to have a coffee at the inn while you read it?"

"I think I'll wait until later. I'd like to look at it alone. I hope you understand."

Eli needed to know what the journalist had compiled in her obviously thick dossier on Moon Grove. "Sure. Do what you have to."

"Thanks." She pocketed the letter and they headed back to the Jeep.

"I'm making a trade. Eli's grandmother for the moonstone ring." Elijah needed help and knew he could count on the Mayor. Redmond was a coward who liked to control the people beneath him and Elijah knew he could manipulate him into doing what he wanted because he knew the workings of Ross's mind. He hated to admit it but they were similar creatures.

"Why are you telling me this?" Ross eased his body into his office chair, knees buzzing, his heart rate kicking up several notches. He didn't want to know.

"Because I want your help."

"Wait. No, I can't."

"You can and you *will*. You owe me for getting rid of Greg. Remember that little task?"

Redmond swallowed the lump threatening to choke him and coughed. "We agreed never to bring that up again. No one knows I've had contact with you."

"Well it would be a shame if they found out somehow, wouldn't it?"

"What kind of help do you need?"

"Your wolves."

"They're not *my* wolves."

"Oh, come on, Ross, do you think I'm an idiot? They're on your payroll. They do what you tell them to do."

"That doesn't make them mine. They come and go as they please."

"Well, I want them at the church by eight o'clock tonight."

"I'll see what I can do." Redmond loosened his tie and

unbuttoned the neck of his white business shirt, sweat beading on his brow.

"No, you'll make sure they're there. It's time to pay up for services rendered. Which reminds me, I also did you favor number two by offing the journalist for you."

"Can we not discuss it over the phone?" The Mayor's eyes darted to his open office door and he got up, crossed the room and closed it. "Why do you want them at the church?"

"That's for me to know." Elijah chuckled, deep and throaty. "You wouldn't want to be implicated in what I have in mind, would you?"

No, I wouldn't. "All right. I'll organize it." Ross hated taking orders from anyone, especially Elijah Blackwood, but he knew his secrets. He'd had the previous Mayor killed and also Wendy Ellis for sticking her nose into matters which didn't concern her. So, he was at the mercy of a deranged psychopath, because no one could ever find out what he'd done.

FORTY SEVEN

Eli pulled the four wheel drive into the station parking lot and climbed out. He rounded the rear of the Jeep, opened Paige's door and helped her down. Snow had begun to fall again. It was going to be a white Christmas. Christmas? Who could think about that at a time like this? It was the holidays but no one could get into the festive spirit with what was going on. The pair headed around to the front door.

Bobby opened it as they approached. "Everything's been taken care of, boss. Clarissa's house is as clean as a whistle."

"Thanks, Bob. Tell the others I appreciate it."

"They know already." He stepped aside to make room for them to enter the warm office.

Paige shivered as she stepped into the snug environment and the heat caressed her cheeks. It was freezing outside. "Hi, Rosemarie, how are you?"

The receptionist stopped typing on the computer and gave Paige a pleasant smile. "I'm good. How're you, hon? Looking forward to Christmas?"

Paige shrugged out of her jacket, took off her knit cap

and peeled her woolly gloves from her hands. "I wish I could say I've had time to get into the holiday spirit but I haven't. Maybe later."

The smile evaporated from Rosemarie's face. She knew exactly what Paige meant. The frightful situation with Elijah was hard to bear. She decided to change the subject. "Want some hot chocolate? I just made a pot."

"Thanks. That would be nice."

Eli walked Paige through to his office. "Have a seat. I'll be right back."

Paige sat down and waited, her eyes roaming the untidy space. Maybe one day, when all of this was over, she'd come in and do a cleanup for Eli. She didn't think he'd mind.

Eli returned to the office with two mugs of hot chocolate, handed one to Paige and sat down behind his desk. "Rosemarie said 'Enjoy.'"

"Thank you." She took a sip. "Mm, it's good."

"Yeah, she says it's a secret recipe but it all tastes the same to me. Don't tell her I said that." He gave her one of his heart-stopping smiles and took a generous sip.

"What do you plan to do about your father? I mean about the meeting tonight?"

"We're going to set a trap for him. We have to stop him. He cannot get his hands on the ring. If he does he'll be unstoppable and Moon Grove will be in danger."

"What are you going to do?"

"The others are heading to church in a while to set things up for tonight. I don't think he'll come alone. I'm sure he's got a pack of his own or knows of other wolves around the area. We'll use what hasn't been tried so far."

"And that is?" Paige set her mug down on the desk.

"How do you know it'll work? What if something goes wrong?"

"All werewolves have an aversion to silver. The pack is going into the church to cover every internal door handle, window frame and lock and any other way out with pure silver. They'll also set up a net in the rafters and at some point we'll lure him underneath it and confine him. It won't kill him but it will incapacitate him long enough for us to bind him with silver chains. It will weaken him and he'll be trapped. Then we'll deal with him."

"Aren't you and your pack sensitive to silver too? What about all of you?"

"We have protective gloves so we won't be in contact with it."

"Do you think he'll bring Clarissa with him? How will you know where to find her, if he doesn't?"

Eli sighed. "No, I don't think he'll bring her. He's too shrewd to put himself in a dangerous situation. Once we have him contained we'll make him tell us where she is."

A worried frown crossed her pretty face. "By what you've told me he seems incredibly strong. Are you sure you're going to be able to subdue him?"

"Nothing's guaranteed. What I can guarantee is that he's not getting out of there alive."

Paige picked up her mug of hot chocolate. "I hope your plan works out. I'd like to get my life back to normal, if I can. Being afraid all the time is unhealthy."

"I know, and that's why we're doing this. It needs to end tonight." Eli remembered that he hadn't finished telling Paige about their connection to each other. He knew now wasn't the time, but he would have to once the situation with his father was dealt with.

Rosemarie's head popped around the open doorway. "Want some cookies to go with the hot chocolate?"

Eli smiled. "Thanks, Rosy."

Her face brightened. "Be right back."

Paige's gaze moved from the doorway to Eli. "Rosemarie is such a lovely person. Does she know about you and the others?"

"Yeah, she's been with us for a long while now. Most of the people in Moon Grove are aware. There are only a few who know nothing about us."

"Is it difficult keeping it a secret?"

"Sometimes."

"Are you governed by the moon?" She remembered reading a paranormal romance once and in it werewolves could only change during a full moon and she wondered if fiction held some fact.

"No, we're not. We can change at will. Only those who've been bitten turn on the full moon and that's only until they gain control of their wolf."

"Oh, ok."

Rosemarie returned with the plate of homemade cookies and set it down in front of them. "Eli's the best Alpha this town's ever had. And he's a good soul, too."

Paige believed that about him. She knew he was a decent person. "Thanks for the cookies, Rosemarie. And, yes, I agree with you." Her eyes moved to him. "He is a good man and I trust him with my life."

The receptionist's gaze met Eli's and her cheeks flushed. She hoped he didn't mind her telling Paige what she thought of him.

"I appreciate the sentiment, Rosy. Thank you." He

gave the woman a warm smile. She was family as far as he was concerned.

"It's the truth." Rosemarie's cheeks reddened even more and she backed out of the office.

"She has a lot of respect for you, doesn't she?" Paige picked up an oatmeal cookie from off the plate and bit into it. It was delicious.

"Yeah, she does." He reached for a cookie and dunked it into his hot chocolate.

Paige glanced over her shoulder. "Where's Craig?"

With all the drama Eli had forgotten to remember to tell her about his death.

"Uh, Craig was working for my father and…"

Paige's face paled. "He's dead, isn't he?"

Eli nodded.

"Was he one of the men that broke into my house?" Paige was connecting the pieces.

"I think so. Elijah had them looking for the moonstone ring. I also think they were the shooters out at your parents' place that day."

"So who was the other person?"

"We don't know, but I'd say he met the same fate as Craig. Elijah wouldn't want loose ends."

"How awful." Paige's body stiffened. Elijah was a true maniac and even though she hadn't come face to face with him he terrified her.

FORTY EIGHT

With everything that had happened in the last few hours, Paige had forgotten all about the letter she'd left in her jacket. She crossed the room and slid the envelope out of the right hand pocket. Staring at the handwriting on the front, a pang of sadness squeezed her heart. Poor Wendy had died because of the secrets the town held.

She walked back into the kitchen and sat at the table, her mug of coffee cooling as she slit the envelope open with a knife and pulled out the folded papers. Her eyes ran over the neat cursive script and her heart did a little shudder. What information did the letter hold? She began to read…

Dear Paige,

If you're reading this letter then something has happened to me. I suppose it was inevitable, given my line of work, that something would one day. I've been looking into the events of Moon Grove for many years, the disappearances, the accidental deaths and animal attacks, and despite what you may think after you read this, everything I'm about to tell is true. My reason for moving here was to investigate what I'd discovered. I've attached copies of certain records to prove it. These documents were entrusted to me by someone close to Ross Redmond and the town council and this person's identity has to remain secret otherwise they would share my fate. I'm sorry I can't tell you who it is, but if you figure it out please be discreet.

You need to be careful of Eli Blackwood. He is not what he appears to be. He comes from a long line of supernatural creatures to which he was born. I know this may not make any sense to you right now, but believe me it will over time. Your father was also part of their world and you… you share his Lycan bloodline. From what I've discovered, you and Eli are fated to be together. You are his Alpha female.

I know all of this sounds absurd, crazy even, but it isn't.

Lycanthropes, werewolves, names associated with the creatures I'm talking about have been here longer than we have. The Mayor has a pack working for him, although he isn't one himself. Eli's father left Moon Grove because he couldn't be the Alpha here, so I assume he went in search of his own pack elsewhere. They gain strength in numbers, Paige. You need to be aware of that.

There is a wolf pack heirloom, a moonstone ring, which is very powerful in the wrong hands. It's been missing for a decade and some believe your uncle Jake hid it. I believe Eli's father may be on his way back to claim it. He's a dangerous man, for want of a more appropriate word. Please be careful! Your life depends on it. If I were you I'd be putting as much distance between me and Moon Grove as I could. Pity I hadn't taken my own advice. Look over the documents; don't just think it's the ramblings of a fanatical journalist. My death should declare the truth of what I've told you. Be safe, Paige, and do whatever it takes to stay that way.

Regards

Wendy

Paige knew everything in the letter was true. But she did trust Eli. She knew he wasn't like his father and that she could depend on him. She unfolded the documents and read each one with care. A copy of Eli's birth certificate with another document attached declaring he was Lycan. His mother's death certificate – she had passed away from a blood disorder. Was she Lycan, too? Paige had assumed it was cancer.

Information about Ross Redmond and how he'd hired Elijah Blackwood to murder Greg Harrison, the former Mayor of Moon Grove, and that Wendy believed he would be her assassin too. The church on the hill held Lycan ceremonies that no one in the town was aware of. It reminded her of what she'd said to Eli about the Masonic Temple.

There had been disturbing deaths within the town, unexplained horrors that had been covered up to prevent an external investigation. Also among the papers in her hand was a copy of the police report about her parents' disappearance only this particular document stated that the investigating officer wasn't sure if the parents were deceased as there had been no bodies at the scene or the nearby woods. Wil Wallace's signature was at the bottom. What had he meant by that? She would never know the answer now that he'd been killed by Eli's father.

A shiver ran through her. She hated being alone in the middle of nowhere, despite the precautionary measures Eli had taken to secure his home. She prayed he and the others would be all right. Tonight could mean the end of all their woes or just the beginning of a far more serious scenario. Paige poured her cold coffee down the drain and sat the mug in the sink then headed to her room. She'd put the letter in a place where no one would think to look… in the freezer underneath the frozen meat.

She showered and changed into something warmer. The early evening had cooled down even more than the afternoon, if that were possible, and she put on two sweaters and two pairs of black leggings plus two pairs of socks. Another shiver ran through her and she wondered what had gotten her so on edge. It had to be the meeting between Eli and his father, what else could it be?

Paige knew she wouldn't sleep so there was no point in trying. She sat down on the sofa, picked up the remote control and pressed the red button. The television flashed to life. The gusty breeze had picked up outside and the screen was pixelating due to the impact of the wind on the antenna. She flicked through a dozen channels and couldn't find a clear screen or hear what the people were saying, so with a heavy sigh she turned the TV off. Maybe she could try reading.

She wandered over to the stacked bookshelf and perused the spines of each book. Eli had eclectic tastes when it came to reading material and after several minutes of pulling books and reading their blurbs Paige settled on a mystery thriller.

Turning the first page, she settled back into the sofa and began the journey with the protagonist. She read until she couldn't keep her eyes open any longer and closed the book and set it on the coffee table. Her stomach flipped over and she had the distinct feeling she was being watched. Without moving her head, her focus shifted to the window. She couldn't see anyone. It wasn't like her to be spooked for no reason. Was someone outside? And if so, who?

Eli and his pack were inside the church waiting for Elijah to arrive. He was late – a tactic to unnerve them, no doubt. Everyone was in position ready to go on the defensive the minute he stepped through the door. Eli knew he wouldn't be alone. His father wasn't stupid. Despite his unusual physical strength and immunity to the common werewolf precautions, he wouldn't be able to fight them all off alone.

The double front doors burst open and Redmond's men entered the hall. Once inside, they turned into wolf form and hurtled toward Eli and his pack. Bobby, Paul, Ryan and Rebecca's wolves erupted through their skin and charged the oncoming assailants.

Fur and blood flew as the wolves bit, clawed and wrestled each other.

Eli raced to the front doors and scanned the outside. No sign of Elijah.

Was this meeting another ploy to lure Eli away from Paige? And where was his grandmother?

He glanced over his shoulder at the onslaught and knew his pack could handle the guys Elijah had sent to attack them. Not wanting to wait another second, he raced to his four wheel drive, jumped in and rocketed down the hill, his gut telling him Paige was in danger.

Paige crossed the room and gazed out of the window before pulling the heavy curtains closed over the sheer ones. Had she imagined it? She let out a sigh and shook her head. Her imagination was running wild, she had to remain calm. Eli had left her a pistol loaded with silver. She knew how to fire a gun. When she was a teenager, her first boyfriend's dad had been a cop and he'd borrowed his father's Glock one Saturday afternoon and had taken her to an abandoned factory to shoot it. She'd hit the empty beer cans every time and her boyfriend had said she was a natural.

She headed along the hallway to her room and pulled the gun out from under her pillow. If anyone was out there thinking about breaking in she'd shoot first and ask questions later. The cold steel and weight of the pistol in her hand brought her comfort. At least she could defend herself. And she would without hesitation. She wandered back into the living room, flicked on the lamp and turned off the overhead light.

Something clattered on the tiled roof and Paige jumped backwards, her eyes glued to the spot above her. *What was that? Was it just the wind under a loose tile?*

Another thump above her. Someone was on the roof.

The wind's howl sounded like a tortured animal somewhere in the night and caused a rash of icy goosebumps to spread along her arms.

There it is again. Paige backed up to the wall and pressed her spine against the paintwork. Her body trembled and she realized that if she tried to fire off a shot she'd miss for sure. *Who's out there?* She thought about calling out that she had a gun but that would only warn whoever it was and leave her open to being shot if they tried to get the weapon away from her. No, she had to keep her cool. Her heart thudded against her ribs and she couldn't take in a breath. Fear finally got the better of her and the advice she'd given herself vanished from her mind. "Who's out there?" she called, her voice shrill and quivering. "I have a gun and I know how to use it."

"I'm glad to hear it. But you won't want to use it on me."

Paige's eyes widened. "Eli!" she breathed. "I'm so glad you're here. Someone's outside."

"I know. That's why I hid the Jeep and hiked back."

Her eyes remained locked on his. "Your father?"

"That would be my guess." He flicked off the lamp and led Paige down the dark hallway. "He didn't show up at the church. He sent Redmond's men instead."

Paige's heart rate accelerated. "He wants to kill me, doesn't he? Because you and I are Alphas."

Eli frowned into her eyes. "How did you know?"

"I had another dream."

His frown deepened. "I thought maybe Wendy's letter."

"She mentioned it but I already knew."

Eli pushed open the door and turned off the light in her room then kept moving down to his. "Where did you hear him?"

She pointed upward.

"Ok. Head into my room and bolt the door, then go into the closet and press the left hand panel beside it. A trap door will slide open. Get inside and press the same spot on the other side. And stay quiet otherwise he'll know where you are."

Paige nodded. "But, what about you?"

"I have to finish this."

She reached up and touched his handsome face. "Please be careful. I – I need you."

He frowned into her sincere, tear-filled eyes and smiled. "Go. I'll be back for you. I promise."

FORTY NINE

Eli heard a thump on the roof and stopped midway along the hall. He eased his tall, muscular frame down the narrow passage to the living room and stopped, his Lycan sensitivities on high alert. Footsteps across the roof tiles. At least Paige was safe. Something he didn't have to worry about so he could focus all of his attention on his father. The footfalls dropped down onto the ground outside his front porch and Eli crossed the room without a sound to the window and peered through the curtains.

He frowned when his eyes met the back of the guy who'd been locked up at the station. *What is he doing here?* Eli was about to open the door when the unnamed man turned into werewolf form and bared his canines.

Eli continued to watch from the corner of the window.

Out of nowhere another wolf appeared. He knew it was his father.

Both wolves faced off, the guy from the lockup guarding the entrance to Eli's house and Elijah pacing back and forth the way a dog does when it's biding its time before a fight.

Eli drew his pistol. He didn't believe in taking chances. If the young guy couldn't take down Elijah he would. No wolf, no matter how strong, had immunity to silver.

The two wolves circled each other, eyes glowing, snarls echoing around the dark trees bordering the property.

Why would the guy want to protect me? A lightbulb flashed on in his head. It wasn't him the wolf was protecting it was Paige. *But why? Who is he?*

Snarls and howls erupted into a physical altercation with teeth and claws gnashing, scratching, fur and blood spraying across the yard as the wolves tumbled in the dirt.

Eli's wolf hungered to break free and join the fray but he suppressed the urge to turn. If the confrontation failed to go the way he hoped it would Paige needed someone to protect her.

Paige hunkered in the back of the small, dark space, hands covering her ears, the sounds coming from outside frightening. She hoped Eli would be all right. Could he defeat his father? What would happen to her if he didn't? She couldn't think about that now otherwise she'd lose it. Her heart trembled against her ribs and she sucked in a sharp, tight breath. She gripped the pistol in her hand for comfort. If Elijah came within shooting distance she wouldn't hesitate to use it.

She was in love with Eli and knew it had nothing to do with the predestined arrangement. He was everything she'd ever wanted in a man. He was kind and gentle and cared about everyone in his life. Once this was over, she hoped they'd have a chance to get to know everything about each other. There were things she needed to tell him and she was sure there were things he needed to tell her, especially about his wife, Michelle. And she had come to terms with what would happen to her once Eli made love to her. She wanted him to make love to her. There was no turning back from her birthright and no way she could walk away from Eli now.

The savage fighting continued. Snarls growing in intensity, claws and teeth ripping, tearing, shredding fur and muscle. Eli was impressed with how the unnamed young man handled himself against Elijah. His determination to keep his father away from the house had been successful so far.

Another wolf appeared at the border of tall pines and leaped into the conflict. It appeared this wolf was a companion of the guy Craig had arrested, but who was it? Neither were familiar to him so why were they here? His gut tightened at the thought of them losing the fight and he pushed his weapon into its holster under his jacket on the coat rail, opened the door, stripped down, and flew into the fight, his wolf erupting as he joined the assault on his father. Three against one were better odds than two.

The battle raged for some time.

Elijah had weakened, Eli could sense it, but his father kept attacking with all the force he had left inside him. He and the other two wolves kept clawing, biting, tearing until the lone wolf went down, his bloodied black form slashed and exhausted, his breathing short and sharp. It was time to end it once and for all. Eli moved in for the kill, the other two wolves vanishing into the trees. Emerging out of his wolf state into human form he gripped the black wolf's neck and tore the head from its body. A fitting end for what he'd done to Jake and the other victim, Harry Winslow. A single tear slid down his cheek at the thought of what might have been and he brushed it away. His father had only cared about one thing – himself. Eli would finish dismembering his body and burning it before telling Paige the fight was over.

The two wolves raced through the dense legion of trees placing as much distance between them and Eli Blackwood's house as they could. Paige was safe and that was all that mattered.

After dressing, setting fire to the dead wolf and watching the remains of his father turn to ash, Eli entered the house and headed straight to his room to the woman he was in love with. He pressed the panel inside the closet and when the door opened Paige rushed into his arms.

"I'm so happy to see you. It sounded terrifying out there." She frowned up at him. "Are you ok?"

"I am now." He gave her one of his breathtaking smiles and pressed his mouth to hers.

Eli's cell phone interrupted their passionate kiss and he knew he had to take the call. "Sorry, I need to get this."

"It's ok. I can wait." She smiled up at him and he rubbed her arm affectionately.

"Hey, Bobby, how'd it go over at the church?"

"Don't worry about that. I found Clarissa and took her to the medical center. She's unconscious in the ER. It's not good. You need to get here right now!"

"On my way."

Paige gave Eli a curious frown. "What's happened?"

"That was Bobby. My grandmother's in the hospital. And by the sound of it it's not looking good."

Her hand flew to her mouth. "Oh, Eli, I'm so sorry."

Eli took her by the hand. "We have to go."

Doc Hoskins was on call and met Eli and Paige at the ER reception desk. "Follow me." He led them along the hall to a room beside emergency, opened the door and motioned for them to step inside. Bobby was sitting beside the bed and stood up when they came in.

"Hey, Eli, she seems to be doing a lot better than before." He crossed the room and gave his friend a reassuring smile.

Clarissa was hooked up to a low-beeping heart monitor and a drip. An oxygen mask covered her face too. She looked so small and helpless lying in that hospital bed.

"Thanks for being here, Bob."

Bobby gripped Eli's arm. "Where else would I be? Clary's like a grandmother to all of us."

Eli crossed the room, sat down and took his grandmother's hand in his. It was ice cold. His gaze returned to his deputy. "How'd you find her?"

"An anonymous tip. Can you believe it?" He stood with hands on hips. "She was locked in a storage locker out at the old sawmill."

Eli's heart sank. His grandmother was too old for that kind of trauma. He ran his loving eyes over her sleeping, wrinkled face marked with cuts and bruises. His father had done that to her. His wolf reared inside him – he was pleased he'd been the one to administer the final death blow to Elijah. It was an appropriate end for the kind of life he'd led and the unspeakable acts he'd committed.

The doctor crossed the room. "Apart from the abrasions and bruising… and being unconscious, of course, your grandmother is holding her own." He ran his eyes over her chart. "She's as comfortable as we can make her. Now it's up to her."

Tears stung the backs of Eli's eyes and he blinked before turning to Doc Hoskins. "Do you think she'll make it?"

The doctor sighed. "I'd like to say yes but Clarissa isn't a young woman anymore, Eli. The kind of trauma she's been through is bound to take its toll on her physically. Let's just focus on the next 24 hours. Ok?"

Tears slipped down Paige's face and she brushed them away before joining Eli. It wouldn't be fair if Clarissa passed away so close to Christmas. Christmas! That was the day after tomorrow.

FIFTY

After a few hours of sitting at Clarissa's beside with no change to her condition, Paige suggested they head to the woman's house to make sure everything was ok and to pick up some fresh nightwear and toiletries for when she woke up. She couldn't contemplate that the older woman wouldn't wake up. It was far too difficult to bear after everyone they'd already lost. Eli looked tired and so was she. The best thing they could do right now was get some rest and come back later. Bobby promised to check in on Clarissa while they were gone and said he'd let them know if there were any changes, as would Doc Hoskins, so there was no need for them to stay.

Eli was reluctant to leave but could see that Paige needed a break. After all, she was still recuperating from being attacked. On the drive back she had an idea. "Let's decorate Clarissa's house for Christmas, the inside at least. I know how much she loves the holidays. She told me the day we cooked together. When she comes home it'll give her spirits a lift."

"That's a lovely idea, Paige, but I don't think anything'll make her feel better. Wil's death will hit her hard."

Paige's voice went quiet. "Yes, I know. I just thought that maybe it would cheer her up, at least for little while."

Eli gave a soft sigh. What could it hurt? "Ok. Let's do it. I'm sure she'll appreciate the thought."

A smile lit up Paige's face. "Thank you. I'm hoping she will."

"Thank *you* for the thoughtful gesture." He reached across and squeezed her hand.

Once inside Clarissa's house, Eli went down to the cellar to find the boxes of Christmas decorations. He carried two up at a time and set them down in the living room. "What about a tree?" You couldn't have Christmas decorations without a tree.

"Is there somewhere nearby where we can get one?" Paige asked.

"Yeah, there is. Why don't you get started here and I'll run into town and pick one up. Shouldn't take too long."

"Ok. Great idea." Paige smiled as she opened up one of the two boxes. "Oh, my, these are gorgeous!" She picked up two, beautiful crystal dove ornaments.

"Clary loves tree decorations. She's been collecting them since she was a girl. There are more boxes downstairs if you want to check them out."

Paige's eyebrows rose. "I just might. See how I go with all of this first. You'd better get going. It's looking gray out there which only means one thing... more snow."

"Yeah, you're right. Don't want to get caught in a snow storm. I'll see you soon." He stepped out of the front door and Paige locked it.

While Eli was tree hunting, Paige managed to hang red, green and gold tinsel and multicolored, twinkling lights around the living room. She also set up the nativity scene on the wood coffee table, decorated the mantel, and made a space for the tree. The room was filled with holiday cheer. It felt good to be doing something Christmassy. Now that there was no longer a threat they could try to enjoy the holiday season, as long as Clarissa pulled through.

Eli unlocked the door with the spare key he carried, in case of emergencies, and pushed the large, snow covered tree into the entry hall.

"Oh, wow! What a wonderful tree." Paige stood with her hands on her hips looking up at the seven foot green fir. "Where'd you find it?"

"I know a guy who has a Christmas tree farm not far from Moon Grove. He owed me a favor so I got this beautiful tree for free."

"Well, let's get it into the living room so we can decorate it."

Eli glanced around the room as he carried the large tree in and was astounded at how much Paige had accomplished while he'd been gone. "Now it's my turn to say wow. This looks amazing!"

"You don't think it's too much?"

"Too much? Clary usually has the whole house Christmassed out. You should see it when she's finished."

"I hope I'll have the chance to."

Eli set the tree in the bucket Paige had placed in front of the living room window. "Yeah, me to."

Paige realized what she'd said and how it sounded.

"I'm sorry. I didn't mean…"

He pulled her into his arms. "I know." He kissed her forehead. "I want to believe she'll come out of it."

"She will," Paige offered with conviction. "She's a strong lady and one hell of a witch, too."

Eli gave her a nonplussed frown. "How did you know?"

"I wasn't sure at first. I mean, I knew she had certain abilities like seeing the future, because of the whole moonstone ring thing, but when she made us some hot chocolate and put drops of verbena in it I looked it up."

"She was only trying to keep you safe, you know?"

"I know. And I appreciate it." Paige picked up the tangle of white lights and passed them to him. "Want to do me a favor and unravel these?"

Eli gave a heavy sigh. "Yeah, ok. Clary always gets me to do this."

"Well, then, you should be an expert at it." She gave him a broad grin.

"Right." He frowned at the mess in his hands. "I don't know why she doesn't wrap them around cardboard or something to prevent them from ending up like this."

"Hey, that's a great idea. When we take them down that's what we'll do. I'm sure there's a box downstairs we can use."

They had just finished putting the star on top of the tree when Eli's phone went off. He glanced at the screen and recognized the medical center's number. "Hello," he said, his stomach tight. Was it bad news?

"It's Tom Hoskins. I wanted to be the one to tell you that your grandmother's awake."

"Thank you, Doc. We'll be right over." Eli shoved his

phone into his jacket pocket and grabbed Paige's hand. "Clary's awake."

Christmas Eve morning, while Paige helped Clarissa prepare for the trip home, Eli went out to the parking lot to talk to Bobby. He'd driven over to check in as promised and was happy to hear that Clarissa was going home. "Doc Hoskins said seeing as it's Christmas Eve and she's recovering well we can take Clary home today. It'll be good for her to be back in familiar surroundings."

"That's good news." A smile spread across Bobby's face. "Yeah, it will. Nothing beats being around family and friends at Christmastime. And with everything that's been going on none of us have really had a chance to get into the holiday spirit."

"Yeah, I know. I had a whole different scenario going on in my head though. I was preparing myself for the worst. I'm pleased she's doing so well after her ordeal."

"She's one tough old lady. And I mean that in the nicest possible way with all due respect," his deputy said.

"I agree with you. She is pretty tough."

Bobby had a question roaming around his head that wouldn't quit and decided to ask Eli. "Who do you think those wolves were that helped you tackle Elijah?"

"I don't know. They aren't from around here. We know all the supernatural creatures living in the neighboring towns. And, just to be clear, they did most of the tackling. I joined in to make sure the job was done."

"And you think the guy was the same one we had in the lockup?"

"He *was* the same one." Eli folded his arms. "What I don't understand is why he came to protect Paige."

"Yeah. Doesn't make a whole lot of sense, does it?"

"No, it doesn't. And the strange thing was he and his wolf companion took off before I could talk to them."

"Well, they obviously didn't want to make themselves known. Remember we couldn't get anything outta the guy when we had him, either."

"But why hide their identity?"

Bobby shrugged. "Don't know. I'd better get going. I still have to do the rounds, although not that much is happening in town."

"Why not call it a day and head home. Be with your kids. It's Christmas Eve. If anything urgent comes up we'll get a call. Tell Rosy to go as well."

"Yeah? Gee, thanks, Eli. I will definitely tell her. Merry Christmas." He tipped his hat, turned and headed across the parking lot.

"Merry Christmas," Eli called out.

Bobby gave him a wave then continued over to the police cruiser.

Something caught Eli's attention out of the corner of his peripheral vision and he swung around. Well speak of the Devil. The young guy they'd been talking about was standing over by the trees.

Eli crossed the parking lot expecting him to take off, but he didn't. "I was wondering if I'd see you again."

"Why?" He pulled his hood over his head and shoved his hands deep into the pockets of his jacket.

"I wanted to thank you for what you did out at my place yesterday. I couldn't have done it without you and your companion."

The guy shrugged. "Just doing what comes naturally."

"Who was the other wolf?"

"Haven't you figured it out yet?"

Eli gave him a curious frown. "Figure what out?"

He smirked, shook his head and rolled his eyes.

Eli grabbed his arm. "Hey, don't do that... what haven't I figured out?" His frown turned into a scowl. He hated not having all the facts.

"About Paige's parents."

"What about them?" Eli's voice tightened along with his gut. Something about his dream popped into his head. He'd been looking at it backwards. He wasn't meant to be heading toward the house he was meant to follow the trail of blood in the other direction to where it began. The bodies were there. Somewhere.

"Her father was killed that night but her mother was taken and held prisoner," the young guy told him.

"How do you know that?" Eli's grip remained on the guy's arm so he wouldn't turn tail and run. He needed to know the truth.

"Because Doc Hoskins helped her get away." His anxious eyes roamed the parking lot as though he was expecting someone he was afraid of to show up.

"From where?"

"You know the town council members are immortal, like us, right?"

"Of course. What has that got to do with anything?"

"They were going to have her killed after they tortured her for information about the moonstone ring. But the doctor couldn't let that happen."

"You're not making sense. Why was Doc Hoskins involved?"

"They'd called him in to make sure she'd stay alive long enough to answer their questions. When he found out she was pregnant he couldn't let them go through with their plans so he came back during the day and took her. They planted the blood at the scene to make it look like she'd been murdered along with Paige's father, so no one would be looking for her. Once they were done with her she could be killed without any consequence because the police already believed she was dead."

Something crossed Eli's face and the young guy smiled. "You're getting it now, aren't you?"

"She had to run. She couldn't come back for Paige."

"See, not such a dumb cop after all." His smirk widened.

Eli's grip tightened and he frowned into the young guy's eyes. "Stop with the wise cracks. That was twenty three years ago."

"Yeah. And?"

"You're about that age, aren't you?"

"Go on. Now you're getting warmer."

"You're the baby she was carrying." His eyes widened. "You're Paige's brother."

"You can let me go of me now."

Eli loosened his grip and the guy shrugged out of his grasp.

"Where's your mother?" A look of awareness crossed Eli's face. "The other wolf."

"Bingo! But you can't tell Paige. Not yet."

"Why not?"

"Because the members of the council will have us hunted down and killed, if they discover we're back in Moon Grove. Our mother knows too much about their activities and their connection to your father, just like the reporter did. And look what happened to her."

"What about your father? Did he have the moonstone ring? Is that the reason he was killed?"

The guy shook his head. "He couldn't get it because it'd been returned to the pack, at that point. But, yeah, that's why he was killed. Elijah thought my dad was trying to stiff him. He was meant to take the ring back to the council but he had other ideas. He wanted it for himself." He pointed to Eli's jacket pocket. "It'd be a wise idea to wear it. No one can get it off your finger unless they kill you for it so it'll be safe."

Eli gave him an uncertain stare. How did he know he had the ring with him? Then he remembered what Ryan had said. The ring gave off a vibration. "I'm not sure I want to wear it."

"Well you should. You're the Alpha and it's better in your hands than the council's, or Mayor Redmond's. He's been after it for years but is too scared of the council members to try anything."

Eli realized the ring was more trouble than it was worth and that the wrong people were prepared to kill for it. Why should he put his life on the line? He already did that on a daily basis. Maybe it should be destroyed so no one can get their hands on it. He had no intention of wearing it and broadcasting to the council or anyone else that he had it. A change of conversation was in order. "Was that you out at the house the day I was there?"

The guy nodded. "I wanted to see where we used to live, you know? It was our family home once."

"And the anonymous call about Clarissa?"

"Yeah, well, I couldn't leave her out there, could I?

What kind of person would I be if I let an old lady die?"

Eli extended his hand. "I appreciate you doing it. Thank you."

The young guy's face flushed and he stared at Eli's outstretched hand but didn't shake it. "Like I said..."

Paige appeared at the hospital entrance. She craned her neck and ran her eyes around the cars and people and when she spotted Eli talking to some guy she waved at him and headed toward them.

"I have to go." Paige couldn't find out about him now.

"Please don't leave. She needs to know you're here."

"Do you want to put her life in more danger?"

"Of course not."

"Then I have to go now before she gets too close."

"All right. But you'll be back won't you? To tell Paige everything?"

"Yeah. We will."

"Can you at least tell me your name?"

The guy thought about it for a moment. "Brent." He turned on his heel and threaded through the parked cars.

When Paige reached Eli she glanced along the road at the back of the guy he'd been talking to. "Who's that?"

"No one. Just a guy trying to bum a cigarette. But as I don't smoke..."

"You seemed to be having a pretty in depth conversation with someone who was just asking for a cigarette," she observed.

Eli shoved his hands into the pockets of his jacket. "You don't believe me?"

"I didn't say that. It just looked to me like, I don't know, you knew each other." She was a psychologist, after all, and had studied people's body language.

"I'm not having this conversation with you, Paige. Either you trust me or you don't." He headed toward the hospital entrance. It did not feel good lying to her.

Paige followed him. "Eli, wait."

He stopped and turned around.

"I'm not accusing you of anything. I was only asking."

"Well it sounded to me like you were."

She huffed out a plume of white freeze. "I'm sorry." She didn't want to fight with him. It was Christmas Eve and they were taking Clarissa home. All should be right with the world. "Let's forget about it, ok? Let's just take your grandmother home and enjoy the holidays with her."

Eli drew Paige close and held her tight. He hated not being able to tell her the truth. He didn't want to keep secrets from her. But he'd given his word, in order to keep her and her family safe, and he would honor that pact. He hoped Brent would keep his word and come back to tell Paige everything. She needed to know the truth and she needed them in her life.

In the meantime, he, Paige and Clarissa would spend the festive season together. It would be a wonderful time of year for them all, at least for a short while. He knew the search for the ring would continue and that once the council knew he had it things would take another dramatic turn for the worse. But until then they could enjoy Christmas carols, eggnog, turkey, and kissing under the mistletoe. Life had to seem normal. At least for now.

Did you love the book?

Let other readers know by posting a
review on Amazon
Visit the author's Amazon page below
https://amzn.to/315OHzU

READ AN EXCERPT FROM
BOOK TWO
WOLF CURSE

ONE

Paige wandered through the house in search of Eli but couldn't find him. It had been a wonderful day of turkey with all the trimmings, pecan pie and other scrumptious morsels which Paige had prepared with Clarissa's instruction, wine and their favorite Christmas carols playing in the background. The older woman was napping, tucked up on the sofa in front of the fire. Now all Paige had to do was find Eli. Where was he?

She'd noticed his Christmas spirit wane toward the end of dinner and wondered what was on his mind.

Paige heard Clarissa's voice echo into the entry hall. "He's out on the front porch, dear. Said he needed some air. Bundle up it's awfully chilly out there."

"Thanks, Clary. I will." Paige shrugged into her jacket, pulled her knit cap onto her head and opened the front door. "Won't be long."

"Take your time, dear, take your time. I'm fine."

Paige closed the door behind her and walked along the porch to Eli standing at the railing. "You disappeared straight after dinner. Everything ok?"

"Come here." He pulled her into his arms and kissed her forehead.

Paige frowned up into his eyes. "What's going on?"

"I've been doing some thinking and I've come to a decision."

Paige's stomach flipped over under her jeans. "What kind of decision?"

He stared into her eyes for the longest time without answering. What was he searching for? A reason to change his mind?

"Eli?"

He gave a heavy sigh. "I can't... I don't want you to be my Alpha female, Paige."

She stepped out of his embrace. "You can't make that decision for me, Eli. It's my choice and I want to be with you."

"I'm sorry, but I have. I can't let you give up your life for me... for this." He motioned at the street, meaning Moon Grove.

"Eli, I love you. There is no choice."

"And I love you, too, but I don't want you to be a part of any of this."

"Don't you think it's a bit late for that? I am part of it." She reached for him. He stepped back.

"It's because I love you that I'm letting you go, Paige." Tears burned the backs of his eyes and he blinked. "Pack up and move back to Washington where you belong and live a normal life."

"No." She stepped up to him, a scowl on her face. "I'm not going anywhere and you have no right to ask me."

"You don't belong here. You never did." His heart ached as he said the words.

Paige gasped and tears welled in her eyes. "Do you mean that?"

"With every breath." He wanted to hold her but wouldn't. He had to make a clean break.

"And you really want me to leave?"

He nodded without answering. He didn't trust himself around her anymore. He knew if she stayed they'd make love and it would be over. She'd become Lycan.

Tears spilled down Paige's face. "I thought..." She didn't finish. She turned on her heel and rushed inside.

After several minutes Eli entered the house.

Clarissa heard him come in and called him into the living room. "Don't do this, Eli. She loves you. And you know without her you'll lose your strength in time. She's part of you."

"I don't care, Gran. I can't allow her to give up her life for me and the pack. It wouldn't be fair to her."

"Even if you manage to persuade her to leave do you really think she's going to stop loving you?"

"In time, yes. She has to." He paced.

"You're bound to each other, my boy. There's nothing either of you can do about that. It was both parents' decision all those years ago. Your mother wanted it for you. She wanted to know you'd have someone after she was gone."

Eli sat down opposite his grandmother. "Why did the Lycan curse kill her?"

A sad look crossed Clarissa's face and her eyes filled with tears. "She wasn't strong enough. It happens sometimes."

"What if Paige isn't strong enough?"

"Oh, but she is. She's proved that already."

Eli shook his head. "I don't know."

"Yes, you do. Go to her. Tell her you're sorry. Tell her you love her and want to be with her. You have no choice. Neither of you do so you may as well make the best of it. At least together you'll be able to keep each other safe."

Eli gave a heavy sigh. Could he ask her to give up her humanity?

www.ingramcontent.com/pod-product-compliance
Lightning Source LLC
Chambersburg PA
CBHW030414180626
46812CB00005B/2004